THE GREY GHOST

Joseph Squatrito
c – 2015

ISBN: 069250477X
ISBN 13: 9780692504772
Library of Congress Control Number: 2015913287
Joseph Squatrito, Staten Island, NY

CHAPTERS

ACKNOWLEDGEMENTS!

FRONT COVER, WWII PHOTOS-Permission file PD-USGOV- MILITARY NAVY.

National Archives and Records Administration Identifier 521011

Wikimedia Commons.

Additional Photos- Queen Mary.com/ public domain file.-All Interior Photos labeled for Reuse under licensing. Some converted from color to black & white to suite format.

PROLOGUE

Sitting on his couch enjoying the DVR tape of the Yankee -Red Sox game James De Marco is interrupted by his wife Carol. " Are we going to be late? Or are you going up stairs, and get dressed?"

" It's the top of the ninth the Yankees are up by a run and Mariano Rivera has just taken the mound."

" It's not like you can't watch the rest of the game later, it is on tape."

" I didn't listen to any of the sports news just so I could enjoy the game, three batters it won't take long. Fifteen minutes and it's all over."

Ranting and raving as she walks down the hall to the stairs leading to the second floor of their home and into her dressing room to put on her evening gown. After all it is the biggest night of her life. Where is James? In front of the television watching a taped baseball game from last night. Fifteen minutes later give or take a few minutes James finds his way upstairs and into the shower. A quick shower and shave he proceeds to the bedroom as he finishes getting dressed. Carol is down stairs doing a slow burn as she waits for him to come down. James yells down. "Carol I need help with these cuff links. Damn arthritis. Fingers don't work anymore, nothing works anymore. Do I have to wear this monkey suit?"

James comes down for Carol's help, talking to himself grumbling like a big bear.

" Why in the hell do I have to wear a tuxedo any how? I have some very nice suits hanging in my closet."

" Because your suits are as old as you. Out dated, out worn and out of style. Do I have to say more, and besides I'm wearing an evening gown so you need to be in a tuxedo. It's a formal affair, black tie that means you."

" Okay but you have to help me with this cummerbund thing, I don't know how to tighten it.

" It's like dealing with a five year old. What happened to your brain you use to be very dapper. The boys have gone to a lot of trouble, not to mention the expense of this party. It's our fifty year anniversary and you are not showing any interest."

" It's not so. I told the boys not to go to all the expense. I wanted to give them the money but they won't take it. I told them just the idea of having a party for you was enough heart felt acknowledgement. I know they can't afford this kind of party."

"You know they would never take money from you. You grew them up to macho always trying to do better than you did.

"Okay, okay let's just go to the party and enjoy the evening. We'll figure out some other way to give them back the money."

James gives Carol a kiss and helps her on with her wrap. Looking for the keys to the car, he finds his glasses which he needs to drive. They exit the front door and James opens the car door for Carol, as he gets in the car, he does a double check. " Carol did I lock the front door?"

" Yes, you did. Can we just go now before we're late to our own party."

James backs out of he driveway and proceeds to the "STAATEN CATERING HALL"

As they approach the building, a long line of cars are waiting to enter the parking lot for valet service. Carol looks at James with those eyes that say we are late for our own party. James says, " It's okay were not that late. There just having trouble getting the old folks out of the cars."

" It's no excuse, if you weren't so interested in that damn baseball game we would have been the first car here. Waiting in the front lobby to greet our guest the way it was supposed to be."

" Your right, I really screwed up this time. Except my apology."

" Of course, let's just go in and have a good time." Said Carol.

Finally James pulls his car up to the valet. He stops and Carol is helped out of the car and up the front steps of the STAATEN. Inside their three sons Jimmy, John and Joe are having a shit fit over the fact they should have been here at least a half hour ago. Jimmy comes over to his mother and says." Mom where were you? We were sick worrying something was wrong, we called the house but there was no answer. We were afraid you had been in an accident or something."

"No nothing like that just traffic, then we couldn't get into the parking lot."

No matter how mad or upset Carol was she was not going to through her husband of fifty years under the bus, as they say. She was not going to spoil the night for the boys by letting them think their father was so irresponsible to make a baseball game the reason for their lateness. John's spouse Mary walks over to Carol and pins a corsage on her gown and a carnation on James' tuxedo lapel. They all walk to the grand ballroom and start to greet their guest as they arrive. Jimmy's spouse Susan is taking pictures of all the arriving guest with her In-laws. Susan is quite a good amateur photographer so placing the job in her hands was a no brainer. Joe's spouse Patricia was making sure everyone got their place cards with their table number on it. The older grandchildren were seated at their assigned table playing video games or just texting while the younger kids were just running all over the room playing. When all the guests had arrived, all the boys and their spouses gathered in front of the microphone and the welcoming announcement was handed over to Jimmy, the oldest of the three sons.

PARTY ON

As Jimmy took the microphone in hand, he thought for a couple of seconds, looked around the room and started his speech. " Wow fifty years where has the time gone? Tonight we celebrate the golden anniversary of our parents, "CAROL and JAMES." Looking around the room, I see so many who are about to celebrate their anniversaries. Life long friends are hard to find, yet my parents have been blessed with a great family of sister, brothers, nieces, nephews, cousins and of course friends. So raise your glass and let's toast, LOVE, LIFE and good HEALTH. SALUTE!"– (Italian toast to drink)

Just then John and Joe take the microphone and John says, " Just a word, we hope, you all have a great time and enjoy the music. There is a great selection of forties music to dance to. My brother Joe would like a word. Joe it's all yours."

" Thank you John this is for dad, we cooked up a little something special, a weekend trip to California. First class on the Queen Mary. Come on up and say a word or two." James slowly rose from his chair and was quite taken aback. Never in his wildest dreams did he ever think he would be back on that ship. All his own dark

1

secrets flashed through his head in a matter of seconds. His knees weakened as he stood there in total shock. Looking around the room, to find someone who could help him with his dilemma. All he saw were his friends and family rising from their seats applauding and yelling cheers of happiness for the old time soldier who gave so much in defense of his country in World War II. As he slowly walked to the front of the room where his boys and daughter-in-laws stood again his thoughts returned to the seen of his old dark secret. Reaching for the microphone from his son Joseph he was chalk white. Joe covered the microphone and asked. "Dad are you okay?" James took the microphone and with a half smile acknowledged he was fine.

" This is quite a shock, I'm at a lost for words. I guess all I can say is. Thank you to my wonderful family for such a gift. I really never expected it and quite frankly I better take my seat before I fall on my ass and really give every-one something to cheer about." Carol quickly came to his aid and together they returned to their seats, walking back James whispered. " Did you know about this?"

Carol squeezed his arm for support and said." Not really, I knew the boys cooked up something for you I didn't know exactly, what it was."

After a couple of minutes James had regained his composure, just then the D.J. announced. " For their first dance James and Carol have chosen the Anniversary Waltz." James and Carol walked to the middle of the dance floor and quite lovingly dance to a round of applause, but as the words of the song rang out.

" Oh how we danced on the night we wed"

James' thought returned to the days before he entered the war and the secret he had been carrying inside of his heart and mind all these years. When the song was over they stopped dancing and he kissed Carol. Carol looked up at James and asked. "What's wrong James, I can always tell when something is on your mind?" " Nothing I'm just a little over whelmed, lets just have a great time and enjoy the party."

The D.J. announced. " Your first coarse is about to be served so I hope you enjoy our selection of dinner music."

In between food coarse the dance floor was filled. As everyone was having a good time. Only James was preoccupied with flashing thoughts he had buried a long time ago. How could he ever know his anniversary party would open so many old wounds, a few trips to the bar took the edge off his dilemma. As the night wore on and the food and drink continued even James started to have a great time. No one was totally aware of his feelings. A group of his old buddies made sure he was going to have a memorable night. When the dance floor became to much for their old tired legs they sat at the head table telling old war stories. Most of the tales were a bit over the top, not nearly the way they happened, Time had turned them into tall fantasy stories. By midnight most of the guest were saying goodnight and the party was winding down to a, " Goodnight Sweetheart" tune by Vito Picone and the Elegants. James stood up at his chair and made one final toast, he raised his glass and said. " To fifty wonderful years with the most understanding and loving woman a man could ever love!"

James' buddies all stood up and in unison said." To Carol, salute."

Carol said, " I think you boys have had a little to much to drink, remember your not twenty-five years old any more. I hope you all have someone to drive you home."

The boys were finished packing all the gifts Carol and James had received and brought over a fresh pot of coffee for the table. They concluded a cup or two of black coffee would help the condition of their father and his cohorts. The owners of the Staaten were quite understandable as to allowing more time to leave the building. They actually, had their staff clean around James' table even offering more coffee. Carol assured them they would be leaving when the coffee was finished. A designated driver was assigned. By the time they all left all the elders who had to much to drink were feeling much better and were sure they could drive themselves home. That was not the case with Carol she insisted on driving home. The boys helped James to his feet and the group all walked to the lobby. There they gave the valet boys their tickets to retrieve their cars. As they waited for each car, Carol was doing a slow burn she was still pissed at James for getting them there late. His drinking in excess put her over the top. Still in front of her sons she didn't show her anger and disappointment in James. When their car was finally brought to the door she tipped the valet as James was helped into the car. On the way home Carol began to tell James just what was bothering her. They were half way home when she realized James had notted off and never heard a word she was saying. She turned the radio up loud, very loud to wake James. Letting out a big yawn and stretching like a big bear coming out of hibernation. Then she turned down the volume so she could express her resentment. James just turned and said. " Are we home yet?" When they reached the house, Carol pulled into the driveway and stopped, allowing James to get out before entering the garage. She hit the power switch closing the garage door, as she walked to the front steps where James was waiting.

" Aren't we going to take the gifts out of the trunk?"

Carol was still fuming inside as she began fumbling with her keys looking for the front door key as she answered. "No. The boys will come in the morning and empty the car and bring all the gifts in the house. You and I have to get some sleep we have a plane to catch."

" There's no way were making that plane, I haven't even packed my clothes and I'm not starting now."

"I already pack for both of us, the boys told me to pack for a weekend trip but they didn't tell me where we were going. So all you have to do is make sure, you have a sports jacket.

" I don't want to go!"

She looked at him as if he was totally nuts. " What! Have lost you mind?"

" No, I haven't. I still don't want to go."

" Is that why you were so quite in the car. The boys went out of their way to plan this trip for you. So your going, even if I have to drag you on that plane. Now go up stairs take off your tuxedo and go to bed. I'll be up in a couple of minutes. Then she let him have it. You've done every-thing in your power to spoil the evening for me. Watching a damn Yankee tape so we would be late. Getting the boys upset, when we should have been there an hour before any of our guess arrived. Getting drunk with your pals and mak-ing a fool of yourself in front of our guest."

" Your right I should have been more aware of your feelings and the importance of the party to you. Please accept my apology."

James went up stairs, in a huff and a grumble all the way to his bedroom. Taking off his tuxedo he looked in the mirror and realized there were memories he had hidden all these years. He was afraid they would show and ruin fifty years of marriage. He thought to himself it's funny, how dark secrets always find a way to surface. What a way to end the evening.

Meanwhile twenty-five hundred miles away a different kind of party was about to take place, only this one was in Las Vegas at Caesars Palace. Eric Von Ellstein is walking over to the V.I.P. checkin. From the corner of his eye he sees a very beautiful lady dressed to the nines. He thinks to himself what I could do with that. Wow, what a body. Just then he hears next in line as he walks to the counter he takes a long last look. His mysterious woman is walking away and her back side is just as enchanting as her face. After checking in he takes his key, and decides to drop off his over night bag in his suite, before prowling the casino floor for what he hope will be a memorable Vegas week-end. Entering the elevator to his suite he passes the famous Cleopatra Barge and Bar never seeing the gorgeous woman that turned his head in the hotel lobby sitting at the end of the bar waiting for her own party to start. Entering his suite he places his carry-on luggage on the bed. Opens it and places his sweaters and underwear in the draws. Then he goes to the closet and hangs up his extra pair of pants and takes off his sports jacket and hangs it up Shaving kit in the bathroom, luggage in the closet and a quick look around just to make sure he is ready to go an embrace the inevitable. As he enters the elevator his thoughts return to the mysterious woman he saw in the lobby, thinking to himself it would be nice to run into her on the casino floor. When the elevator stopped on the main floor of the casino he was far more observant of his surroundings. He turned right and walked towards Cleopatra's Barge. He instinctively did what all men do as they pass the barge. They reach up to touch the large wooden tits of the naked woman that hangs over the front of the barge for luck. In the old days of sailing ships many ship builder would add a naked woman with large breasts, at the front of their ships. Sailors believed this was a good luck omen against rough seas. Today it was simply a gesture for good luck on the casino floor. As he walked towards the bar he saw his mysterious woman. She was sitting alone having a drink, as he got closer she turned towards his direction, and smiled tilting her head. He immediately smiled back and sat down next to her.

" Bartender, a Dewars and water and give the lady another, what ever she's drinking. A Chocolate Martini I think, yes?"

" Quite observant or was that a good guess?"

" Sometimes I do get it right, Hi I'm Eric, Eric Von Ellstein and you are?"

" Kristy with a K.

" Are you alone Kristy with a K? I saw you in the lobby as I was checking in."

She thought for a second and smiled saying. " That's funny, I saw you too. Now tell me the truth how did you know what I was drinking?"

" It was easy, first the shape of your glass and second the color. It was either chocolate or coffee. Most woman never pick coffee, it's not the first time I've sat with a beautiful woman at a bar. I've been around the block a few times. Now it's your turn, how come your sitting here and not on line to get into the disco club?

" I happen to prefer live music and a more subdued atmosphere. Do you dance?"

" Actually, I do. Although I'm not sure about a dance floor that moves. I never understood why they would put a four piece band in the front of the barge, a dance floor in the middle and tables and chairs in the back and then the damn thing rocks side to side."

" Hello, it's sitting in water, that's what a boat will do."

Eric finishes his drink, smiles and says. "Okay there playing a nice slow song lets give it a whirl." He takes her by her hand and signals the bartender, to pour another round. He escorts her onto the barge dance floor. As they are dancing he thinks how good she feels in his arms this is a classy woman who knows how to work it. When the music stops they walk back to the bar where their drinks are waiting for them. Kristy is quite impressed with her new friend. Not only is he very handsome, but he knows how it treat a woman. After some small talk Eric asks her. " Are you hungry? Would you like to join me for some dinner? I haven't eaten yet and one more drink without food is not going to be a good thing."

" Sure I would love to have dinner with you, to tell the truth I haven't had anything since lunch and I'm getting a little light headed myself."

" Good we could go to the Spanish Steps for steak or we could go up to my room and order. I have butler service. It would be a lot less of a wait for our food and you could order anything you'd like."

" You have butler service, in a room?"

" I have a suite with a full dining room. I could call from here and order, do you know what you 'd like?"

" I have to be straight with you if we go up to your room it will cost you two hundred and you can think of me as dessert.

" How about I offer you five hundred and you stay for the night, and tomorrow if you like what I have given you, I'll give another five hundred to hang out with me."

" Lets finish our drinks and have another slow dance I liked what I was feeling only order the food first. I'll have what ever your having."

Eric picks up the house phone and orders room service to be delivered to his suite. Then he waits for a real slow grinding dance where he can show Kristy his moves. They often say you can fall in love on a dance floor. A slow dance just brings out the chemistry in some people, body motion can be very seductive. It seemed Eric's plan was working quite well. Coupled with the five hundred dollars she was promised for her night's work, Kristy was hot to trot and he knew it. To his way of thinking she was going to be the best piece of ass he has had in a long time. When the dance was over they made their way to the Centurion elevator and up to the penthouse floor. As the elevator doors closed Eric used his key card, which was the only way you could get up to that floor. Kristy immediately remarked, " Very impressive."

Eric only smiled and said nothing, when the elevator stopped at the top floor a second key card had to be used to open frosted glass sliding doors with the gold leaf Caesars Crown in the center of each door. This was more class than Kristy had ever seen before, she turned to Eric and said. " If I knew you had this much clout I would have asked for a thousand dollar to spend the night, and you would have agreed. I've never slowed danced with anyone who got so hard so quick on a dance floor."

Eric just smiled and pointed to the double doors down the hall indicating which penthouse suite was his. He knocked on the door and a butler in full tuxedo answered the door saying. " Good evening sir, room service just called to say your dinner will be here in ten minutes. I prepared the dining room just the way you like it. May I prepare a drink while you wait?"

Eric thought for a second and then said. " I'll have a Dewars and water and the lady will have a Chocolate Martini or is that to sweet before dinner? "

" Make it a vodka Martini instead."

As the hotel butler served up the drinks a knock at the door revealed their dinner had arrived. The best surf and turf the hotel kitchen could deliver. The butler prepared the dining room table set out the complete meal and excused himself saying. " Just ring if you need any additional service, sir."

Eric pulled out the chair for Kristy as if she was a lady he was trying to impress. Not a lady of the night, he had just paid for her time and yet there was something different about this woman. He had been with many a woman of the night and knew their ways and body language. To him a hooker was just a low life spreading her legs or giving a good blow job for money. Most were on drugs or alcoholics just supporting their habit. Vegas was experiencing a new breed of woman coming out of California, the educated well dressed woman who had been screwed over by a cheating husband, who had left with the money, jewelry, car and a girl half his age. He had a feeling Kristy fit right into that category. She was classy and educated, she knew how to make you feel as if you were special and not just a dollar bill or in her case five hundred dollar bills. He poured a glass of wine for both of them and he toasted the evening and began eating their meal. Eric had ordered jumbo shrimp cocktail, porterhouse steak with lobster. Side trimmings of mashed potatoes, roasted vegetables, and for dessert well he left that up to Kristy. The conversation during dinner was very enlightening, he found out that she was attending UCLA, when she met her husband. She was in her first year and he was a Senior. Two years later they got married and life was great for the first five years, he had a good job plenty of income but by year seven it was a nightmare. She had to sell all her jewelry for a lawyer who got her nothing from the divorce. She tried different jobs but the pay was not what she needed to live in L.A. so she started her Las Vegas enterprise of night work. She knew most money men who came to Vegas for the weekend were looking for a classy woman, who could hold a conversation and yet have the appearance that turn them on. She fit the resume to a tee. After dinner she asked Eric if he was ready for dessert. Eric smiled and said. " I'm a bit stuffed for dessert. What do you say we hit the casino for a while and digest our meal?"

Kristy replied. "If that's what you want, I'm on your clock just remember it's less time you'll have to spend with me."

"Guess I'll just have to buy more time and if you bring me luck at the tables well I'll just have to take better care of you financially."

They left the suite and took the elevator down to the casino floor. Eric walked over to the Roulette table and asked for a marker of five thousand dollars. He showed his V.I.P. Casino Card. The dealer showed it to the pit boss who immediately acknowledged the okay to give him chips in five and twenty-five dollar denominations. He handed Kristy a couple of twenty-five dollar chips and said. "This is for you, go play the slots and it has nothing to do with our arrangement."

She took the chips and walked away, once she was out of sight she cashed them in and put the fifty dollars in her purse and walked over to the Cleopatra Bar and sat down and ordered a drink. The bartender asked if she was still with Mr Von Ellstein, she nodded yes. He told her he would put the drink on his bill from before.

She sat there listening to the music from the band and nursed her drink. She was by far the most beautiful and voluptuous woman at the bar. Several men came over and tried to hit on her. Asking if they could buy her a drink, or have the next slow dance. Her answer was always the same. " Sorry my dance card is full for the night, Maybe the next time I'm in town." After a while when she finished her drink she went back to the Roulette Table and stood behind Eric, who was not having a good evening at the table. He was down to his last twenty dollars in chips. She rubbed his shoulder for luck and said. " Put it all on thirteen black."

Eric followed her lead and waited for the spin to stop. Thirteen Black! Eric collected eight hundred and seventy five dollars, then Kristy said." Press your bet it's going to hit again but first tip the dealer twenty-five dollars."

Eric pressed his bet by added one hundred dollars on top of his chips and waited for the wheel to stop. Thirteen Black! Eric collected forty three hundred seventy five dollars he was even for the night. Everyone at the table cheered and Eric gave Kristy a big hug and kiss. She whispered in his ear. "Do it again."

" Are you sure, that's a lot of money."

" This Time put a dime or (ten dollars) on it for the dealers."

Eric smiled and added another hundred and ten dollars and waited for the wheel to stop. Thirteen Black! Eric started jumping up and down cheering which was very uncharacteristic of him because he is always so in control of his emotions. He then collected seven thousand eight hundred and seventy-five dollars in winnings. Paid back his marker and had the winnings credited to his account. Then he told Kristy she was his good luck charm and he would take good care of her this weekend. With that they both went up to his suite and had a nightcap. Eric was so jacked up it took several drinks to bring him back to earth. Kristy excused herself and went into the bathroom to freshen up. After a while she came out in only her black lace bra and panties. Her body was as he had imagined, perfect. Every curve of her bust, hips and thighs were mesmerizing and as she walked into the bedroom and removed her bra and panties she was gorgeous from head to toe. Eric followed her into the bedroom only to find her under the sheet of the bed sitting up covering herself as if this was the first time she was about to have sex. She watched Eric remove his shirt, then his shoes and finally his pants. Standing there in his underwear she could see his strong well built body, she slowly looked down from his broad shoulders to the ripples in his stomach and what appeared as a large bulge of his package. As he removed his underwear she smiled and knew he was going to give her all she could handle, walking towards her she rolled back the sheet revealing her breasts that were absolutely perfect. She laid back and waited for Eric to mount her and penetrate her warm moist womb. She took every inch he had to give as they moved in a slow satisfying motion that lasted for hours. He thought to himself, oh my God, she's the fuck of the century. When they were totally spent from exhaustion they fell asleep intwined with one another.

As the night was winding down in Las Vegas, the casinos and clubs were starting to thin out and the party scene was coming rapidly to a close. Couples were heading to their rooms to sleep or continue with a little sexual delight of their own. Even Sin City comes to a close in the wee hours of the morning. Although casinos and coffee shops never close, their open twenty-four hours a day. Only a skeleton crew are at work attending to the few die hards that refuse to give in looking for a little late night action. Or just a cup of coffee to clear their head from all the booze they consumed before going to bed and wrapping up their evening.

RETURN TO THE QUEEN

With a three hour time difference back east everything was starting to come alive. The sun was rising and a new day was dawning as the alarm clock was about to go off waking Carol and James. With the first sound of the alarm Carol was up and shaking James saying. " Come on James we have a plane to catch, the boys have sent a car to take us to the airport it will be here in an hour."

As she walked out the bedroom she could hear James grumbling like an old bear being awoken from a long winters sleep. He yelled out. "I need and hour just to shit, shower and shave. When am I going to eat breakfast? You know I have to have food before I leave the house. Carol!"

" Will you please get a move on and get cleaned up and dressed, the car will be here before you know it. Just grab a glass of orange juice. We can eat on the plane."

As Carol rushed to get ready, James was still grumbling as he gets into the shower. "Plane food yack, got to eat that garbage, fight the crowds, wait on line, take off my shoes. What has this world turned into? Where's the freedom I fought for in World War II. Carol there's no hot water."

The car pulls up right on time and the driver phone the house letting them know he's out side ready to help with their luggage. A couple of minutes later Carol opens the front door and signals to the driver who gets out immediately to help load the car. James finishes his orange juice and they walk out of the house locking the front door after setting the alarm system. As they entered the waiting limousine the driver checks his log for airport and the airline. then he says. "Good morning, a beautiful day for flying. American Airline, terminal A, Newark International. Have I got it right?"

Carol answers. " Yes that's right." Then she turns to James and says. " Relax James it's not going to be as bad as you think."

"I hope your right, because I really don't want to be taking this trip."

Saturday morning traffic is light due to the fact most people are home from work for the weekend, their car makes excellent time as they arrive at terminal A. The limo driver finds an open spot right at the curb and stops. A skycap comes over to help with the luggage, the driver pops the trunk and pulls out the two carry-ons. The skycap checks their airline tickets and says." I've got the bags, just follow me sir." He brings them to the first class V.I.P. counter, no waiting next in line. James tips the skycap who after they have checked in, brings them to the front of the security line, again no waiting.

A quick check of the luggage and the removal of cell phones, coins and all metals along with shoes and belts and James' nightmare is over. Before long they are calling for first class ticket holder to board, again no waiting. As they pass the final boarding check and start their decent onto the plane James says, " This first class stuff is pretty damn good, I could get use to this."

" See it turned out to be better than you thought, wait until they start pampering you in the first class section of the plane."

" I sure hope we can get a good breakfast, I'm starved."

The smell of fresh brewed coffee fill the first class cabin along with the cinnamon rolls still being baked. As they prepared to take their seats, James placed the luggage, in the over head compartment. Taking his seat he tells Carol. " Something smell good hope we don't have wait to long to be served."

With that the flight attendant came over and took their drink order and told James breakfast will start as soon as they are in the air, and the captain has turned off the seat belt sign. It could not be soon enough as far as he was concern the aroma was making him anxious for lift off. The cabin doors were closed and the plane was pushed back from the terminal gate. Just then the intercom came on and the captain said. "Good morning folks this is Captain Douglas from the flight deck were number three in the take off pattern. Won't be very long before we're air born, with a beautiful flight all the way to Los Angles, six hours and ten minutes of blue sky. So sit back and enjoy the ride."

All James could think about was breakfast, and before he realized he was being served hot coffee and a cinnamon roll along with a menu to choose from. Carol asked what James was having and his answer was." If everything on this menu is as good as the hot cinnamon roll, I want everything."

When the flight attendant returned to take their order Carol said. " I'll have the egg white omelet with a side of bacon and a roll with butter. The Hungary bear wants everything but he'll have what I'm having maybe you can add a waffle just to make him happy. After breakfast was served and completed James was ready for a little nap, the early morning rise and rushing completely wore him out. Carol reminded him if he started to snore she was going to slap him silly, James just grumbled and sunk his face into his pillow and covered his head with a blanket and snoozed away a couple of hours which was a great help in making the flight seem shorter. This was his first time sitting in a recliner chair in first class. He thought to himself I can really get use to first class accommodations. Then he began to think about the first time he was on board the "Queen Mary" and Michelle. The true love of his life. Michelle was quite the vixen, a real wild cat. She knew how to boil James' blood. She would get the hairs on the back of his neck to stand up as well as his penis. It was the perfect sexual chemistry between them. Michelle knew when she turned on the charm he could never say no to her desires. She loved having sex at the most un-opportune times, when getting caught was at it's highest level. It just added to her sexual pleasures. As he stretched his arms only to wake up to the smell of fresh brewed coffee and chocolate chip cookies. Those memories of Michelle brought a smile to his face. "Well, look who finally woke up." Said Carol.

" I'd still be sleeping if it wasn't for the smell of those cookies."

" Here comes the flight attendant now."

The dessert cart was rolled down the aisle as coffee and warm chocolate chip cookies were being served to the passengers. When the cart finally reached Carol and James' row. Carol asked the flight attendant. "How much longer before we reach Los Angles?"

" This is the end of our food service, so it won't be long now."

The plane started it's decent into the Los Angles area James told Carol. " I can't wait for the return flight home, I've decided this is the only way we should travel, First Class."

Looking out the window, James was filled with mixed emotions he was starting to get excited about seeing the old girl. Would all the secrets he keep to himself all these years come back to haunt him or would this turn into a very joyful trip down memory lane. Finally the wheels touched the ground and the sound of the brakes and tires screeching to a slow movement brought cheers from all the passengers. Before long the plane came to a halt and the doors were opened and all the passengers got out of their seats and reached for their carryon luggage in the over head compartment. Slowly and in an orderly fashion they started to disembark the plane. Following the crowd and reading the signs that lead them to the luggage pick up area. They were looking for the door when they spotted a man holding a sign that read Mr. James DeMarco. Carol pointed to the sign and they walk over saying." Hi we're the DeMarco's are you our driver?"

"If your James and Carol DeMarco I am, Hi I'm Wilson let me take your luggage. I have a car waiting and I'll be your driver all the way to Long Beach, please follow me right this way."

He leads them out the door marked south where his black limousine is parked in a holding area. Wilson pops the trunk for the luggage and opens the door so Carol and James can sit while he puts the luggage in the trunk. Closing the trunk he walks to the open door and says, "There's cold drinks in the mini fridge, and snacks on top just help yourself. We have a two hour drive maybe more. The traffic on the freeway is very heavy this time of the day. If you need a pit stop before we get started the bathrooms are right through those doors, I have no problem waiting, once where on the freeway there's no exiting for restrooms." Carol looks at James and says. " Maybe we should go it's better to be safe than sorry."

With that they both leave the car and walk back into the terminal and find the restrooms. A couple of minutes later their journey is resumed and they begin to take in the sights of Los Angles. Leaving the airport the surrounding neighborhood is not the glamorous idea they both had of what California would be. The low rise buildings and the mom and pop stores looked very much like any small town back east. The expression on James' face lead Carol to say, " I guess the Rodeo Drive and Beverly Hills we hear about must be in the opposite direction."

" Well, it certainly is not this area of Los Angles, not much to look at maybe the view will get better as we travel south. If I didn't know better, I'd swear we were back in Spanish Harlem. Even the graffiti looks the same." Said James.

The only view they saw was cars, and cars and more cars moving like snails on the freeway. It was just as Wilson feared the Los Angles Freeway was bumper to bumper a complete parking lot. The drive to Long Beach would certainly be long and boring, but all things considering the trip was as pleasant as it could be. After all they were sitting in a limousine and could stretch out and close their eyes and listen to music and sleep.

Carol said, " Just think if you were driving us to Long Beach, you'd be one pissed off puppy right now."

" You got that right, sweetheart!"

Eventually they reached their destination. As the limousine took it's place in line to the drop off area. Wilson let them know he would be back for them on Monday afternoon about 2 o'clock so they would beat the traffic back to the airport. When he reached the final drop off he stopped the limousine, got out opened the door and popped the trunk to get the luggage. James tipped him. Wilson said. "Thank you sir and I'll see you both on Monday."

James and Carol took their luggage and continued to the gangway elevator, just then James stopped in his tracks and looked up at the old girl and said. "This is not the way I remember her."

A new paint job had just been completed, the hull was painted black with white trim and her triple smoke stacks were painted red, she still looked like the fastest ship on the ocean and could be ready on a moments notice to start a new adventure. The wooden hand rails shined like the day they were first installed.

Back in Las Vegas the night people were starting to wake to bright sun of the new day, even though it was afternoon the hustle and bustle of the Vegas life was at it's peak. Eric had already gotten up and took a hot shower to revitalize himself from the nights love making. Kristy was quite the woman, she satisfied him as no other woman had ever done, letting go of her was going to be extremely hard. He called for room service and had a full breakfast ordered to the room, then he went into the bedroom and started to wake up Kristy.

" Come on sleepy head, it's time to get up and take a shower breakfast is on it's way."

The morning butler assigned to the suite was notified that breakfast had been ordered, and it was time to prepare and set the dining room table. The fine china with the Caesars Palace logo were place at the head and first side chair of the table. Eric did not like sitting far from his guest, sitting Kristy at the other head seat was to far for the quiet conversation he preferred, especially after a long night of drinking. Again he called to her, "Kristy it's time to get up." She sat up in bed rubbed the sleep from her eyes and grabbed Eric's bathrobe and opened it pulling down his pajama pants and started to kiss and stroke him saying, " I see exactly what I want for breakfast, yum, you taste better today." She didn't stop until Eric had given her all the nectar she desired. Eric looked at her smiled as he pulled up his pants saying, "Breakfast of Desire!" Eric was the man in every woman's dreams. Handsome, rich, classy and a very good lover. Kristy had no intention of letting him go. Eric went into the dinning room to sign for the food being delivered, while Kristy showered and dressed. During breakfast Eric asked Kristy. "Are you an adventurous soul? Would you like to spend more time with me, I'm going to California for a couple of days and returning on

Monday. I'm going on a ghost hunt, so be prepared to get scared out of your wits."

"I'm up for a good adventure, Ghost, really I'm in."

" Are you sure, I could pay you what you have coming or I'll give you another thousand to tag along."

" When do we leave on this ghost hunt?"

" Later this afternoon, first I'd like to go to the pool and get some sun. My limousine will pick us up about four, do you have a bathing suit?"

" Of course I do, but I'd like to get a casual outfit or two most all my clothes are evening wear."

" Perfect, here's the five hundred dollars I promised you, and a thousand more for helping win at roulette. Go the Caesars Mall get what ever you need and meet me at the pool. I'll be at the private Venus Pool where you can go topless if you want an even tan. I'll leave your name at the checkin desk, look for me on one of the canopy beds."

" Wait a minute, you mean I have to pay for my own clothes, just to go on a ghost hunt with you. That doesn't seem fair, does it?"

" Okay, okay buy what ever you like just charge it to my suite. I guess I owe you that much, if it wasn't for you telling me to play thirteen black I would never have gotten my money back, plus the winnings."

Kristy took her money and left to go shopping while Eric slipped into his speedo and robe and went to the pool. An hour later Kristy entered the Venus Pool, at first glance she looked like any other sexy chick that frequented Caesars Palace. Wearing her designer sun glasses, a bathing suit wrap and wedge heel pool shoes. When she found

Eric sitting under a canopy bed and removed her shoes and wrap. She looked like the Goddess Venus come to life. The string bikini revealed her statuette body. Every curve was even more inspiring in the light of day. She sat at the edge of the canopy bed and handed Eric her suntan lotion.

" Can you help a girl out and apply some lotion to my back?"

Then she rolled on her stomach and loosened her strings and removed her top. As Eric applied the lotion he began to think how it was having sex with her, how she felt, how she moved and how wet she was after each climax. He was starting to get an erection just touching her flawless body. He knew something strange and different was happening to him with this woman. Was he falling for her and not even realizing it. Then he signaled the pool waitress and ordered two frosty drinks lace with vodka, in the hope it would calm him down in more places than one. When the drinks came Eric just signed for them and added a tip for the waitress. When she left, Kristy sat up crossing her legs in an Indian fashion facing Eric with the sun at her back. She smiled and said, "The bulge in your speedo is growing you better jump in the pool and really cool off."

"Your right, this drink is not cutting it." He said as he made a fast move and dove into the pool. Kristy knew she was getting to Eric in a big way and she had no intention to let go. After a few minutes in the cold water Eric's erection had calmed down. He exited the pool and walked back to Kristy still sitting on the edge of the bed. He grabbed a towel, dried his hair and wrapped the towel around his shoulders. Then he said.

" How did you make out at the mall? Did they give you a problem with signing for your clothes?"

" No not at all. They did verify if you were in the hotel suite, and everything signed to you was comped. See so it didn't cost you anything, so I bought an extra outfit."

" WOW! I didn't think they would comp clothes at the mall. You learn something new every day."

" Maybe you should buy a suit when we get back from California."

" That's something to think about. I did see a sharkskin suit I liked. Let's just enjoy the sun for know."

Back in Long Beach James was having his own struggles, but of a different nature. As he and Carol were about to enter the elevator from the pier to the check-in lobby he turned to Carol and said, " Take the luggage and meet me at the top, I want to walk the gangway steps just like I did during World War II."

" Are you losing your mind? Those steps will kill you."

He shook his head no, and left her in the elevator as the doors closed. She waited for him at the top, when he appeared he was out of breath, beet red face holding his chest.

" Damn fool," she said.

James just looked around catching his breath. " This is not the Grey Ghost that I remember!"

The Queen Mary had been restored to it's art decor original 1936, grandeur. James couldn't believe his eyes. As they waited in line at the registration desk memories he had long forgotten began to emerge in his thoughts. Then his day dreaming was shattered as the clerk behind the desk called. " Next in line."

Carol and James walked over to the desk and said, " Hi James and Carol De Marco we have a reservation for two nights."

The man paused for a minute looking at his computer for their reservation and replied,

" Got it, Mr. and Mrs De Marco two nights in a suite, all expenses paid you can just sign at any restaurant, bar, event tour. Here is a brochure with a map of the ship, listing all we have to offer as far as restaurants, with dinner and dancing and tour times. Do enjoy your stay and if there's anything we can do for you just ring us twenty-four hours a day." He rings for the bellman. " Robert will help with your luggage and take you to your suite." He hands over the key and says, " Grand Suite M101."

They follow the bellman to the elevator that brings them to the top deck, as the doors open the hallway is absolutely exquisite. The walls are lined with pictures of the dignitaries that stayed on the ship during her glory days. The carpeting was plush and spotless even the door handles shined. James was in awe of what he was seeing and he didn't even get to his suite yet. When they arrived the bellman opens the door to their suite and Carol says, " Oh my God. This is elegance personified, just look at this!"

They entered into a living room (parlor) with oak paneling that shone like mirrors, with art decor pictures of days gone by. A velvet couch and side chairs, coffee tables and plush carpeting that led to a bedroom with a king size bed, full walk-in closets with beautifully appointed wardrobes for each of them. Two bathrooms on each side of the bedroom, His nicely appointed with a sink toilet and shower. Hers with a full size free standing tub and a bid-day next to the toilet. The vanity sink had an attached cosmetic table with a lighted mirror and pull out chair. This was truly the way the rich and famous traveled in the nineteen thirty's. The bellman place the luggage at the foot of the bed and asked, " Is there anything else I can do before I leave sir?"

James hands him a ten dollar tip saying, " I think we can take it from here."

" If you need anything just call the front desk, V.I.P. service goes with the suite twenty-four hours a day."

James calls out to Carol, " I'm starving lets go and have lunch we can unpack later. The brochure says there are two open restaurants for lunch a sandwich shop and a full lunch cafe."

" Okay if we don't go now you'll only grumble till we do, lets go."

While James and Carol are trying to find their way around the Queen, Eric and Kristy are packing up clothes for their trip to the Queen. Even though their reasons are totally different from James and Carol.

" You really think this trip is going to turn into a ghost hunt?" Said Kristy.

" Do you think I'd leave Vegas if there weren't any merit to the story? Believe me I've got it on good source's this is a true adventure in the paranormal. We just have to be very careful how we get into room B.340. They don't allow anyone into that room after the last person swore they saw ghost of people that were murdered in that room."

" Is that why your bringing all this camera equipment?"

" Yes, I want to capture on film whatever we find."

" Okay then, let the adventure commence."

After Eric packed all his equipment into a large duffel bag he called down to the bell captains desk to send a bellman up to get the luggage and duffel bag. Then he called for his driver to bring his limousine to the front door of Caesars Palace. Five minutes later with the bellman loading the luggage trolly, Eric hands him a tip and says, " My limousine is out front we'll meet you there."

Eric and Kristy leave the suite and head to the main elevator in the Centurion Tower while the bellman enters the service elevator. As the Centurion Elevator reaches the casino floor they must pass Cleopatra's Barge and Bar where Eric and Kristy first met. Eric stops Kristy and escorts her to the bar then he calls his driver and gives him instructions about the luggage and the equipment in the duffel.

" I think a farewell drink is in order before we start on our little adventure, after all this is where we met and had our first drink." Says Eric.

" I think your right, we should have a farewell drink!"

Eric orders two 'Long Island Teas' and a ceremonial toast to their new relationship. At four o'clock the bar has an open hot buffet for anyone drinking so they decide to stay and have a cocktail hour. They move to a table in the back near the barge where it's more private with less noise. Ten minutes later two large heated tables with chrome cover tops are wheeled to an area between the bar and the barge. Two men dressed as waiters with white glove are dishing out hot hors- d'oeuvres. Kristy decides to get up and get two plates filled for herself and Eric. When they've had their fill they continue on to the casino for a couple of quick spins of the wheel. Eric pulls out a roll of hundreds and asks for hundred dollar black chips. The pit boss immediately comes over to welcome Eric to the table. After a few words Eric says, " With black chips you have to play black numbers."

So he covers black thirteen with five chips, then he puts one chip on twenty-eight, seventeen, fifteen, eight and thirty-five all black numbers. The dealer spins the wheel and wishes him good luck. When the wheel stops the dealer announces twenty-four black. Eric turns to Kristy and says, " Oh my God! How did I not play twenty-four!" A thousand dollars lost on one spin of the wheel, he gets another stack of black chips and says, " Can you come back to the street?"

A street in roulette is a block of numbers in a row, double zero, three, thirteen, twenty-four and thirty-six would be a roulette street. Eric covers all five numbers with a black chip but this time he adds four more chips on thirteen and twenty-four. The dealer spins the wheel and when it stops announces black thirteen. Eric has now won seventeen thousand, five hundred dollars plus the five hundred on the thirteen is still his. The pit boss comes over to check the winnings and needs to go to the money cage for more chips. Eric responses with, " Just credit my account, less five thousand, and he gives the dealer a two hundred dollar tip. Tell the pit boss, I have business in California and will be back in two days. " Is that wise, giving him all that money without a receipt." Says Kristy.

Eric laughs and informs her not to worry. "I do this all the time, they know who I am. That money is as good as in a bank. Maybe better."

Eric pick up the five thousand in chips and they walk to the casino cage. At the window the teller smiles and says. " Looks like you've had a run of good luck Mr E."

He puts his arm around Kristy and says. "My good luck charm, and she's sexy too."

" How would you like that in a casino check, or all cash?"

" Cash! I need some walking around money. All hundreds. Thank you very much." Then he slips Kristy Three hundred dollars and whispers. "Buy yourself something nice when we get back."

Exiting the hotel they find Eric's driver waiting outside the limousine. He opens the door they enter he closes the door. Soon they are driving towards Las Vegas Blvd and heading west towards California. Kristy is looking out the car window when she turns to Eric and asks.

" Do you really think I'm your good luck charm?"

" For sure. Every gambler is superstitious."

Inwardly she smiles and asks. "Are you a professional gambler or do you work for a living?"

" It really shouldn't matter to you where I get my money. As long as you get your money there should be no question asked."

" I didn't mean to pry. I was just curious, you never talk about yourself."

" There's nothing to talk about. I inherited a few dollars and invested wisely."

" The way you gamble it had to be quite an investment."

" You have to remember, if your in the right place at the right time the rewards are endless. In your line of work, you must have been with plenty of business men with plenty of connections and big bank rolls."

" None that I wanted to be with more than one night or even one roll in the hay, sort of speak."

" So what makes me so special?"

" I don't know. Chemistry maybe, the way you operate with confidence and style." Then she realizes she is never going to get a direct answer from Eric. He's always going to answer a question with a question and never truly reveal himself to her. So she sits ever so quietly and stares out the window wondering what her mysterious Mr Von Ellstein is all about. Then she rolls to her knees and starts to pull down Eric's zipper. He immediately presses the button to close the black out glass separating the driver from the passenger seats of the limousine. As the glass is rising the driver takes one last look through the rear view mirror and sees Kristy in her knees facing Eric. Then he smiles knowing Eric is about to get a limo blow job. Kristy unbuckles his belt and open the button to his pants. Pulling them down passed his knees she begins to work him until he is fully erected. Then she proceeds to slip her lips around him, and take him as deep as she can while holding on as tight as she can. Not allowing any chance he may get soft on her. Kristy was a real artist at her trade and she worked him until he popped his rocks. Then she began to kiss Eric with all the passion of a woman in love. He starts to believe no matter what happens on that ship. Bringing Kristy along for the ride across the desert was worth it.

Carol and James decide on lunch at the Promenade Cafe and are quickly seated The hostess hands them each a menu, and walks away. The waitress takes their order and leaves. A short while later she returns with their drinks and lets them know their order will be out shortly. As they wait Carol begins to ask James some thoughts she has held back for many years.

" Why did you never include me, when you told the boys your war stories?"

" I never thought you'd be interested and that you would see through some of the exaggerations I added to spice up the stories."

" What's the real reason you didn't want to make this trip?"

" Too many war memories."

" I thought you were going to tell me the ship was haunted."

" Oh but it is."

" Is that why they called it the Grey Ghost?"

Carol had no idea of the history of the "Queen Mary" so James started to fill her in saying. "When she was christened in 1936 not only was she the grandest ship afloat but also the fastest. Her cabins were the largest of any ship on the water. Queen Mary was twice the size of Titanic. A year before her maiden voyage, the ship was completely sold out. Every dignitary and royal wanted to be on that trip. The buzz around England was of such grandeur that everyone had to see it for themselves to believe it. Of course the Queen did not disappoint anyone. She was as elegant as every story being told. The exterior paint was of the highest quality for ocean travel. Her black hull, white decks and red smoke stacks shone like no other ship afloat. The art deco interior with her marble columns, inlay silver, paintings, carpeting over whelmed every passenger. Her biggest problem was not the hype it was the era. In 1936 Hitler was in power in Germany and he decided to take back all the lands or countries Germany had lost during World War I. His Nazi regime was coming to power and world domination was his goal. He started his invasion of Poland in September of 1939, followed by Austria, Netherlands, Belgium, Luxembourg and France. During those years people were not traveling as much for fear of war. In1939 England finally declared war on Germany. The next two years it was only England and the

French and Norwegian resistance commandos fighting against Germany and her ally Italy. That year was her last crossing from England to America..

She docked in New York City and was kept there for safety reasons. After Pearl Harbor when America entered World War II she was commissioned as a troop ship, stripped of all her glamour and elegance. All her art deco, paintings, furniture, carpeting, dishes, silverware and stemware were crated and stored in large warehouses. Every inch of her inside and out was painted battleship grey. Hence the name Grey Ghost. I went over on her right after graduation from West Point. We had no idea of the hardship we were about to endure. They put sixteen thousands eight hundred troops on her at one crossing, a record that still stands today. Every place they could put a sleeping bag on the outside decks a soldier slept. Only officers, doctors and nurses had inside cabins. They squeezed six into a cabin that was made to accommodate two, and we were the lucky ones. There was a working hospital, a prison and the indoor pool was drained was used as a morgue. The pool deck was so far under the water line that the walls of the pool were freezing without the heated water..

The worst of it was not enough bathrooms for all those soldiers. Every man had to pee over the side, and crap in paper bags. When the ocean got rough which was almost every day men vomited all over the decks, the smell was awful. It really wasn't something you wanted to tell your sons or share with your wife."

" I could see why you were a little taken aback, not wanting to come. Do you still want to go on the tours or will they upset you?"

" I won't know until I go, but I am intrigued about how there set up. I really don't want to go on the "Lady Di" tour, what am I going to see dresses and shoes. That one I pass."

" I'm sure I can find other women who's spouses' feel the same way as you, it's easy to start a conversation about fashion. I'll be fine you can take a nap or what ever."

" Fine, lets finish our soup and sandwich and go find history."

After lunch they signed up for the ship tours, they began with the wheel house as it was call in the old days. Today it's known as the bridge where the Captain is in control of the ship, with his officers. In the modern ship's bridge the Captain's chair is in the center an it's the command center for all decision. A small joy stick controls the movements of the ship, Queen Mary's large wheel controls the rudder and moves the bow to the right or to the left, and a separate free standing double handled instrument tells the boiler room for more power or to reverse the shaft so the blades will slow down the ship. James was in awe that the wheel house was in the same condition as he remembered it. Every piece of chrome and brass still shined and every wood finish looked as if it was brand spanking new. All the people on the tour listened to the tour guide as he explained all the instrumentation. He explained how the ship builder installed a much larger rudder than what was needed. They learned from the Titanic, steering clear of icebergs in the North Atlantic Ocean in the middle of winter was very important. A large rudder could save the ship from disaster if a hard over was needed. (Hard over is the term used to get the maximum degree of turning power.) Today all modern cruise ships and ocean liners have no rudders. Azur-pod propulsion can turn right or left this give the ship the ability to move sideways. Next on the tour was the World War II prison where Nazi officers as well as deserters where held awaiting Court Marshall. Again James was amazed that it was still true to form the way it was used during the war. He started to get flashback memories of an American AWOL soldier who was murdered in his cell. Some said it was the prison guards. They followed the tour guide to the aft of the ship where the hospital was erected. Again James was mesmerized as to the detail of the hospital ward, but nothing could have gotten him prepared for the operating room. It was glass enclosed and a full scene with manikins dressed as doctors, nurses and patients about to conduct an operation on a wounded soldier or prisoner. All the equipment being used dated to pre World WarII. As he stared something was starting to happen, the manikins became real and a full operation was under way. They had lost this patient and as doctor covered him with his sheet from behind her surgical mask appeared Michelle. The love he had lost so many years ago, he couldn't believe his eyes. He started to breath heavy holding his chest.

" James what's wrong? Your chalk white and sweating." Carol said.

" I'm all right."

" You look as if you just seen a ghost!"

" I have to go top side and get some air, stay with the tour next you'll be seeing the "Lady Di" exhibit. I'll meet you back in the suite."

Just as Carol predicted almost all the men left the wives at this point and the women had no problem making new friends. Every woman remembered how beautiful Lady Dianna was and when they first saw pictures of her wearing one of the elegant gowns on display. Each gown was accompanied by matching shoes, jewelry, and hand bag.

James went directly to the suit and sat in one of the velvet arm chairs, closing his eyes he envisioned Michelle the true love of his life. He met her when he was at West

Point, she was a young army nurse working in the hospital there. Her father was Colonel Frank O' Brian head master of the college. Michelle was a real wild cat who played by her own rules and she was crazy in love with James. She had her father pull every string and call in every favor to get her on the Queen Mary at the same time as Lt. James De Marco who had just graduated. James was assigned to active duty alone with the other sixteen thousand soldiers on "Queen Mary. It was at a small club that he saw her sitting at the bar when he asked her to dance a slow dance. She excepted and it was love at first touch. The tighter he held her the more turned on he became. He could feel every curve of her body and the soft yet firmness of her breasts. She knew exactly what he was feeling because she could feel him getting an erection. She moved as close as she could letting him rub against her. Then she looked up at James and smiled. He looked into her eyes and kissed her. She didn't hesitate for a second when she kissed him back. They both felt the chemistry between them, her smell was intoxicating. When the music stopped they were still holding each other on the dance floor. After a few drinks he took her to a motel and they make love all night. She told him she never had sex with someone she only knew by name, but he was different from anyone she had ever been with before. She couldn't explain it and she didn't understand why, it just was. He felt the same and it wasn't just the way she looked that turned him on. Michele was a classic beauty with a body to compliment her moves. They say you never forget your first true love, so it was for James. When Carol returned from her tour she found James asleep on the couch, she thought it was just a long day of travel and that he needed a nap. She let him sleep while she unpacked their clothes and put them away, then she took a hot shower to relax and fell asleep on the bed waiting for James to wake up. Without their knowledge a strange thing started happening in the suite, lights were turning on and off, the room suddenly got cold and the end tables started to shake. James was sleeping and found himself sitting at the edge of the couch, rubbing his arms to get warm.

Talking out loud to himself " I don't know but it must be thirty degrees in here, I'm go to the front desk and find out what's the problem."

James opened the door leading to the hallway and it was a comfortable warm 'seventy -four' degrees. Then as suddenly as it came, it went, the room was 'seventy- two' degrees. There was no real explanation for what happened other than an old ship.

Still unaware Carol was sleeping in the bedroom, he walked into the bathroom to freshen up. A quick shower and shave, but when he was finished with his shave the lights start to flicker. Each time they'd go on and off he appeared younger, until he sees himself as a young Lieutenant in full uniform. He rubs his eyes in disbelief, he's back to World War II and his first crossing on the Grey Ghost. About the same time Eric's limousine was pulling in the drop off area, there were several other cars ahead of them so they had to wait their turn. Kristy looked at the ship and said. " Is this the adventure you were telling me about? This ship is a relic. Next your going to tell me it's haunted by ghost."

" Of course, why do you think we came?"

" Take me back to Vegas, the inside is probable a dump."

" Excuse me, am I not paying for your time? Don't mistake my kindness for weakness, because I'm taking you inside that old ship and fucking your brains out. So shut it and lets go register, Kristy with a K, I have a suite reserved."

It was the first time Kristy saw a different side to Eric. She began to think maybe she didn't have a hold on him after all. He snapped back at her like a rattle snake when she challenged his position. Kristy was unaware of Eric's hidden agenda. The driver stops the limousine and gets out opens the door and takes the over night luggage and duffel bag with Eric's equipment out of the trunk. Eric and Kristy pick up the bags and walk to the elevator. When they reach the top the doors open and they walk directly to the registration desk. Kristy looks around at all the art deco interior and says,

"Wow this is really elegant, marble every where, it's like a step back in time."

Eric shows his credit card and says to the front desk clerk." I have a reservation for a suite, Eric Von Ellstein."

" Yes! Mr. Von Ellstein I have it right here, suite M124." He rings for the bellman and hands him the key. " Take the luggage to suite M124."

When they get to the suite the bellman opens the door and takes the luggage into the bedroom, hands Eric the key and the brochure of the ship.

" Is there any thing else I could do for you sir." As he waits his tip.

Eric walks him to the door and hands him a hundred dollar bill, but holds on to it and whispers in his ear.

" Get me the key to room M.340 and I'll give you another hundred."

" Pardon me sir but we never rent out room M.340, getting the master key could cause me my job."

" Two hundred more."

Then Eric looks him straight in the eyes and the bellman is unable to resist."

" I can't get the master key until after my shift is over, and that won't be until after midnight."

Eric hands him the two hundred dollars and smiles.

" Take this now just in case I'm not in my room when you bring back the key, I know you won't disappoint me."

OPENING THE VORTEX.

Eric takes a look at the brochure in his hand and tell Kristy. " Lets get dressed and have dinner at the Sir Winston Restaurant and afterwards we can have drinks and dance at the Observation Bar and Lounge."

" Fine by me, I'll take a shower first so I can dry my hair while you shower and we can dress together."

" Sounds like a plan, maybe after we can have desert back here before we go ghost hunting."

While Kristy is showering, Eric sneaks out and heads to the pool deck to try and get a handle on the vortex. That is rumored to be the place where all spirits enter and leave the ship. A large group of people are on tour and are listening to the tour guide give his speech about how haunted the pool deck is. Eric realizes this is not the time for him to be in that area, so he immediately returns to the suite without Kristy realizing he was even gone.

James steps out of the bathroom feeling his uniform and when he looks up there standing in front of him is Michelle in her nurses uniform. Before he can get a word out to ask how is this all possible she kisses him and leads him into the bedroom. Everything is just as it was nearly sixty years ago. James realizes he is no longer in the elegant suite of the Queen Mary, but back on the grey ghost.

" Wait Michelle, I don't understand!"

" Hurry we don't have much time." As she starts to take off her uniform.

" We could get court marshaled if we get caught."

" I've waited the whole trip over to be alone with you. Tomorrow we dock in South Hampton. You'll be going over to France and I'll be in some field hospital."

" How is this possible, I'm young again and your young and alive!"

" We've been given a second chance, I've been waiting for you on this ship for all these years." She opens his jacket and loosens his tie and belt and pulls him to the bed and they make love. Just as they did so many years ago. Michelle was his one true love, he could never resist her, she had that magical power over him. The chemistry between them was to intense, James had never felt it with any other woman including Carol. He keep it bottled up inside for all the rest of his days. Just looking at her in her bra and panties turned him on, as they kissed he knew he was in heaven. He slowly pulled down her panties and penetrated her. She was hot and moist just as he remembered her. When they were finished making love he looked her in the eyes and told her he could never love anyone the way he loved her. Then in a flash she was dressed and told him she had to leave but she'd come back for him later tonight. He grabbed her hand and won't let go.

" Why do you have to leave?"

" The vortex is starting to open, I'll be back for you before the evil comes through."

" Evil what evil?"

20

In a flash of light everything was back to normal, The Grey Ghost was no more. James was sitting on the couch in the art deco suite he thought he left behind. When Carol finally came in looking for him she said. " Why did you let me sleep so long?"

"I didn't realize the time, We could still go to dinner, I'm all showered and shaved and dressed. All I have to do is put on my sport coat."

" I'll grab a jacket just in case it's cold in the restaurant.

Carol turned and went back into the bedroom for her jacket and James sat back down on the couch holding his head. He thought he certainly must be loosing his mind. How in the world could this be happening, if he tried to explain it to Carol he'd have to reveal his secret. He decided not to say anything. He thought it was just low blood sugar. His lack of food and not taking his meds at the proper time was the cause of wishful dreaming. He was sure a good meal at the famous " Sir Winston Restaurant" was exactly what he needed. When Carol was ready they left the suite and went directly to the Sir Winston. Entering the restaurant the hostess asked if they had a reservation James replied.

" No but we are guest of the hotel staying in Grand Suite M101.

She picked up the house phone and spoke to the front desk, the night manager said.

" Mr. and Mrs De Marco are V.I.P.s of the hotel and please accommodate them with a table, top of the list of reservations.

The hostess informed them it would only be a few minutes to prepare and set a table for two. When they are finally seated Carol looks around the room and comments,

"What an elegant room this is, the wood work and marble."

" Don't forget the food, this is a five star restaurant!"

Then he opens the menu and looks at the wine list, " Wow! Five star prices too."

" James do not sign this bill to the room, the boys have paid enough. I don't think they could ever imagine these prices."

" Just like a mother hen always worrying about her young, I get it, I'll pay cash and they will never have to know we were here. What do you feel like having?"

" The lobster dinner, comes with a salad and bake potato. That's what I'm having."

" I'm going to have surf and turf, with salad and potato."

After he gives the waiter their order he asks for a bottle of ' Pinot Blanc.'

Just then Kristy followed by Eric walks by on their way to their table. James feels a cold presence pass through him, he could not explain it but the look on his face told Carol something was very wrong.

"James are you all right, your chalk white again. Haven't seen another ghost again have you?" No pun intended."

" Carol don't make fun, there are serious things going on here that I can't explain. This is one of the reasons I didn't want to come on this trip. I don't think I'm going to make it off this ship!"

"Your letting your imagination run away with you. Your old memories and this haunted ship thing, are getting to you. Just relax, have dinner and you'll feel a whole lot better."

"Maybe your right, a couple of glasses wine always help to settle the nerves."

21

As they were enjoying their meal, every time James looked up at Carol, because of the angle setting of the tables Eric was in his line of sight. For some strange reason that he could not comprehend he could'nt stop looking at Eric. Their was a force drawing him to Eric. Then Michele appeared between James' line of sight to Eric and the force he felt disappeared. It was as if Michelle had come to his rescue, breaking Eric's aura.

When dinner was over James paid the check with cash. Carol smiled acknowledging her wishes. Then they continued to the 'Observation Bar and Lounge. A room in the sophistication and style of the 1930s'. The art deco bar was worth the trip, everyone who entered the room had to stop and take it all in. From the mural over the bar featuring the dancing figures of a bygone area to the silver trim along the bar top that had a mirror finish to it. The walls had silver inlay between the marble covering, even the stools, tables and chairs were a perfect complement to the decor. This was a gathering room for all the swells of that era. No ordinary Joe, would be found here, no sir. This was a place for celebrities, dignitaries and the very rich. No second class citizen would be among those drinking and dancing the night away.

While James and Carol were enjoying their trip down memory lane, Eric had other ideas for himself and Kristy. They sneaked down to the lower level to the pool deck. At this time of night the pool deck was off limits. When they entered it was dimly lit and the musty stale odor was every where. The pool and water soaked tile gave off a mildew smell even though the pool was empty. During the day fresh air was pumped in to accommodate the daily tours. Kristy was reluctant to go, not wanting to get into any trouble, but when she went and smelled the air she said.

" This place stinks, it's disgusting down here. Lets go."

" Are you kidding, this is the place where the spirits enter and leave. The vortex is right behind that sealed wall. Years ago there was a locker room for men and woman to change into their bathing suits and then later shower and get dressed. When people began to see and hear things, that's when the legend started to grow, and when a few unexplained murders happened. The ship's captain had the wall erected sealing off the lockers. The pool was still open to the first class passengers who found warm robes in their closets to wear over their bathing suits. Clean towels were provided to dry off exiting the pool. Then World War II broke out and the ship became a troop carrier, and the ship's pool was drained and used as a morgue. Because the bottom of the pool is so far below the water line the cold walls keep the bodies from smelling and decaying."

" How do you know all this stuff?"

" I told you, this is my passion. The best is room B.340 became the haunted spirit room. More people were killed in that room after the lockers were sealed. It was as if the spirits needed a new place to dwell. Why they picked that room no one really knows. That's why we have to get into that room. I have to see for myself, don't you want to be a part of this adventure?"

" It does sound a little scary, okay I'm in."

" Let just hope we get that key at midnight, until then what would you like to do?"

" What have you go in mind?" Said Kristy.

" We could go have a drink at the Observation Bar or we could go back to the suite and I could fuck your brains out. Wait, what about we get room service to send up a bottle of vodka set up, with fruit and cheese and we can party and drink at the same time."

" Sounds like a plan to me, lets see if your a man of your word."

Eric gives Kristy a hug to reassure her that all is well between them, then they turn to the elevator and start to walk away. With their backs to the pool and locker room area a strange phenomenon started to occur, many color lights began to slowly open a portal to a different dimension. This was what Eric was hoping for, proof positive to see with his own eyes that the legends of the Grey Ghost were real.

When they got back to the suite Eric called for a vodka set up. He was told it would take about fifteen to thirty minutes.

James and Carol were having the time of their lives dancing to the old big band song the band was playing. " Oh my God, we haven't danced like this in years!"

" We better sit down Carol or your going to have to carry me back to the suite. "The Old Grey Mare, aint what he use to be."

" Okay lets just finish our drinks, catch our breath and call it a night

"Carol there playing," Moonlight Serenade" we got to dance to this. Come on we'll take it nice and slow.

" Two minutes ago you couldn't breath, now you want to dance. Your killing me James, or do you have a death wish?"

At the end of their dance they returned to their table to finish their drinks and just listen to the great songs of 1940s.

Eric and Kristy were making their own music as they decided on a little fore play until the vodka showed up. Rolling around on the bed Eric started to strip Kristy of her clothes. First it was her blouse, then he pulled off her shoes and pants. He mounted her and started to dry hump her. In her bra and panties she began to really turn him on, he took off his shirt and kicked off his shoes.

" Stop your going to start something and not want to stop when room service, delivers the vodka set up."

" Your killing the mood Kristy!"

A knock at the door was enough to stop Eric in his tracks. He immediately answered the door and signed for the delivery. Then he poured two large vodkas on ice and brought them into the bedroom along with the tray of assorted fruit and cheese. With Kristy sitting up in bed what better place to have a party than on a bed with a half naked woman, who in a black lace bra and panties could make any man clamor for more. As they were drinking Eric took a strawberry dipped it in his vodka and passed it down Kristy's cleavage. Then he started from her bra and licked upward to her neck, he began sucking on her neck giving her a large hickey. He grabbed her by her hair at the back of her head and feed her his vodka. Looking in her eyes he kissed her with all the passion of a man falling in love. He fed her his strawberry after she took a bite he sucked on the rest. Then he put his drink and hers, on the night table next to the bed. He unhooked her bra allowing her voluptuous breasts to fall free. he laid her back down and started to caress her nipple until it grew and hardened, then he did the same to the other. He kissed her stomach and edged his way to her panties, pulling them off until she was totally free to except him inside her. Removing the rest of his clothes he mounted her and slowly started to penetrate her. This was not the action of a man who was paying for her time or her sex, but of a man who was trying to satisfy his love. She responded by tightening her inner muscles to hold a firm grip on Eric's penis, Kristy was the consummate professional knowing fully how to use all the tricks of her trade. She was determined to make it as hard, as possible for Eric to leave her after the weekend was over. Kristy was digging her hooks into Eric without him even realizing what was happening. Actions speak louder than words by his response to her she felt she was winning the battle. They were so engrossed in their love making they never heard the knock at the door in the next room. Eric's wishes were granted as the bellman quietly opened the door and slipped the key to room B.340 into the do not disturb pouch on the inside handle of the door. He could hear the moans Kristy was making and did not want to disturb them. He couldn't help himself as he quietly walked through the living room and peeked in on them having sex. Eric's intuition make him look at he doorway and he saw the bellman sneaking a peak at them, he rolled Kristy on top as she pumped away riding non stop. Her naked body was an extra perk Eric felt he deserved for bringing him the key. Then as quietly as he entered the suite he left.

Eric knew the later they went on their adventure to room B.340, the less chance there would be of someone seeing them sneaking into the room. Continuing to have sex with Kristy made perfect sense in Eric's mind.

When James and Carol finally got back to their room they were totally exhausted and went right to bed. A short time later Michelle appeared in their bedroom, a chill woke James. It was the same chill he had experienced before. Even in an unclear stupor of sleep he knew Michelle had come for him. He walked into the living room and again a light flashed in front of him and again he was a young Lieutenant. Michelle grabbed his arm and said, " We have to get off the ship before the vortex totally opens or we will never have a chance to be together."

James didn't understand it but he followed Michelle as they walked down the gangway on to the dock. As James looked around they was no longer in Long Beach. A jeep was waiting for him, the young soldier driving gave him his orders, James read them and said his goodbyes to Michelle. As the jeep sped away James looked back to get a last look at Michelle but she was gone. So was the ship they had just gotten off, there was only country behind him. They were not in England but in northern France. He sat facing forward in the jeep and pondered what was happening to him. The jeep was kicking up plenty of dust the faster the young driver went. It was if he understood the urgency of James' orders. The further north they drove the colder it got. The young soldier stopped the jeep and handed James his winter field jacket saying.

"You better put on your winter jacket sir, we're running right into winter. It gets mighty cold up here in December."

James had no response, he just reached for the jacket and put it on over his short uniform jacket. While they were stopped the driver put the canvas top back over the windshield and buttoned it down as if expecting snow. When they reached a base camp the jeep stopped in front of a large tent with a wooden sign saying headquarters. James got out and went inside. Lucky for James this was a well equipped winter tent with a pot belly stove heating the entire tent. James could not feel his hands, face or feet. There he found two majors and a colonel. He saluted and stood at ease waiting orders. Colonel Meyers was in charge and they all gathered around a map on a large wooden table.

" Lieutenant I need you to hold this position." Pointing to the map. " We have good intelligence that a large tank division is moving into the Ardent Woods. The position I have shown you is ten miles east of Bastogne. We're sure the Panza Division will use the main road at that point before spreading out to surround the area leading to Bastogne. Time Lieutenant every hour of every day you can hold back that German Panza Division gives Patton time to reinforce that area. This may very well be the turning point of the war. I'm going to give you three squads of men. Two of which will be bazooka (anti-tank rocket launcher) men and three fifty caliber machine gunners. There's a small town called Bastogne' which has been our headquarters in that area. They are almost out of supplies and food. It's imperative we hold that town. You have to slow down that German column until General Patton can come northwest from southern France to support the town and the area with his third army. Make no mistake this is a very danger-ous mission but one of great importance. You were selected for this mission because we were told you were the best tac-tician coming out of West Point. Make us proud son, make us proud. Get some food and a good night sleep you leave at first light, but first get yourself a pair of winter boots from the supply tent. Meet up with Sergeant Ryan he'll give you a briefing on your men, that's all for now. Good luck and God be with you all."

" Thank you sir, we'll fight to the last man." (Salutes, and leaves.)

OPENING THE VORTEX.

The first thing James did was find the supply tent, food and sleep could wait what he needed most was those winter boots. As he entered the supply tent he looked around and asked for size nine boots. The orderly in charge said. " I have them right here sir along with a pair of winter pants to go with your winter field jacket. I guess they knew you'd be coming."

As James was about to turn and leave the tent the soldier said. "Lieutenant, don't you want your Thompson Machine Gun?"

" Can't do much fighting without one of those." Said James.

" Officers tent is three tents over to the left. You can get food and a clean cot sir.

At first light James meets up with his Sergeant, all the men are ready to go they board the trucks as James gets in his jeep and signals to move forward.

" How far is the jump off point Sergeant?"

" About ten miles, after that it's on foot to the woods. The word among the men is most of our soldiers have been killed or captured. What do you know sir?"

" Not much sergeant, all I know is we have to hold our position to give time for General Patton to reinforce Bastogne."

" Sounds like the lambs being lead to the slaughter, Sir."

When they reach the ten mile mark the column stops and the men gather their equipment and ammunition and form three groups. Each bazooka gunner has one man with extra rockets to carry and a soldier with a Thomson Machine Gun for security.

The second group is three 50 caliber machine gunners with three ammunition men. The third group was the remaining thirteen men not counting Sergeant Ryan and James. Twenty- seven men in all against a tank division, it was looking more like a suicide mission. The night before James had studied the map and topography looking for a good location to catch the Germans in a cross fire. As they walked closer towards the woods they came upon a bombed out mill, with a main house made of stone a work shed also made of stone and a horse barn with a stone foundation. The main road passed between the main house and the mill. James realized there would be more cover there than in the woods. He immediately got some of the men to clear out some of the fallen stone to setup a clear line of fire shot for one of the bazooka gunners. The other would be across the road behind the tool shed and open fire on the German Panza Tank closest to them. James hoped the element of surprise would be a major factor.

James moved the men into their positions, he knew that at least two maybe three Tiger Tanks would be leading the infantry. With the remaining tanks bringing up the rear.

The bazooka gunners would have to be the first to fire, taking out the two lead tanks with the 50 caliber machine guns giving them cross fire power and time to take out the third tank. The rest of the men and the last 50 caliber machine gun would be the second line of defense, in order for this plan to work the bazooka gunners would also have to take out the advancing rear tanks. Then the German infantry would be left in the open with no real cover. They dug two fox holes for the 50 caliber machine guns, the men inside the hole would be less of a target when the

Germans returned fire, and they could camouflage their position until they opened fire. They brought over as many large stones as they could find from the falling walls of the buildings. Placing the stone on each side of the machine guns creating a small wall for additional cover. A bazooka team would then be placed inside the bombed out main house after they took out a lead tank. They would wait until the tanks passed their positions and then they would take out the lead tanks. When the tanks exploded the 50 caliber machine gun would open fire on the German ground troops. Now all they had to do was go over the plan so every man knew what he had to do to make it work, and wait for hell to arrive. Their nerves were starting to get the best of them when in the quiet air they could hear the sound of the advancing Tiger Tanks.

" Saddle up men, it's show time. Lets give them hell!" James said.

The plan was working to perfection, taking out the two lead tanks and catching the infantry in a cross fire giving the time needed to attack the third tank that was in a wishbone formation. The Germans just kept coming the second line of defense opened fire and the first wave of attack was over as they started to fall back. James knew the second wave of attack would not be so easy as the element of surprise was now over. It gave time for James to regroup his men after killing hundreds of German infantry soldiers and taking out three German Tiger Tanks, James had not lost a single man.

" Men the Germans are going to regroup and hit us with every thing they've got. I expect they will pound the shit out of this location. As soon as they get their plan of attack ready. So lets drop back behind the stone buildings and use them as shelter. The bazookas have got to get behind the tanks and take them out if were to have any chance. Any ideas?"

"Lieutenant how about if we crawl back out to the fox holes cover ourselves and wait till they pass and open fire."

" Do you really think we can fool them twice from a fox hole?"

" It's worth a try."

" Okay but only one team will go, the other bazooka will stay with the main group so I can move them as needed. Also after you take your shot fall back the 50s will give you all the cover fire they can."

Before the light of day the Tiger Tanks bombarded the location and buildings until they felt secure enough to advance their infantry. When the bombardment stopped we took our positions in the remains of the stone walls for cover. The fighting was intense on both sides as James was starting to loose his men. Although the bazooka gunner took out a fourth tank as planned, it took their last two rockets. The first hit the steel tracks and the second was a perfect broadside hit. With no rockets left they decided to abandon the fox hole and try to make it back to the stone house for cover. They never made it back even with the machine gun cover that was provided. The battle raged all through the day and ammunition was getting low. A fifth Tiger Tank was taken out with the last rocket. Two of the 50 caliber machine guns were completely out of ammo. Half of James' men were killed and they knew it wouldn't be long before they were over run. When more Tiger Tanks arrived to support the German Troops they knew all would be lost. By night fall with only a few men left the German tanks poured it on with more direct shelling. A stone wall finally gave way and collapsed on top of James. The last thing he saw before loosing consciousness was Sergeant Ryan and the last of his team killed by machine gun fire from one of the Tiger Tanks. Two days later as the men from the fifth division searched the battle ground an American soldier heard what he thought was someone praying he found James barely alive and yelled for a medic. When James woke up he was in a field hospital and his eyes were covered in a bandage, when he heard a voice that could only belong to Michelle, he spoke out.

" Michelle is that you, where am I?"

" Don't try to get up, you are badly hurt and have a very bad concussion"

She went to his aid and lowered his head to the pillow. Then she sat by his side and held his hand. She increased his pain medication and he past out. She knew sleep was the best medicine at this point, he needed to rest and regain his strength. She never left his side. Even when her shift was over. She sat at his side and held his hand. Days later the doctors removed the head bandages from James' eyes. He could hardly see at all, everything was a complete blur. The doctors reassured him in time he would get back his vision one hundred percent. It was his other wounds that would give him pain he rest of his life, Both his legs were crush under the weight of the stone wall that fell on him, he also had four broken ribs and an arm all on the same side. What he needed now was lots of tender loving care that only Michelle could give him. Weeks later Colonel Meyer came to see him and told him.

" How are you feeling Lieutenant? Are they treating you okay here, is there anything I can do for you?"

" My men, (pause) did any of them make it sir?"

" I'm afraid not."

" I'm sorry I failed your mission, you put your trust in me and I got my whole squad killed."

" Nonsense my boy, you held your position for more than two days. Twenty -Seven men against a Tiger Tank Division, Bravest thing I've ever heard. The two days you delayed the Germans from advancing saved hundreds maybe thousands of men in the 101 infantry division until Patton's Third Army got there to reenforce them. That's why your getting the Metal of Bravery, Bronze Star, and the Purple heart. You just get well your fighting days are over. Your going home a hero and your country thanks you. When your able we will ship you over to a real hospital."

Six weeks later the cast on his arm was removed and his ribs were totally healed, now all he had to do was wait for the cast on his legs to be removed so he could start to try to walk again. Orders came through for James to be moved to the nearest Red Cross Army Hospital. As James was being placed in an ambulance he was trying to say his good byes to Michelle.

" I just want you to know I could never have made it this far if it wasn't for you. I love you with all my heart, there will never be anyone that can take your place. I'll miss you Michelle."

"What! Did you think you were getting rid of me that easy? I had my father pull some strings and I've been trans-ferred to the same hospital."

" Maybe you should consider a new guy, why get stuck with a broken down soldier who can't even lift his legs."

" After all this time, now your feeling sorry for yourself. I'm doing this for me, your just a pain in my ass. If I don't see this all the way through until you can walk again, you'll always be a pain in my ass. Oh one other thing, I'll kick your ass from here to Paris and back if you ever talk to me that way again. I told you a long time ago I was in love with you. When I gave myself to you on that ship, I knew you were my first true love and you'll be my last and there will never be anyone in between."

"Michelle, I can't see to find you, I can't walk to hold you!"

" I'll find you, and I'll walk to you and I'll never ever let go. Do you understand if it takes forever, I'll be waiting there for you. When we get to the hospital I'm going to work you so hard, your legs will be like new and the doctors said your eye sight will return in time. I'll see you in a few days."

Michelle gives him a kiss goodbye, and the medics slide his stretcher into the ambulance. Closing the doors as Michelle waved watching James slip away from her once again. When James got to the Red Cross Hospital he was very well taken care of but nothing could replace the loving care Michelle had given him. A week later Michelle finally walked into the hospital after seeing her commanding offi-cer, and the head of nursing. She immediately looked for James. Finding him a semi private four officers to a room was considered deluxe accommodations. As she walked in all the other officers started to whistle at her, she was the first young nurse they had seen since coming to this hospital. So when she went over to James and gave him a kiss, she heard the remarks.

"Where's my kiss? I'm a captain he's only a Lieutenant."

" I'm the best looking guy in the room."

" I can see I'm going to have to close the curtains every time I come into this room," said Michelle.

" Hey pipe down you guys, this is my girl Michelle."

They all knew of the heroics James had gone through for his men and that he still had no eye sight to speak of. So all the jokes were all in good fun and humor. Michelle was station to a different floor so she looked in on him every chance she could. All her free time was spent with James giving him all the support she could, as time passed James' eye sight started to slowly come back. The agonizing time on his back was starting to take it's toll on James. His nerves were wearying thin, and he was slipping back into depression. A few days later Michelle came in with great news, his casts were going to be removed the next day. Michelle informed him that the real work to the road to recovery was about to begin, his leg muscles were totally weakened from the long healing time and would have to be strengthen back to support his weight and movement. Bright and early the next morning the doctors sawed off the plaster of paris mix which held James' legs for two months. When the casts were removed the doctors began to bend his legs at the knees to get movement into the joints, then they wanted James to try and do it on his own. He could hardly lift them at all. Then they sat him in a wheelchair and told him an orderly would take him outside for some sunlight and fresh air. Michelle found him outside, in back of the hospital. There was a large patio that leads to a beautifully manicured lawn with flowers and trees.

" Well, look who they let out of jail! Enjoying the sunny day? I brought some food, I thought we could have lunch together."

James was very quite and reserved, he appeared in deep thought.

" I can't lift my legs on my own."

" Of course not, they haven't been mobile in months. Now's the time to build them back up where they can support your weight while you walk. Tomorrow you start therapy we'll get those puppies going. Each day Michelle would work on his legs. First she would lay him on his back in bed and hold his feet and pump his legs like he was riding a bike, after and hour she would rub a creme to ease the pain This went on until it was time for him to work his legs on his own. James was getting his strength back as well as his eye sight. Which was now almost totally recovered just like the doctors had told him. It was now time for James to try and walk on his own, he was placed between two parallel bars for support, just in case his legs gave way he could hold onto the bars. From there he works on a stationary bike, each day getting better than the last. At last after months of therapy he started to walk with two canes for support. James knew the time was getting close when he would be sent back to the states leaving Michelle behind. They moved James down to a rehab therapy floor were he had more freedom to move around and come and go on the grounds of the hospital. He was spending as much time with Michelle as she could give to him. She still had to work her shift in nursing after all she still was in the army. Word came down that the last allied push into Germany and onto Berlin was about to take place and all army doctors and nurses were going to move up closer to the front. With Germany as their last strong hold the allies anticipated the German Army to fight with everything they had left to defend mother country. All doctors and nurses awaited orders and when they finally came Michelle knew it would be the last night she might ever spend with James. She secretly sneaked him into her room for a night of love making a memory that would have to last forever. As they entered Michelle's room James was very taken aback. Suddenly his fear that his legs were not strong enough to support his body during sex. Even though he was walking better every day with just a cane. Then he said, " Wait, maybe this isn't such a good idea."

" Don't you want to make love to me?"

" Of course I do, but."

" But what?"

" What if my legs can't support you. Or they give out on me."

" Don't worry, I won't let that happen. You just follow my lead. Let me control the movements, we've made love before and I know how to satisfy both of us."

Then she was as gentle in her love making as he was the first time they had sex together. James handled her like fine crystal. Every movement was to totally satisfy her. Like all unselfish true love, when your mental outlook is for the other person first before yourself. The sexual memories will last forever.

She tried to explain the danger of the time and place she brought James to was catching up to the time and place when they left the ship. He didn't quite understand what she was saying about what was happening on the Grey Ghost. At that exact moment in the future world Eric and Kristy were finishing their lustful sexual desires. Eric was now ready to shower and dress and begin the adventure he most anticipated. While Kristy was in the bathroom he began to look for his camera and flash light and tape recorder. When Kristy was finished dressing and came out of the room she looked at Eric.

" You look like your going on a safari with all that equipment." She said.

" I want to be able to prove anything we encounter. We may be making history, proving that the legend of the Queen Mary is true."

They very quietly moved down the hallway to room B.340. When they got there Eric inserted the key and turned the lock, it gave off a very loud knock as it had not been tried for many years and was somewhat rusted inside. As they both slipped inside Eric turned on his flash light and recorder, then he looked for a light switch hoping it would work. When he found it to his surprise it worked giving off a little light, it was a big improvement over just the flash light. Kristy remarked about how musty and stale the air was with a pungent odor of blood.

" Let's get out of here, this room is giving me the creeps!"

" Quiet we don't want anyone to know were in here."

Eric continues to look around. The room was just as it had been left. A wooden bed with simple bedding and a pillow, a night stand with a small lamp, a table with a medal bowl for water to wash in, a single wood chair and a mirror on the wall. The room was filthy and the dust was an inch thick. Eric was taking photos and had his back to Kristy when she let out a scream. Eric turned and covered her mouth with his hand.

" Didn't I just say keep quiet?"

" Did you see the dead man in the bed with an axe in his head?

" Where?"

" Right there." Pointing to the bed.

" I don't see anything, I think your loosing you mind."

" That's it I'm out of here, let me out of here."

Just then two white lights form hands and start pulling Kristy through the mirror as she is screaming Eric is frozen and can't move all he can do is snap picture after picture. In a matter of seconds Kristy is completely gone. Eric runs out of the room closing the light behind him, locking the door and races to his suite to dump all the equipment because he knows exactly where Kristy has gone. If there was anyway to help her he would have to race there before the vortex closes.

Michelle can feel the danger that is happening on board the ship and cannot stop the two worlds from colliding. She can only play out her time with James until the parallel universes aline. She made the best of the night with James and the next morning Michelle makes ready to leaves for the front. At the same time James is brought out of the hospital and loaded onto the Red Cross Trucks. As they pull away James is waving goodbye to the only woman he ever really loved. She waits until the trucks are out of sight and returns to the hospital that is staffed with a skeleton staff, unable to take any new casualties of war. The only news they are getting is the fighting is intense with many wounded soldiers on both sides. The worry for Michelle's safety has out grown the pain his legs generate each day. When James' orders finally arrive at Calis he is leaving half heartedly for fear of what Michelle is enduring at her field hospital. He has a couple of days before his transportation would arrive to take him from the port of Calis across the English Channel back to Southhampton England. He recruited a young Private he had met in the hospital while he was recovering from his wounds. Michelle had given him special attention to help him get well. When James told him of his fear for Michelle he immediately volunteered to help. They were now an army of misfit soldiers on a mission to find Michelle, and they only had a couple of days to do it. Together they stole a jeep, two Thompson Machine guns just in case they ran into any German soldiers. James found a map in the jeep and decided to follow the main road east that lead to Berlin. He knew sooner, or later he would run into Allied soldiers or American soldier that could give them information as to base camps or Red Cross Hospital Tents. They traveled several hundred miles east when they realized they were getting low on fuel, without gas they were in big trouble because neither of them could walk any distance at all. Lucky they came upon a refueling convoy for tanks and trucks, when they stopped and asked for a fill up. The Sergeant in charge said.

"Sure Lieutenant, but where are you going?"

" I'm looking for a field hospital. My girl is a nurse stationed there."

" There's a field hospital about ten miles up the road, when you get to the fork in the road bare left a couple of mile further into that road you'll see a large hospital tent. Your all fill sir, good luck."

Every tent Hospital has a large Red Cross painted in the top but Hitler is loosing the war and gives orders to kill everyone. The rules of the Geneva Convention mean nothing to him, he is showing his madness to the high command who are starting to doubt his orders. German Messerschmitt fighter planes were attacking everything they saw on the ground. Convoys, base camps, tanks even hospital tents were being destroyed. No one or nothing was safe from Hitler's orders. When James finally found the hospital tent, Michelle was not there. No one had seen her at that location.

James knew he was running out of time and if he wasn't back to the pick up point, he'd never get a transport back to the ship waiting in Calais. With no idea of where she could be he decided to return. Missing the ship was the easy part, being court marshaled for steeling a jeep and putting a soldier in harms way would give him a ride home in the prison cells on the Grey Ghost. Soon he was on a ship leaving Calais for England and the waiting Grey Ghost. At the same time tragedy had struck, Michelle was attending a convoy of wounded American Soldier when Messerschmitts came roaring out of the sky and attacked the convoy. With guns blazing almost everyone was killed. Michelle was badly wounded and taken back to the very hospital tent where James had been looking for her. The doctors there worked franticly to save her but her wounds were much to intense for a field hospital with limited operating equipment. Michelle died without ever knowing James was there looking for her. Colonel Meyers came himself to see how she was doing, he was best friends with Michelle's father ever since their days at WestPoint.

" I want this nurse handled with kid gloves, her body is to be on the next transport flying back to England and placed in the Queen Mary bound for the states."

Michelle was placed in a body bag suitable for transportation. The swimming pool on the Queen Mary was empty of water and because it was at below sea level without heated water the walls were cold enough to be used as a morgue. All American soldiers of high rank were shipped back to a American Military Cemetery. Her body was placed on the first transport back to England and sent to the docks to be loaded onto the ship. When the jeep that brought James to the Queen Mary for his return trip stopped along side a canvas truck, he had no idea his beloved Michelle was inside one of the body bags. As he walked up the gang way to enter the ship he had a strange feeling and when he looked back two Soldiers were unloading the truck. It was the first time he thought to himself he would be on the Grey Ghost without Michelle. The trip back was very lonely, James worried for Michelle, he constantly thought what might be happening at the front as the allied command pushed forward into Germany. On his lay over waiting for transportation he was hearing all sorts of chatter from different soldiers who claimed they knew what was going on at the front. How much of it was true and how much of it was just bull shit, he had no way of telling. Every night he'd feel Michelle's life force around him, how could he know she was in a body bag in the ships morgue trying to get to him. Her spirit roamed the lower decks not knowing where exactly where she was. She had never been on the lower decks when she first crossed the Atlantic Ocean on her way to England. The Hospital, Cabins and main Mess Hall where on the higher decks and the only ones that were familiar to her. This was her new world and for the first time ever she did not aspire the confidence she always had in life. Getting to know the other spirits that roamed the lower decks was all new to her. It would take years to feel free to roam the entire ship. The vortex was small and did not have the power it had taken on as the years went by. The more it was feed souls the stronger it's hold was on the person it was trying to possess.

Such was the case with Kristy, when she was taken from room B.340 she found herself fighting for her life. She didn't understand what was happening, only that she was whirling around as if she was caught in a wind storm. Eric knew exactly where to go, to find her, he ran as fast as he could to the pool deck. When he got there the Pool was filled with sea water, he could hear the screams from Kristy but he could not see her. In his haste to find Kristy he left all his equipment in the suite. His large flash light would have come in handy if he had brought it, but he had no idea how dark it was going to be. Then the vortex started to open and a strange light, the same as the one he'd experienced in room B.340 shown on the pool. A scream for help rang out as Kristy came to the top of the pool water fighting for her life. What Eric didn't know was Kristy was a champion swimmer in college and almost made the Olympic team.

Every time the spirit force pulled her down under the water she fought her way back to the top. As she gasped for air, she screamed for help, then she saw Eric standing at the edge of the pool. He was frozen just like he was in the room when she was being pulled through the mirror. Again she was pulled under and again she kicked her way to the top, only this time she screamed for Eric's help. This time she fought with all her might and she kicked and kicked until she reached the edge of the pool. Little did she realize it was Michelle who was now back on the ship giving her the strength to beat the force created by the vortex. She pulled herself out of the water and started to scream and beat her fists on Eric's chest.

" What's wrong with you? You just stood there and watched me almost drown and you offered me no help. What kind of a monster are you?"

" I couldn't, you just don't understand. My legs were frozen, my body couldn't move. I don't want the vortex to take you, I want you to stay with me. I've never felt this way before about any other girl I've ever been with."

" What are you talking about?"

Then in a flash she was back in Eric's suite, lying in bed snuggled under the sheets exhausted from her sexual affair. Michelle was able to move her back in time, she now knew the danger Kristy was about to face. She now had two problems to contend with, how to get Kristy off the ship alive and safe and how to keep James on the ship with her forever. She had to find a way to close the vortex and keep the evil spirits from invading the ship and seeking a new soul to satisfy their hunger for new blood but how, there must be an answer somewhere. Michelle was determined to find it, but where to look that was still the determining factor. There were many good spirits on the

Grey Ghost all of whom made up the legend that the ship was haunted. They occupied the hallways and provided the sounds that many passengers would hear. Never was there any evil doings from them, all their sightings were late at night when most passengers had a few to many drinks and were unsure what they thought they had seen. This created a buzz of conversation which led to the infamous legend that still grows as the years pass. The vortex would only open once or twice a year and when it was about to happen the spirits would move to a different dimension and out of harms way. Before World War II the Queen Mary was the most elegant way to cross the Atlantic Ocean. The ship was filled with celebrities and dignitaries from all over the world. Even when the rumors began about the ship being haunted, it was a happy place to be. Movie stars that traveled on board loved the mystery she projected as well as the art deco interior of the times. The ghost sightings were always the same. The Lady in White, a Child about six that was said to have drowned in the pool and various Engine Room Sailors that died because of the extreme heat and the hard work of shoveling coal for the boilers to create steam for the engines. The turbine engines made the Queen Mary the fastest ship on the ocean, no German ship or submarine could catch her on the open sea. She believed none of these spirits were connected to the vortex, they died on the ship and their souls were forever bound to roam the hollow decks of the Queen Mary. She sensed no evilness whenever she encountered them in passing, this further made her believe the strength of the vortex had to be coming from the men who died that were prisoners being held on the ship as it crossed from England to America. Some were deserters, others were Nazi Officers and some were just spies.

The one thing they all had in common was, they all committed murder in one fashion or another. Many of the prisoners were brought on board wounded and the thinking was to have the ship hospital attend their wounds, only to have them die on the operating tables or from loss of blood. The doctors and nurses felt it was a waste of time, energy and most of all needed blood supply. Most of the officers believed it was a righteous kill and never questioned why they had died. Believing she was on the right track, she still had to find the common denominator she was looking for.

At the same time Kristy was waking up from her exhausting sexual romp. Totally naked she made her way to the bathroom while sitting on the bowel she started to get flash backs. All that had happened to her were coming in waves of still photos, she couldn't distinguish what was real or just the effects of to much alcohol. What she did feel was the aura of Michelle around her. A small voice kept telling her not to go through any of the ghostly experiences with Eric. When she came out of the bathroom Eric was sitting up waiting for her return, when he saw her naked body he began to get excited for her. He rolled back the covers inviting her into his bed for another round of sexual pleasure. She smiled and thought to herself as long as he wants me sexually he's not thinking about going on his ghost hunt, and that suited her just fine. He poured the last of the vodka into a glass added ice and a squeeze of lemon, then he offered Kristy the glass to share the last of the vodka. She excepted and took a sip or two, giving it back to Eric who finished the drink and began to kiss and touch her voluptuous breasts. As he worked down her body his erection could not wait an other second, he had to slowly penetrate her hot moist vagina. The harder he pumped into her the more aroused she became, the intensity of their body chemistry was incredible. Orgasm after orgasm Kristy begged Eric to stop, she thought her heart could not take anymore. He was out to prove she was totally under his power, he wanted her as his sex slave. When he finally climaxed and started to ejaculate she lifted her body arching her back for the deepest penetration he could give her. She held that position and tightened the inner vaginal muscles squeezing every ounce he had to give. When they were done again they fell into a deep sleep. When Kristy finally woke up Eric was all showered, dressed and ready to go on his quest for ghost hunting. Kristy sat up in bed and said.

"I'm not going on any ghost hunt. You'll have to go without me, I have a bad feeling about it. I'll wait here for you to come back with your pictures or stories."

" No way, stop being such a girl. We started this together and we'll end it together, so go take a shower and get dressed and you'll see how much better your feel about all this."

" My mother always said to listen to that little voice in the back of your head it's the angels talking to you. Every time I didn't listen, it was a bad situation for me. I'll be right here when you get back."

This was not what Eric was expecting and it pissed him off to say the least, he began to throw the empty bottle of vodka to the floor and knocked over the coffee table and fruit bowel in a fit of rage. Then he took the key to room B.340 and stormed out the door.

GOOD-VS-EVIL

Eric really scared the life out of Kristy, it was the first time she had seen him that upset. She took a quick shower to refresh herself and got dressed. She still couldn't make heads or tales out of the way she felt but she knew she had to get out of there and off the ship before Eric came back. She started to pack her over night case, taking the clothes out of the closet and draws and folding them as quickly as she could and placing them in the overnighter. Then she remembered her makeup case and tooth brush and went into the bathroom when she came out Eric was standing there.

" Where are you going?"

" I told you I wasn't going on your ghost hunt and I meant it, so I'm packing and leaving the ship."

" I'm sorry I scared you or made you upset, I should have understood but I was hoping we were going on this adventure together. If you don't want to go to room B.340 I'll go alone. You don't have to leave the ship, how are you going to get back to Las Vegas?"

" I was going to take a cab to the airport and fly back."

" At 2:00 in the morning, do you really think there's a commuter plane this hour of the night?"

" I don't know. I guess I wasn't thinking clearly, it's just you went crazy and that's a side of you Iv'e never seen before. You scared me half to death."

" I never gave you the rest of your money, why don't you stay here, I'll go take some pictures and when I come back we'll talk things out. You can't just sit around an airport for five or six hours until the commuters start running. If you still want to leave in the morning I'll have a car take you to the airport."

Eric was a master at manipulating peoples minds to get what ever he was after. So reminding Kristy of the money she had earned on her back screwing his brains out was only one factor for staying. The other was the time she would have spent alone in an empty airport. Without the influence of Michelle who was back with James trying to stabilize the time periods and aline the parallel dimensions. With that Kristy decided to stay and Eric left the suite on his hunt for the paranormal he so wanted to encounter.

Michelle knew she didn't have much time until James would be brought back to the present time so she immediately went to the prison deck and searched through the files of prisoners with a murder trial awaiting them or prisoners who had died or were killed on the ship as she was crossing the Atlantic Ocean back to America. There was hundreds of files to look through, so she decided to look first at the ones who had died or were killed figuring their souls and spirits would still be a part of the ship. After looking at a dozen names she found a very interesting name, Otto Von Ellstein. He was second generation Austrian American on his father side of the family, who had killed his Sargent with his bare hands while being captured as a deserter. He claimed he wasn't deserting only trying to see his sickly grandmother who live in a small town on the Belgium German boarder. He was being sent back to face a war tribunal for his crime of murder but he was killed in his cell crossing the Atlantic. He was one of the many crimes that were never reviewed or questioned by the higher commanding officers. Michelle figured he was the grandfather of Eric Von Ellstein, but what did that have to do with the vortex and Eric. Was he looking for his grandfather's ghost? Could that be the reason for his obsession to wanting to find out if the Queen Mary was really haunted? She decided to look deeper into the files, how Otto Von Ellstein was murdered. Most of the prison cells were reconverted rooms large enough to sleep four men a set of bunk beds on each side of the cell. There was a single toilet bowel, a small sink with a cabinet to hold soap and four tooth brushes. A towel rack that held four individual towels. It seemed one night with the other inmates fast asleep someone got into the cell without awakening the others and strangled Otto Von Ellstein in his sleep. The guards and officers felt it was pay back for the well liked Sergeant Kelly, Otto Von Ellstein had murdered in the same fashion. The morning he was found dead in his bed, everyone claimed to have heard or seen nothing during the night. Could it have been the ghost of Sergeant Kelly roaming the ship looking for his own revenge. Maybe the Sergeant was mistaken for one of the boiler room sailors that had died on the ship. The night was running out and soon the sun was about to rise above the horizon bringing another days activities to the Queen Mary. Michelle had to work fast to get James back to his normal time line in his dimension.

Without hesitation she took James to the exact place and time she first transported back in time. James walked out of the bathroom and sat on the edge of the bed staring at the mirror across the room. Just then Carol awoke and asked what was wrong.

" James what's the matter with you? You look sick, do you feel okay?"

" What! Yeah I'm okay but I had the craziest dream, I swear I was young and back in the war."

" It's this ship, to many memories and a bit to much to drink will play tricks on your mind. Why don't you lay back and rest awhile and I'll take a shower and dress and then you can do the same. After we'll have breakfast and you'll feel better."

" Okay your probably right, but it felt so real."

James took Carol's advice and laid back down, if it was only a dream why did he feel so exhausted. He couldn't remember all the events of his dream, but he knew Michelle was with him. When Carol came out of the bathroom fully dressed and ready to go, James was fast asleep. She decided to let him sleep so she went into the parlor room and sat on the couch and read a magazine. About an hour later James can out of the bedroom looking for Carol.

" What time is it, did I fall asleep again?"

" I don't think you feel asleep the first time, anyway it's about an hour later than the first time you got up. Go get cleaned up and dressed I'm really hungry."

After James showered, shaved and got dressed he told Carol he was feeling much better and they should go have breakfast and plan their day. James was very eager to get back on the tours he was unable to finish. He wanted to get back to the hospital deck the prison area and of course the pool deck. He wasn't sure how Carol would react to going on those tours again so he decided to break the idea slowly over breakfast. The Sunday Champagne Brunch on the Queen Mary is a world famous dining experience Carol and James knew coming aboard, it would be their Sunday choice. Entering the Grand Salon for the first time was truly like stepping back in time. It was the dining room for the first class passengers on Queen Mary at the height of her grandeur. The room had been restored to the elegant art deco form of the 1930s.

The massive oak columns trimmed in brass shined like new, the back wall had a twelve foot high art deco mural framed in brush brass figurines that accented the days of high society and royalty. The one hundred varieties of food represented the port of call Queen Mary sailed too. A white glove service was displayed at every carving station and table while serving the champagne. From breakfast to desert the quality of choice was impeccable. After being seated at a table for two Carol and James started their stroll around the room filling their plates making selection after selection. When they returned to their table Carol reminded James to go easy on the champagne, considering the rough night he had consuming to much alcohol the night before. Not wanting to ruffle Carol's feathers he decided to wait for a better time to discuss his idea to return to the tours of choice. When James returned to the table with his third plate Carol remarked.

" I hope your not planning on eating for the rest of the day?"

" Not to worry a good long walk to the end of the pier is the museum."

" What museum would that be."

" The museum that houses the Spruce Goose, Howard Hughes wooden plane that only flew for ten minutes. He built it during WWII as a troop transport but it never got finished until after the war."

" If we're walking to the end of the pier I'm changing my shoes, these high heels will kill me walking there and back."

While James was finishing his dessert, Carol went to their suite and changed from her heels to more comfortable pair of shoes. When she got back to the Grand Salon, James was waiting and they set off on their next adventure. As they were leaving Kristy and Eric were entering, when they passed each other James got a cold chill up his spine as if death had just walked passed him. He turned back to get a second look at the couple that had just past them and Eric was doing the same, only it was Michelle presents he felt. After they were seated, Kristy looked around the room.

" Wow! This is quite a room, the art deco is absolutely gorgeous."

" Wait until you taste the food, if you can't find something you like here well then it don't exist."

" I was looking at all the tables, unbelievable variety of food."

" Let's get a plate and start eating."

As they both found the plate station, they began as most people do with breakfast and work their way into lunch and desert. When they returned to their table a waiter was pouring the champagne. Eric lifted his glass and made a toast, " Here's to a very enjoyable weekend."

Like James, all that had happened to Kristy was very vague. Almost dream like, only the bad feeling they both had and could not truly understand was in the back of their minds. Then Eric slipped a thousand dollars to Kristy and said.

"This is yours, I'm sorry you don't want to stay until tomorrow. I ordered a limo to take you to the airport, it should be here in about two hours. We still have plenty of time to work our way to desert."

Eric felt by being polite and charming he could win her over to stay. A few more glasses of champagne couldn't hurt his cause either. As time passed Eric fed Kristy more champagne then she could handle, even desert was laced with a large glass of Cognac.

When it came time to leave Kristy had a hard time getting up from her chair.

37

Eric very gallantly helped her to stand and get her bearings. He walked her back to the suite to get her weekend bag. Entering the suite she said, "I think I need to lie down the room is spinning. I guess I shouldn't have mixed the cognac with the champagne."

Eric helps her to the bed removes her top and pants leaving her in her bra and panties. He slips her under the covers and closes the light and the door as he leaves and enters the parlor. He sat on the couch and pondered what to do with Kristy.

At the same time James and Carol had left the ship and started their walk to the end of the pier. It was a beautiful clear day and the building that housed the Spruce Goose seemed closer than it really was. Half way there James began telling Carol he wanted to go on the late afternoon tour of the hospital deck the prison deck and the swimming pool area. He needed to clear his mind of the memories he was having. Maybe standing there in front of what use to be, could jar the thoughts he was having and the feelings he was enduring. Carol looked at him and just smiled shaking her head as if to say what ever. The closer they got to the old museum the more it looked as if it had been left in a run down condition. They walked to the main gate but it was closed and it seemed there was no one around. Then from the side of the building a man appeared, he looked like a worker maintaining the building.

" Can I help you folks?"

" We were looking to see the spruce goose, this is the museum?" Said James.

" It was the museum, before they moved the plane."

" When did they move the plane?"

" Nineteen ninety-two."

" Where did they move it too?"

" The Evergreen Aviation and Space Museum, up in McMinnville Oregon."

" Oregon! I can't believe I didn't hear about that."

Carol grabbed James by the arm and started to pull him away saying, " You can't know everything that's going on in the West Coast, when you live on the East Coast. Maybe it just didn't make the news back home or you just missed it."

James turned to the man and said, " Thanks for the information, I really would have loved to see it. Always heard it was a monster."

" Biggest damn seaplane you ever saw, that's why it only flew for ten minutes. Even with eight engines it couldn't stay air born."

On their walk back to the Queen Mary, James started to tell Carol all about the Spruce Goose. How it was made of wood, a ship with wings was the idea, a troop carrier that could deliver the men and supplies right to the shores. Only problem it never got completed until after the war was over. There was a big senate investigation why it took so long to complete. Howard Hughes faced a possible jail sentence for miss appropriating government funds. It really was a war between PanAm and TWA. Howard Hughes owned TWA and was looking to expand into PanAm territories in South America."

" I guess the only good thing to come out of this walk will be a little exercise and a breath of fresh air. By the time we get back were both going to need a nap." Said Carol.

" Not me, I'm going on those tours only this time I'm not going to have any panic attack. This time I'm going to figure out why the memories of the war seem like only yesterday, as if I was reliving the war, all over again.

"If you're that determined to go on those tours again, maybe I'll sit on the outer deck and finish that book by Joe Squatrito. "Where Evil Lurks" it's turning out to be one terrific read. The starboard side of the ship provides a spectacular view of the city.

When your finished with your tour that's where you'll find me."

" Okay sounds like a plan, I'll see you later. Love yah bye."

Carol went back to their suite to get her book and a sweater, it was getting breezy on the top deck. She found her book and put on her sweater and continued to the top deck. Walking down the hallway she passed Eric as he was entering his suite, he gave her a smile and a big hello, then he said.

"How are you enjoying the old girl?"

His conversation caught Carol off guard and she answered." What! I'm sorry were you talking to me?"

" Yes, how are you enjoying the ship? Very elegant, a real throw back to the old days of travel." Said Eric.

"The art deco and the restoration of the interior is beyond surprising." Answered Carol.

" Enjoy the rest of your day."

Carol went on her way to the outside top deck and Eric went into his suite. She thought to herself what a mysterious man, why would he go out of his way to start a conversation with me. Eric looked in on Kristy to see if she was still asleep, when he was about to leave the room he heard her say. "What time is it?" How did I get in my bra and panties?"

" It's about three o'clock, I tried to wake you an hour ago but you won't have it, you were lights out. As far as being in your bra and panties, I took off your clothes and put you under the covers. I hung your top and pants up in the closet. Oh by the way, you missed the limo to the airport. The driver waited for a half hour then he left, you couldn't make the plane anyway."

" You couldn't wake me up! What a head ache, I'm never mixing champagne and cognac again."

" There's a plane leaving at seven from San Diego airport to LAX change planes and on to Las Vegas. Do you want me to call for the limo again?"

" I don't know, I can't think straight. I need a hot shower, maybe the steam will help wake me up."

Eric watched Kristy get out of her bra and panties as she made her way into the bathroom. After all the time they spent in bed together and all the sex they had he still couldn't believe how voluptuous her body was. He was getting horny just looking at her.

Kristy took her shower and felt refreshed, walking out of the bathroom her hair was wrapped in a towel to keep from getting wet and her body was also wrapped in a towel as she looked for her bra and panties. She bent over and unwrapped her hair shaking her head to get her hair air raided then she through her head back and ran her fingers into her hair bringing it back into a style. Reaching for her panties she dropped her towel revealing her body. Then Eric said. "Wait five hundred dollars."

" Really. NO! I have to leave.

" A thousand dollars, you have time. We'll make it quick."

" There is no quick sex when it comes to you."

Then he took out the thousand dollars and fanned it waving it back and forth. " A half hour of your time, that's all I want. A half hour of work for a thousand dollars, even you can see the benefit of that."

" A half hour, no more no less. You got a deal."

She climbed on the bed got up on her knees and started to take Eric's shirt off, then she unbuckled his belt and opened his pants and pulled down his zipper. She could see in his shorts he already had an erection. She thought to herself this is going to be the fastest thousand dollars she ever made. Eric was hoping once she got started enjoying what he was about to give her, she wouldn't want to stop and she would disregard the time. He knew from past performances she loved sex as much as he did. Each one had their own agenda why they were their, but the sexual attraction they had for each other was incomprehensible, their body chemistry was like gasoline and a lit match. Explosive! Eric was right the more he worked her body the more she climaxed the more she climaxed the more she wanted. He knew how to play her like a fine violin, time meant nothing to her at that point. Again Eric had Kristy totally under his control.

Michelle knew she was loosing the fight to keep Kristy safe from Eric and the vortex. She needed to come up with a new plan. The day light hours were getting short and the last tour was under way. Once darkness came upon the ship the vortex would start to reopen, she needed to keep the evil spirits in the lower pool deck. Finding the answer to that problem would be extremely difficult. Keeping Kristy from going back to the pool deck might be even harder. The evil spirits wanted a new soul and someone had to fill that order, but who. If she found a way to save Kristy would they go after someone else. James was following the tour and on the first stop was the prison, he tried to remember all that had occur during his crossing to and from the war. When he stopped in front of one particular cell he remembered a prisoner had died in his cell. The word was he had been strangled in his sleep for killing his Sergeant while being captured for desertion. He couldn't remember the name of the prisoner, it was on the tip of his tongue. He was sure if he didn't dwell on it, eventually it would come to him. As the tour continued on James had found himself standing in front of a glass enclosed make shift Hospital ward and operating room. This time the uniform manikins were not coming alive in front of James as they did the first time James was on the tour. He did not see his beloved Michelle or even hear her voice in the back ground. Still trying to remember the name of the prisoner who was murdered in his cell he was drawing a blank as to his name. He was sure it would prove to be important if he could only remember. The group moved on to the next part of the tour and that was the pool deck where all the accounts of ghost sighting began. The infamous legend of the Queen Mary and the vortex started on this very deck. Long before the war legend had it that spirits came and went from the vortex that was in the locker room area. People swimming late at night swore they would see strange lights coming from inside the locker rooms. It was then that the sightings of a woman in white, a child about ten years old and sailors would be seen in various section of the ship. These stories were never proven and as a result the legend stories grew. Only room B.340 where a man was found dead from an axe wound to the head. Even though the door to the room was locked from the inside, it was keep very quite. Afterwards the room was cleaned and rented again as if nothing had happened. But time after time passengers complained about lights going on an off, screams in the middle of the night. Even sighting of the man found dead would appear and disappear. Eventually room B.340 was off limits and would never be used again. There was never any evilness to the stories until the Queen Mary was turned into the Grey Ghost a WWII troopship, hospital, prison and a morgue. Out of the clear blue the name Otto Von Ellstein popped into his mind, as he said to himself that's the name I've been trying to remember. Of course he had no idea Michelle was there giving him the name she linked to Eric. Then James said to himself where did I just hear that name, he was sure it was since his arrival on the ship. Then it hit him, when they were leaving the Grand Salon after having brunch the host was escorting a couple to their table.

As Carol and I got closer I could hear her say, " Right this way Mr. Von Ellstein, I have a table by the window with a beautiful view"

It couldn't be a coincident, the young man had to be a direct descendent of the murderer Otto Von Ellstein who was found strangled in his cell. Without his knowledge Michelle was leading him down the right path to help stop the vortex from taking another soul. She hoped together they could stop Eric from returning Kristy to the Pool deck. James followed the tour for their last stop which was the wheel house as it was called back in the early voyages of Queen Mary. Today it is known as the bridge, everything was the same as James remembered it. Thinking of the old days he completely forgot about Eric and was enjoying his trip down memory lane. Eric had some thoughts of his own, if he couldn't persuade Kristy to return to the pool deck he would need a new victim so the vortex would reveal itself again. He left Kristy in the suite fast asleep from exhaustion, and went walking on the upper outside deck. As he walked he planned his next course of action. Seeing the woman he had a few words to earlier sitting on a lounge chair reading a book, he decided to stop and renew their conversation.

" Well hello, nice to see you again."

Carol looked up from her book and politely said, " Hello to you again."

" Reading a good book?"

" Yes! It's a very good book."

" Where Evil Lurks" what a great title especially on a ship like this. I'm Eric Von Ellstein." As he extended his hand.

" Nice to officially meet you. I'm Carol De Marco.

" Are you here alone?"

" No. Why do ask?"

" I've seen you at least three times on the ship, and you're always alone."

" I'm here with my husband, who happens to be on the ship's tour. He's a WWII veteran. In fact he crossed over and back on this very ship. Our sons and their wives gave us this trip for our 50th anniversary."

" I'm here with my girlfriend Kristy. Fifty years is a long time together, congratulations. Would you and your husband like to join us for dinner tonight? A golden wedding anniversary is something to be shared with a young couple. You know, hope and inspiration. So what do you say?"

" Thank you for the invitation, but I still have to check with my husband,"

" Of course, talk it over and if you can make it, we dine about nine o'clock. Just call my suite and let me know. We're in suite M124, hope to hear from you. Enjoy the rest of your day, reading. " Wow, "Where Evil Lurks" what a great title for a book."

Just like that, Eric was gone and Carol was left thinking what the hell was that. A very nice and polite young man but why would he want to spend time with us. Where old enough to be his parents.

When Eric got back to the suite, Kristy was getting dressed and she asked. "Where did you run off too?"

" You were still sleeping so I took a stroll outside on the upper deck and meet a very nice older woman named Carol. We talked for a while she was telling me how she and her husband were celebrating their 50th wedding anniversary. If you decide to stay, I invited them to have dinner with us tonight."

Kristy thought for a while and then she said.

" If I stay tonight and return to Las Vegas with you in the morning, do you promise not to involve me in any of your frightful ghost encounters?"

" Of course, if you don't wish to go back with me to prove my theory then you don't have to."

" Okay I'll stay, but remember no ghost business."

With that arrangement he knew he had half of his problem solved. The hard part was getting her to agree to stay, the easy part is getting her drunk enough not to know what was happening until it was to late to change.

When James got back to the suite about an hour later he got a jacket and went looking for Carol on the top deck. It was late in the afternoon and the sun was going down and so was the temperature. He found Carol still reading her book and sat down on the lounge chair next to her.

" I see you were smart enough to go to the suite and get a jacket, wish you would have brought a blanket out with you."

" I knew it would be getting colder, you've been out here a long time. I could go back to the suite and get an extra blanket from the closet."

" If you want to sit out here and watch the sunset, then yes I'd love a blanket. I'm getting cold even with this winter sweater."

" I'll be right back with a blanket."

" Your a sweetheart!"

" After fifty years your just starting to notice my good qualities."

They both got a chuckle and James went in for the blanket. When he got to the suite he had a thought so he called room service and asked if they could deliver two cups of hot tea to the outside upper deck. The telephone operator answered by saying that would be no problem, she even asked if he would like a few cookies or muffins. James returned to the upper deck with a blanket and a big smile on his face. Carol immediately picked up on his expression and said. " You look like the cat that just swallowed the canary!"

James opened the blanket and covered Carol, " Your going to swallow those words in about five minutes" he said.

Five minutes later hot tea and cookies were delivered from the room service kitchen. The surprise look on Carol's face was priceless as she said. "You never stop amazing me, this was very thoughtful and very surprising."

She bit into a chocolate chip cookie and said, " Oh you have to try one of these, there till warm. Just delightful."

" Try the tea, just the way you like it, with sugar and lemon."

They shared their blanket, hot tea and cookies and enjoyed a beautiful sun setting view.

Carol asked James how he enjoyed the tour, he answered by telling her. " It was very informative and brought back some memories of things that had occurred on my crossing back to the states after I was wounded. I remembered one particular incident that happened where a prisoner was murdered in his cell while he slept. I remembered he killed his Sargent as a deserter, Otto Von Ellstein was his name."

" Von Ellstein, are you sure?"

" Yes, quite sure. Why?"

" I just had a conversation earlier this afternoon with a young man.

He introduced himself as Eric Von Ellstein. I had seen him three maybe four times before on the ship, he always stopped and said hello. Then when he saw me reading he stopped told me his name and even asked if we would like to join him and his girl friend for dinner. I said I'd have to talk it over with you."

" I'm thinking this younger Von Ellstein has to be the grandson of Otto Von Ellstein, but why is he interested in you? It sounds to me like he's trying to play a new trump card in what ever game he's playing." Said James.

" Maybe it's just a coincident were on the ship at the same time, and he's just a nice person wanting to extend an invitation."

" See that's you, always looking on the good side of a situation. Sometimes you have to look at the other side, not all people are kind and loving. Evil does live in the hearts of men."

" Okay you've made your point, what do you want to do?"

" I don't really know, one side of me is saying I don't want to sit across the table with a man who's grandfather was a murderer. Yet curiosity is killing me, why he wants to spend the night with us. There has to be another meaning to his madness. I have to think this through."

" You have plenty of time, he said they have dinner about nine o'clock and if we want to join them just ring his suite."

Afterwards James got very quiet as he sat on his deck lounge and watched the sunset. Carol had no idea his brain was traveling a thousand miles a minute trying to figure out what his next move would be. He was hoping Michelle would whisper in his ear and tell him what to do. A short time later Carol said. " I'm getting cold again, and if where going to eat after nine o'clock I think we should share a sandwich. The cookies and tea are not going to hold us until then. How does soup and half a sandwich sound?"

" I think your right we should get a little something and hot soup sounds very inviting right now."

They folded the blanket James brought from the suite and went inside to the Promenade Cafe. Where they both ordered a hot bowl of New England Clam Chowder, and they shared a Grilled Vegetable Wrap. During their late lunch Carol could see a worried look upon James face, it seemed to her he wasn't enjoying his meal even though she thought the chowder was the best she's had in a very long time. Then she said to James.

" Try the chowder before it gets cold, it's very good. Maybe you'll be able to think clearer on a full stomach."

" I'm not sure if a full stomach is the solution to the problem, but your right the chowder is excellent."

" Your worrying yourself to death over something that happened a long time ago. You can't change the past, what happened during the war to soldiers were the effects of war. Men do strange things under the stress of war and you can't hold someone responsible for the action of another man, even if it's his grandfather."

" Okay you've convinced me, maybe we should have dinner with the young Von Ellstein and hear what he has on his mind."

When the waiter finally brought over their wrap to share, James was in a different frame of mind. He seemed less up tight and was enjoying himself in conversation with Carol.

When they finished their meal they went back to the suite and tried to relax and nap.

It was always easier to take a nap on a full stomach, so while Carol sat in the parlor and read her book, James went into the bedroom to nap. Michelle came to him during his sleep and brought him back to the war. Only this time it was not his past but that of Otto Von Ellstein. It was as if they were over looking the past and observing what really happened. This was totally a new experience for James. He held Michelle's hand as tight as he could afraid to let go. Michelle sensed his despair and said. " Don't worry I won't let you go. We're here to find the truth."

Sergeant Kelly enters an old abandoned farm house where his squad of nine men are trying to get some well deserved shut eye. A few hours later he says.

" Okay rise and shine, it's time to move out."

Lots of grumbling among the men as they felt they needed more than the few hours of sleep. As Kelly walked past his men barking his, " LETS GO!" he stopped and kicked the bottom of Von Ellstein's boot.

" Your lead man so move your ass and lets go, were moving due east right into the heart of Gerry Land."

" Me again Sarge, why do I always have lead?"

" Because I don't like you and if anyone is going to get their head blown off in this squad I rather it be you."

" Why do you dislike me so, is it because my family comes from Belgium and not Ireland?"

" No, it's because you have a big mouth and never know how to keep it shut."

Otto Von Ellstein picks up his rifle and puts on his helmet and storms out of the farm house and takes the lead about a hundred yards ahead of the squad. Even though Von Ellstein is a good soldier he always got the shit details. His hate for Kelly is growing stronger but the straw that breaks his back has not yet occurred. The next day they cross the Belgium boarder and can hear the American Bombers Planes unloading on German railroad lines, munitions factories and airports. The flashes of light on the horizon let them know their getting closer to the city of Salzburg. As an advance squad their mission is to report back to headquarters the German Troop movement, now that General Patton's U.S. 4th Armored Division has reenforced the Belgium City of Bastogne. The German Panzer attack during the Battle of the Bulge has stalled and the German troops are in retreat. During the battle thousands of allied troops were captured and sent back to German P.O.W. camps. Von Ellstein was well aware that Patton's 3th army would make a major push Southeast from Bastogne into Germany. His personal problem was his grandparents. Who had a farm twenty miles west of Salzburg. If the American bombers don't destroy their farm house Patton's tanks surely will. His situation was the direction they were to follow, it was three miles south of his grandparents farm house. Even if he tried to slip away during the night he'd have to cover six miles round trip on foot before dawn. That would leave him very little time to get his grandparents to some kind of safety. So when he had a far enough lead distance he rushed back to Sergeant Kelly saying he saw a column of German soldiers heading north into the dense forest. When Kelly got the report he called into headquarters and waited for a response. A few minutes later he got orders to follow that lead, saying they believed a German Panza Tank group was trying to regroup with foot soldiers for another offensive. After receiving his new orders Kelly opened his map and drew a line northeast from their position. It was almost directly over the Von Ellstein farm house.

" This is our new direction, were to keep a safe distance and report back if there is a regrouping of German soldier and Panza tanks, Von Ellstein you have the lead, three hundred yards a head of the squad. If you see any tanks your to report back to me immediately."

This time there was no remarks or grumbling about being the lead soldier. He knew his plan was working and the closer he got to the farm house the better his chances were to help get both grandparents to safety. It took the rest of the day and part of the night to get through the dense forest, on the other side they came to a large open meadow. A moonless night made for very poor vision and in the darkness they couldn't see what they might be running into. Kelly decided to use the trees as cover and spend the night at the edge of the forest. Following the new path sent from headquarters by the next afternoon they would be less than a half mile from the Von Ellstein farm house. He remembered how stubborn the old timers were about leaving their home and farm in the past. Even if he couldn't get them to leave, giving them a heads up what to expect as far as danger would be a big help. He remembered a sub cellar where his grandmother stored her jars of fruits and vegetables. His grandfather cured his meats and kept his barrels of wine cooled as the temperature was always on the chilly side even in the warmest of days. It was well vented so air was never a problem and the door leading to the sub room was surrounded by crates and boxes so it was very hard to find unless you knew exactly where to look. As long as they brought down some warm clothes, bedding and blankets they could hide there until the danger passed. Otto Von Ellstein thought by explaining that his grandparents farm house was so close warning them would be no problem.

" Sarge, can I talk to you in private for a minute."

" What on your mind, Von Ellstein?"

" By tomorrow afternoon we'll only be less than half a mile from my grandparents farm house, it will take me no time at all to warn them of the danger coming there way."

" No!"

" Less than an hour, there and back."

" I said no and I meant it. You want to go off on a wild goose chase to a farm house that could be held by the Germans. You don't even know if their alive. You could be walking into a trap, that eventually would bring us into."

" Why are you being such a prick about this? I'm just trying to save two lives."

" I don't care about their lives, I don't care about your life. I only care about my life and the men behind me that's why your always in front of me."

" And they gave you stripes, your not fit to lead men in combat. When we reach the point closest to the farm house I'm going."

" You go and I'll shoot you for desertion."

By this time the conversation had gotten so heated that all the men in the squad could hear and knew what they were auguring about. Some of the men even sided with Von Ellstein their thinking was what's the harm. So we lay low for an hour while he warns his people. The majority thought like Sergeant Kelly, they didn't like him so fuck him. Then one of the other soldiers said, "If Von Ellstein is shot for desertion who's going to be the new point man, you want to have your ass shot off to warn Kelly."

That night Von Ellstein slipped out under the cover of darkness and headed to the farm house. He knew Kelly would never let him go, he'd rather shoot him for desertion. His only hopes was to get there and back before the light of dawn. Once he crawled far enough away he started to run in the direction of the farm house. Knowing time was of the essence he ran harder and faster with each step, he finally got in sight of the house it was in complete darkness. He approached it with extreme caution in fear that the Germans might be using the farm house for cover against any approaching enemy. He walked around the house looking in the windows to see if any German soldiers were occupying the house, when all looked clear he pounded on the door until a light from within appeared. He called out to his grandfather who immediately recognized his voice and opened the door.

"Otto my boy what are you doing here?"

" I've come to warn you that the American 3th Army is headed this way to engage a German Panza division. You must prepare yourself, get warm clothing, blankets, food and get down to the sub cellar and hide until the danger has passed."

Just then his grandmother came out of her bedroom, seeing her grandson was all she could wished for. She ran over to him with loving arms and hugged and kissed him in celebration of his return. " Otto I'm so happy to see you, I dreamt you were coming and here you are."

" Grandma your both in danger. A battle my occur here and the farm house could fall under a rein of bombing. Bring everything you need down to the sub cellar now, before the shelling starts. I love you both, I have to go before I'm missed if I don't get back before dawn I'll be called a deserter."

He hugs them both and kisses them and leaves. Running back as fast as he can before dawn. His heart is for filled knowing he has given them a chance to prepare and survive.

As dawn is breaking he has reached the edge of the forest where his squad is still at rest. About fifty yard away from camp Kelly was waiting he raised his rifle and shoots Von Ellstein in the shoulder knocking him to the ground. Lucky for him the bullet went clear through and out his back, as he laid on the ground holding his shoulder, Kelly yelled out to the rest of the men who were awoken from the sound of Kelly's rifle.

" Somebody go get that deserter before I put another bullet in him."

Two of the men ran out to Von Ellstein, one of them was the medic for the squad so he bandaged the wound and they helped him to his feet. As they walked him closer to Kelly suddenly he bolted and charged at him, his hands reached out to grab him around his neck and he tackled him to the ground. There combined body weight hit the ground with a tremendous force, unfortunately Kelly's neck hit a large rock. The force broke his neck. When the rest of the soldiers pulled Von Ellstein off of Kelly, he was dead. Corporal Smith was the next highest ranking soldier and he ordered Von Ellstein arrested for murder. Then he call headquarters to report the incident and waited for further orders. A few minutes later Corporal Smith was ordered to stay put at there present location and wait for a truck that would bring them back for further questioning. By the time the truck arrived each man had a difference of opinion what really happened, some saying it was an accident others saying it was murder. They quarreled in the truck all the way back to headquarters, the fact still stayed the same Sergeant Kelly was dead at the hands of Otto Von Ellstein.

Higher command sent Otto Von Ellstein back to England to stand trial for murder, there he would face a war tribunal for his so call crime. A complete mixup occurred with the paper work and Von Ellstein found himself on board the troop ship called Grey Ghost. There he was placed in the prison deck at the stern of the ship with many Nazi prisoners. One night as the ship was returning to the states a prison guard approached Von Ellstein and said.

" So your the deserter who killed Sergeant Kelly."

" I didn't kill anyone it was an accident, after he shot me, I tackled him and he fell on a rock and broke his neck."

" Sergeant Kelly was my basic training Sergeant and my friend."

" I told you I didn't murder him!"

The next night Otto Von Ellstein was found murdered in his cell. He had a broken neck, black and blue marks showed he was being strangled before his neck was broken. No higher command cared about a deserter and the murderer of a well liked Sergeant. His body was placed in a body bag and placed in the pool morgue before being` thrown over board. His wife and family only knew he was missing in action and presumed dead. He never knew he left a pregnant wife, who delivered a son which he had never seen. Although his body was cast to the bottom of the ocean to be feasted on. His soul never left the "The Grey Ghost". Was he looking for revenge all these years or was he looking for a family member to clear his name and put his soul to rest. What happens when a soul enters the vortex, what exactly is inside of it and why does it require a new soul each year. Did Eric Von Ellstein come to the ship to find answers and put his grandfathers soul to rest or is he the new gate keeper bringing what could be considered a lost soul to be feed to the vortex and give it the strength to carry on all these years. James was determined to find out, his voyage back to his time and place in the ship was now filled with new meaning. When he finally woke from his nap, he walked from the bedroom to the parlor only to find Carol fast asleep on the couch. Although her reading glasses were on the coffee table, she had a firm grip on her book.

" Wake up sleepy head."

Then he gently shook her saying. " Carol wake up, I've decided to except the dinner invitation from your mysterious Mr. Von Ellstein."

Then he walked over to the phone and asked the operator to ring Mr. Von Ellstein's suite. " Hello Mr. Von Ellstein?"

" Yes this is Eric Von Ellstein, can I help you?"

" This is James De Marco, you extended an invitation to dinner this afternoon to my wife who was reading on the outside deck."

" Yes, charming lady. We had a very pleasant conversation."

" If you wouldn't mind moving the time up an hour, we'd love to except your kind invitation. Us seniors need to eat a little earlier than you young folks."

" Sure I understand, I'll call reservations and change the time to 8o'clock, if there is a problem with getting the time changed I'll call you back. If you don't hear from me we'll see you both at eight."

James hangs up and goes back to Carol who is still asleep, only this time he makes sure she is awake to inform her of the news about dinner. " Were on for dinner with your new friend and his lady for eight o'clock Rubbing the sleep from her eyes, she drops her book to the floor and reaches for it.

" Still reading that book, "Where Evil Lurks?"

" Actually I finished it, excellent story should be the summer read of the year."

" You were sleeping so peacefully I was sorry to wake you."

" When I finished reading I closed my eyes for a minute and just passed out. What time is it anyway?"

" Six thirty, dinner is at eight."

" Are you sure you really want to go to dinner with this Von Ellstein person?"

" When I was sleeping I started to dream about his last name, and suddenly I remembered the story about what really happened to Otto Von Ellstein. This ship keeps bringing back memories of the war. Could it be I have suppressed all these memories for all these years?"

" Who knows what triggers a memory, maybe a name, a place or a time."

" I won't worry about it now, I'm to intrigued about what is on this young man's mind. I think he has a motive behind this invitation."

Carol got up and started to lay out her clothes before taking a shower and doing her hair. James yelled out. "When your finished in the bathroom, I'll shower and shave."

At seven forty five they were ready and walked out of their suite on their way to meet Eric and his lady friend for dinner. Entering the Sir Winston Restaurant, James gave his name to the host and he lead them to an empty table and explained Mr. Von Ellstein had called ahead he would be a little late. Before they were seated a bottle of champagne was brought to the table, the waiter explained if there was something different they preferred to drink he would bring it right over.

" This will be fine" said James.

The waiter popped the cork and poured two glasses, placed the bottle in a silver bucket of ice and left.

" How long do you think were going to have to wait?"

" Relax enjoy your champagne, I'm sure it won't be long."

Ten minutes later Eric showed up and introduced Kristy as his lady friend, then Carol introduced James as her husband. After being seated the waiter poured two more glasses of champagne. Eric apologized for being late explaining he had a long distanced phone call. " He's being very gallant in taking the blame for being late, it actually was my fault. It takes forever for my hair to dry, it's so thick." Said Kristy.

The waiter comes over and hands out the menu and refills the champagne glasses, and walks away. The conversation is light as they make their selection to the entree. The waiter returns and takes their order, then Eric asks. "

When I spoke with Carol today I asked if you were a World War II veteran, she said you were."

" I was a Lieutenant fresh out of West Point when I came over on this very ship.

Ten months later I even came home on her."

" I've been searching for information on my grandfather for years, he was listed as killed in action but no mention as to where his body was buried.

The waiter comes with the food and the conversation stops for a while, enjoying their meal the girls change the subject and talk about how wonderful the Princess Diana tour was, both agreeing her gowns were absolutely gorgeous.

It didn't take long before Eric was back on the subject about his grandfather, he started asking question if James knew how to find information about Otto Von Ellstein. After thinking for a while James said. " Now that you mention his full name I do remember hearing rumors about a Private Otto Von Ellstein, he was a patient at the same hospital I was in outside of Paris. I was rehabbing when he was brought in shot by his Sergeant returning to his squad, he was mistaken for a German soldier. When he was helped back to camp a fight broke out between the two men. As your grandfather tackled Sergeant Kelly he hit his head on a rock and his neck was broken."

" I never found any information about that."

" How bad do you really want to know about what really happened?"

" His spirit haunts me night and day." Said Eric.

" Your grandfather was with me when I was being transported back to England. I was being sent home and he was facing a Court Marshall for murder. Some how, his papers got mixed up and he was sent to the Grey Ghost with me. He was held in the prison on the ship. Back then the larger rooms were converted to hold four prisoners at a time. He very well might have been placed in a cell with three German Prisoners of War. Why he was placed in a cell with them no one ever really knew. Was it a mistake, or was it deliberate. One night he was murdered in his cell. He was strangled and no one in the cell heard a thing, or so it was reported. Some said it was the prisoners, others said it was the guards. The higher command never looked into what really happened, so they cast his body into the sea. After all he was labeled a murder and a deserter. I believe his body went to the bottom of the ocean but his spirit is still here, maybe he is part of the vortex of the ships legend."

"I have to get back into room B.340." Said Eric.

" Your not getting me back in that room!" Said Kristy.

They all started talking at the same time and Carol exploded. "Please, don't tell me you all believe in this ghost stuff. Have you all lost your minds."

Kristy said. " You won't believe what happened to me in that room, I was pulled through the mirror by the hands of a ghost and was fighting for my life in the pool."

" That pool hasn't been filled with water in fifty years." Said Carol."

"All I know is I was fighting for my life in a pool filled with water, and if I wasn't a champion swimmer in school I would never have made out alive. No thanks to my brave hero over here who stood there and did nothing to help."

" I couldn't move, it was as if my legs were frozen. I wanted to help, something just held me back."

" I think you both were in a time warp, and thrown back fifty maybe sixty years ago." Said James.

When they were finished with dinner they started to plan what they were going to do. The girls both agreed they wanted no part of trying to find the ghost of Eric's grandfather. They were going to stay together in Carol's suite and support each other. The waiter brought over the desert menu after the table was cleared of dishes." I'll give you a few minutes to look over our desert list. Anyone ready for coffee or an after dinner drink?"

James said." How about four Cappuccino laced with brandy for starters."

When the waiter returned to take their desert order the girls both declined, James ordered a cheese cake with cherry topping, Eric ordered a double brandy saying.

" I'm going to need a little shot of courage going back in that room."

James knew he had an edge because Michelle would be there to protect him, so he volunteered his help saying. "I'll go in with you, together maybe we can find the answers your looking for."

FACING YOUR OWN DEMONS

Eric felt very relieved he found someone with knowledge of what really happened during the war. He started to ask James questions why he is being haunted and why he couldn't help Kristy when her life was almost taken from her? James could not give him a direct answer, he really wasn't sure. Even after all that Michelle had showed him, he believed the answers were in room B.340. What evil waited for them there and was all that Eric was telling him bull shit just to lure him into his den of demons.

After dinner was over they waited for the check, when the waiter brought it over to the table Eric immediately reached for it saying, "My treat, I invited you to dinner." James wanted to leave the tip but Eric would not hear of it, when he paid the bill they all got up and went back to James and Carol's suite. There James changed into more comfortable clothes, when he came out of the bedroom only the girls were there, Eric decided to do the same. He went back to his suite and got out of his suit for clothes that would be more suited for what might lie ahead of him. They waited and waited for his return, when he didn't return they went looking for him in his own suite but he wasn't there. They all went to room B.340 and knocked on the door there was no answer, Kristy started to panic thinking he must be down on the pool deck where the vortex is most powerful. James said,"Pool deck." Kristy responded. "I'm not going down there, once in a life time is far to many times."

" Okay, I'll go down there myself and if he's there I'll bring him back."

James went down to the pool deck and looked all over the room, Eric was nowhere to be found. Now James started to wonder if the vortex had already taken him, he call for Michelle to help him. Weather she sent him a message or not he didn't know, but all of a sudden he got the bright idea he may be on the prison deck. He raced there as quickly as his old legs could carry him, he found him sitting on the floor in the exact cell is grandfather was murdered in. James entered the cell and asked. " What are you doing down here?"

" I don't really know" said Eric.

James helped him to his feet and said. " Lets get back to the girls. Kristy is frantic something has happened to you, after what happened to her when you both went into room B.340."

Eric nodded his approval and together they went back to James suite where the girls were waiting. When they opened the door both Carol and Kristy were relieved. James told the girls there was no activity on any of the decks where he was looking for Eric. He then said. " I believe it's the time, there's an other hour until midnight. Where just going to have to wait. Lets go to the "Observation Bar" and have a few drinks, I think we all could use it."

They all agreed a few drinks would take the edge off their fears, it's like the old saying. " He has his beer muscles on" meaning we all do things we might think better of, when we've had a few to many. The " Observation Bar," was very crowded and it had the feel of the art deco era nineteen thirties when the 'creme de la creme' meet for their nightly social. This was not turning into one of those nights, this was a night of facing the demons that roamed the ship after the midnight hour After ordering a round of drinks James began to feel dizzy, Carol was afraid he was getting one of his episodes from his heart problems. She thought maybe it was to many drinks, his doctor told him a drink wouldn't harm him, but tonight he has had a few to many for a man with a heart condition. He shrugged it off as nothing, Carol knew better.

The alcohol and the excitement of the evenings events were starting to catch up to him.

Eric said. " It may be better if I go it alone, you seem a little under the weather."

" I'll be all right! Just a little indigestion."

Carol insisted he go back to the suite and rest, maybe if he rested he'd be able to help Eric later. The waiter brought over their drink order, two scotch on the rocks and two chocolate martini's. When James started to sweat, Carol said. That's it were going back to the suite, you need your meds. They left without even taking a sip of their drinks, by the time they got back to their suit James was having pains in his chest. Immediately Carol gave him a heart pill "Ranexa" it opens the arteries and relieves "Angina." James went into the bedroom to lie on the bed. Carol followed him in and said. " There's no way I'm letting go on any ghost hunt with Eric. Your health is more important right now."

Back at the "Observation Bar" Eric and Kristy were still drinking and quietly talking about what to do, Eric said. " I have to go back to room B.340, can you wait outside and if I don't come out in fifteen minutes let James know."

" I'll go with you but there's no way I'm going in, waiting outside that's it right?"

" I swear, I wouldn't put you through that again. We still have time, lets just relax and have another drink."

The heart pill James took was starting to take effect and his color was returning, he started to think he might be able to help by the time Eric made his move to find his grandfather's spirit. He knew Carol would have other thoughts on that, he laid in bed he began to call for Michelle in his thoughts. Hoping she could aid them against anything that came out of the vortex. The more he called for her, he began to realize she was not going to help Eric, he didn't understand the dangers of being dragged into the vortex even for a spirit. If Eric was determined to find his grandfather spirit he'd have to go it alone. At the midnight hour Eric entered the evil room B.340 while Kristy waited outside. She checked her watch and noted three minutes passed twelve, fifteen minutes weighted like hours, it seem the time never moved forward. Inside the room Eric was much more observant to his surroundings. This time he stayed in the center of the room and waited for what ever was about to happen. Just like before the lights started to flicker and then they went out. They started to flicker again, as before a man's body lay in the bed with an axe buried in his head. Furniture began to move and the walls appeared to come alive. When the mirror began to show flashes of light he panicked and left the room telling Kristy what had happened.

" Your never going to find the answers your looking for unless you face your demons" said Kristy.

He bent over holding his chest taking deep breaths, when he regained his composure he said. " Your right, go stay with Carol and James. What ever happens if I don't return by morning you have the key to my suite take your clothes and leave the ship."

As she began to walk away, he grabbed her arm and said. " Remember day light, you'll find five thousand dollars hidden in my suite case, right side panel."

" Don't talk that way, you'll be back and I'll be waiting for you." Said Kristy. Eric opened the door and went back in ready to face the unknown. Again the room showed all the signs of the demon threat, only this time he was ready to ride the wave of destruction. When the mirror opened it's portal he didn't run he just turned his back and let it happen. Just like Kristy he was pulled in and found himself on the pool deck. He began to call for his grandfather to appear, there was no response. He walked around the pool calling out the name of " Otto Von Ellstein." Suddenly he was flipping in the air and found himself hanging by his feet with his arms spread straight out as if he was the sacrificial lamb. A loud piercing voice said, "You had your chance to be the new gate keeper and what did you do, you let the bitch go free. Foolish boy you let the power of the pussy rule your mind, all you had to do was hold her head down under the water and she would have been ours. Now you come here to clear your grandfathers name a murderer just like us, you think we would let him leave the vortex?" Up side down Eric could see the pool filling with water, in a matter of minutes it was filled. Eric's body hung over the pool and each time he was submerged and pulled back up a spirit came out of the pool with him. Again and again, all the evil murderers from World War II who died while on board ship were being summoned back to the vortex.

Finally Otto Von Ellstein's spirit emerged when he looked at Eric it was as if he was looking at himself fifty year ago he immediately got him down and freed him from the evil hold he was in. " What are you doing here?"

" I came to tell you we know you never murdered any-one during the war. The fight you had with Sergeant Kelly was provoked because he shot you for desertion when in fact you were returning to camp. He fell and broke his neck on a rock. You were murdered for the wrong accusation."

" You have to leave, I can't save you if you stay."

" I came to save you from the vortex."

Back at James' suite Kristy and Carol were a nervous wreck worrying what was happening to Eric. James was still in his bedroom, just lying in bed thinking of how he could reach Michelle. When she appeared to him she told him. " Before I help you, I want to know why you never looked for me after the war. Why did it take you fifty years to return to me?"

" When we docked in Clifton, Staten Island I was sent to the Marine Hospital where all returning veterans who needed additional medical attention were processed. Six months of rehabilitation to strengthen my legs so I could walk on my own. Marine Hospital was located on Vanderbilt Avenue. The road that circled the water front was Bay

Street it was flat and level to the docks where many ships embarked on their way to the war. The docks at the town called Clifton were the jump off point for the first O.S.S Commandos who also went across the Atlantic on a cruise ship "Monticello." It was a much smaller ship compared to the "Queen Mary" carrying only five hundred soldiers and crew. The "Monticello" was part of a thirteen ship convoy that left the docks from not only Staten Island but also New York and Brooklyn. Vanderbilt Avenue ran from it's lowest point at Bay Street up hill to it's highest point at Targee Street. The grounds of Marine Hospital were huge and manicured. The entrance of the hospital lead to a large circular driveway. The main hospital floor had old world charm, with marble columns and flooring that led to a marble reception area.

Each elevator was maned with a soldier who controlled the lifting operations. Every floor was marble and tile with large windows and sixteen foot high ceilings for good ventilation in the summer months. The building that surrounded the hospital were much smaller with no ambiance, only two stories not like the hospital that was five stories high. Most were barracks for the Marines that were their to protect the hospital, doctors, nurses and patients. A road ran around the hospital and barracks, the last barrack on the right side of the hospital was turned into a rehab center with a large patio porch with a magnificent view of the bay, and coast line of Brooklyn and Fort Hamilton a U.S. Army fort. Staten Island also had it's own, Fort Wadsworth also an Army fort. Both protected the entrance to New York Harbor against any German Ships with large cannons that could destroy any enemy ships. Marine Hospital also had two large cannons on their grounds facing the harbor with two Sherman Tanks posted on each side of the entrance to the grounds. The back and left side of the hospital grounds ran up hill with many thirty and forty foot oak trees that provided great shade in the hot summer months. While the cool breezes that blew in off the water made for many enjoyable moments while enduring the hard work of rehabbing weak damaged legs.

I met Carol there she was a volunteer aid. She was attending nursing school and had only one semester to go before the war broke out. She worked with me and we developed a friendship. There was many times she asked about the war, how I got wounded, what kind of action did I see. The curiosity of war is a strange fascination most returning soldiers cannot understand or explain.

I looked for a year after the war was over, I contacted the war department they had you listed as missing in action. I tried to contact your father but even "West Point" had no follow up address, he was in complete denial and would see no one. When I finally found Colonel Meyers he told me you were killed in action by German Messerschmitts when they attacked the Red Cross Hospital Convoy you were stationed to. He had your body shipped home and said you were buried at one of the cemetery's out on Long Island. I even went to the Calverton National Cemetery on Long Island where I found your grave in the military section. You were the true love of my life, it took years to put your memory to rest. It wasn't until I reached that point in my life that I could get serious with my relationship with Carol. The thought of coming back to this ship after fifty years scared me half to death, if it wasn't for Carol insistence to come on this trip I would have never returned. How could I have known your spirit was here on the very ship that held all our memories. Michelle was very quiet as she listened to James explain why it took so long for him to return to her. She told him she had a better understanding, war is hell even if your not the one who gave your life for your country. Then she said she would try to help Eric who was about to face a demonic spirit he never expected. She told James it would take time to round up all the good spirits connected to the ship and ask if they would stand with her to face the evil spirits of the vortex. The first spirit she approached was the boiler room sailor who died from the intense heat when his heart gave out.

For years he was mistaken for a navy sailor because he was dressed in bell bottom jeans and a white tee shirt but it was the white sailor hat that completed the look. When Michelle explained the situation he was glad to help considering he was the first spirit to roam the halls of the ship. Michelle asked his advise as to weather or not to include the child dressed in white, the sea man told her he didn't think she should be included. He said there was enough spirits of American soldiers, who didn't make it across because of injuries. He felt Michelle had a formidable group behind her to face any evil force. The problem was rounding them up. Seaman Jones, who knew, most keep to quiet sections deep in the bowels of the ship. Where they keep hidden from visual view. All had lost their life in the hospital ward or during surgery. Even though the operating room had at that time, what was considered the most modern equipment available, the doctors still had the problem of the ship's movement. There was never any advance notice of heavy waves or the zigzag changes in course to avoid any German Submarines that were always looking for troop ships. Even though "The Grey Ghost" as she was dubbed was the fastest ship on the ocean, every precaution was taken to avoid enemy torpedoes. Queen Mary was the most hunted ship in the Atlantic Ocean, she was equipped with the best sonar so she could out run any approaching submarine. As each spirit was explained the dangers of the vortex demons taking over the ship. The spirits that were found agreed to face the problem head on as a group just as they did in the war. In the lower decks some of the spirits were not so agreeable they felt the vortex was there for many years and they were never in any danger. One spirit said." What makes them so sure the vortex was trying to take over the ship?"

Another said. " Why should we risk anything for a murderer?"

Seaman Jones explained, the soul we're trying to save is not a murderer, and does not belong in the vortex with all the evil inside it. A spirit shouted, " What happens if we go in and don't come out?" The bickering went back and forth among them. Seaman Jones knew he was running out of time and loosing the argument with this group it was time to move on to the next deck.

Back at the pool deck Michelle was there trying to win her argument, why the spirit of Otto Von Ellstein should not be brought into the vortex she said. " This man was falsely accused of a murder he didn't commit, the death of Sargent Kelly was an accident."

All the spirits that were lifted out of the pool waited for their entrance into the vortex. Suddenly the booming voice from the vortex appeared, it was the prison guard that killed Otto Von Ellstein in his cell as he was sleeping. He said. "You took the life of Sargent Kelly, he was to be my gate keeper after the war so I took yours. A "Soul for a Soul " is the code we aspirer by. If your grandson would have done what he was summed to do, you could have stayed buried in the ocean waters but he let the girl go now someone has to take her place. Who speaks for Von Ellstein?"

" I speak for him!" Said Michelle

" What do you have to say that we haven't already heard?"

" You've waited fifty plus years to bring the grandson of Von Ellstein here to be your new gate keeper. He has not for filled your needs because he is not truly evil. The love of his grandfather spirit got you the release of the evil spirits that were released from the pool, not your own power. If you had that power you would have used it years ago. Your making these new spirits side with you so you can control the vortex. Let the Von Ellstein spirit go back to the ocean knowing his family now knows the truth about what happened, he did not commit murder. Take your evil herd back to the vortex and leave Eric alone to go back to his life."

" No! Someones life has to be taken, maybe I'll take the life spirit of your friend James."

" Never! I'll never let you take him."

" You an army nurse, think your strong enough to stand against me!"

In a flash of light, James was standing in front of the vortex, Michelle immediately brought him to her side of the pool.

"Bringing him to your side will not help, I can take him any time I want."

Just then sea man Jones appeared with several other spirits to give Michelle addition strength. She told James to stand behind her and the group of good spirits that have come to join the fight. Michelle said. " We have been on this ship longer than any of you. What gives you the right to try and take over this ship?"

The evil one finally revealed himself as a wielder who was working on the construction of the Queen Mary when one of the steel beams broke loose, struck and killed him. It was the fault of an other wielder not doing his job correctly. Queen Mary's keel plates were laid on December,27th 1930. The work was long and hard, but for the first year all went well. It was thought because job #534 (Queen Mary) as it was known then was almost twice the size of the previous larger ocean liner "Majestic" Cunard Company believed the ship would be finished in early 1932. In the early months of 1931 the depression started to effect the economy and business was slow for Cunard as a result there wasn't enough money coming into Cunard to finish the work on the ship. On December 11,1931 all work stopped on job #534. Britain's depression began a few years later but it was thought to be a result of the great depression of 1929 that America was going through. Franklin D. Roosevelt was elected president on November 8th,1932 based on his promise to create jobs and federal programs to end the depression. By 1933 it became a worldwide depression, as a result of the government passing the Smooth- Hawley tariffs to protect domestic industries and jobs. World trade plummeted 65% as measured in dollars. and 25% in total number of units.

On March 8th of that year Roosevelt signed into law his New Deal which created forty two new agencies to create jobs. FDIC, SEC and Social Security are still in effect today. Britain followed his lead they saw the ship, job #534 as a matter of national pride. A member of Parliament, David Kirkwood said. " As long as job #534 lies like a skeleton in my constituency, so long will the depression last in this country. To me it screams Failure, Failure, Failure!" The British government finally gave into the pressure and in 1934 agreed to loan Cunard the money to finish the ship known as job #534. In April 1934 work started again, four hundred workers marched back into the shipyard to the tune of bagpipes. One hundred thirty tons of rust had to be cleaned from the hull. Hundreds of bird nest had to be broken and removed. Some of the laborers were keep on even thought they were not skilled workers, this made for dangerous situations. He told his story.

" When the steel beam that was being used as a cross support broke loose the corner edge cut through me like a hot knife cuts through butter. My quick reflexes allowed me to move back so my head was not crushed like a walnut. I was cut from my shoulder across my chest to my thigh, I had several crushed ribs and breast bone. I was immediately rushed to the nearest hospital where a team of doctors began trying to put me back together. After hours of surgery it was determined I had to many organs that were damaged, it was only a matter of time until I would die. They should never have tried to repair me, all it did was prolong the inevitable. I was a young strong man in my prime with everything to live for. I was engaged to be married to the most beautiful girl in our town. We were to have a wonderful life together, she came everyday to the hospital. She sat next to me held my hand and prayed, read books to me, fed me and washed my face. After a while they transferred me to a bigger hospital where they gave me intervenes blood transfusions in the hopes my internal bleeding would stop. I prayed for life, my life, but soon my prayers turned to bitter pain and I began to fear the worst. I began to curse the man responsible for my injury. Just before my death I began to curse the ship, I wished my spirit would haunt the ship and all that sailed on her. When I died I went back to the shipyard but the hull was completed and she was gone. On September, 26 1934 the hull slide down greased runners into the Clyde River. Acting as breaks 2350 tons of drag chains were attached to the hull. Job #534 slid 1196 feet into the Clyde River. From there she was towed to a Quayside or " Fitting out basin" where engines and the interior of the ship were fitted, with twelve decks the lowest being for the crew only. The ship was divided into three classes. First class cabins were located in the middle of the ship for a more stable ride, second class cabins were to the stern and third class in the bow. The public rooms in first class were large filled with art deco of the era. Cunard spared no expense to make these rooms magnificent. When the ship was close to being finished the board of directors of Cunard went to King George V to attend the launching with his wife Queen Mary who would preform the ceremony and christen the ship. Cunard asked permission to name the ship after England's greatest Queen. In their minds it was "Queen Victoria" King George thanked them and said.

" My wife will be delighted"

On launch day two hundred thousand people in the rain showed up to see their newest ship being christen. Two and a half foot letters were attached to each side of the ship that read " QUEEN MARY" then they heard these words.

" I name this ship " Queen Mary" I wish success to her and all who sail in her."

A bottle of champagne hung down from a large swing rope, and when she crashed the bottle against her hull the horns sounded. Then she pushed electric buttons which released the hull, into the river which had to be dredged and widen to accommodate her size.

"I have taken many life forms since the year of my death always searching for a way to get back onto the ship and strengthen the vortex to stay open long enough to retrieve my comrades. Come to me and I will show you a new dimension where your life forms will be reborn."

Suddenly a voice arose from the group that were taken from the pool." Show us this new dimension were all is possible and we will follow you to the ends of the earth."

They all screamed out. " SHOW US."

Lightening bolts flashed out from the vortex like the hands of evil and latched onto each spirit and pulled them into the vortex and they were gone, so was the vortex. Everyone cheered believing they had won over the evil vortex. Only Michelle reminded them this was not the end, but maybe the beginning. She told all the good spirits they needed to plan how they could keep the vortex from opening again, but first James and Eric would have to return to their suite while plans were set in motion. In a flash they both were gone from the pool deck.

NIGHT MOVES

In the blink of an eye James was back in his bed and Eric was outside his suite wandering the corridor as if what had happened on the pool deck was all a dream. He opened the door to his suite entered and looked for Kristy, when he could not find her he realized she must still be with Carol. He went into his bathroom to wash his face and recompose himself. Looking into his mirror he was still woozy and not sure what had just happened. He was getting flashes of images like still photos but couldn't connect the dots. The more he thought about it the more it became obvious he had just experienced what most people read about in books or see in the movies. This was way beyond what he imagined as an adventure. For the first time the images he remembered had him scared to death. Then he remember Kristy not being in the suite so he went to James' suite in the hopes she was still with Carol. Leaving his suite he found himself bouncing off the walls as if the ship was in heavy seas, a rocking motion he could not explain since the ship was tied to a stationary concrete dock, stuck in many feet of mud. He was walking in slow motion. It was like his mind was taking four steps forward and three steps back, he felt like he was stoned on some kind of drug. He could not understand the feeling of weightlessness, as if he were in space. Then in front of him the air began to take form, a circle with colorful clouds surrounding the entrance. Eric began to fight the motion as he entered. Was this a new vortex to a new dimension of time and space or was he just dreaming. Once inside the portal closed behind him, Eric was no longer on the ship. Walking down a cobble stone street that appeared to be any street in old London at the turn of the century. In fact he was in the East end of London. Mitre St. was in the impoverished district of White Chapel. A man with a few extra schillings could buy any woman of his desire. In the evening all the pubs and street corners were the meeting places for sexual pleasures. Even though it seemed he wasn't there to the people going by, he could see and hear every conversation. The news boy held up his evening edition screaming.

" JACK THE RIPPER STRIKES AGAIN"

Eric walked over to the news boy and held out a hand full of change, the boy took a U.S. Dime and handed over the evening edition of the "London Times." Eric looked at the date at the top of the newspaper it read September 30, 1888. Eric could not believe his eyes, he had been thrown back in time. Reading the headline he continued to the story, it told of two prostitutes Elizabeth Stride who was murdered on Berner St. and Catharine Eddowes also murdered on the same night on Mitre St. The very same street Eric was standing on. Could this be a coincident or was the vortex trying to tell him something. He sat on a wooden box he found in an alley way between two buildings that lead to the other side of the block. Continuing to read the article which described how the mutilations of the bodies were the same as two previous bodies, also, " Ladies of the night" found a month before. The first victim was Polly Nichols found dead on Buck Row, August, 31,1888 there were multiple stab wounds as well as slash wounds made from a knife with a serrated edge. Her throat was cut from ear to ear. The same patten followed the second victim Annie Chapman found at 29 Hanbury St on September 8,1888. The London police believed they had a serial killer on the loose, all four murders were committed in the same district. Police warned all woman not to be out at night alone.

Eric needed a place to flop for the night, but he was a strange looking man to the people of that era. His clothes did not fit the times, his hair was cut too short and his speech was all wrong for the cockney spoken in that part of London. He decided to ask the first bartender in the first pub he walked into were was a good place to get room. The "Wild Boar" was the sign that hung outside the pup, he entered. Inside, the room was packed with both men and women drinking up a storm, while music played a merry tune. He walked up to the bar and placed a ten dollar bill on it, the bartender looked at the ten and asked. " What can I do for you mate?"

"I'm not from around here as you can see. I need a clean room to sleep in, one were I don't have to worry about being stabbed or robbed in my bed. Now give me a cold beer and a shot of your best whiskey."

" Coming right up."

He drew a beer from the tap, or as cold as you could get as the barrel that sat on a block of ice the drained into a hole in the floor and poured a shot of his best rye whiskey.

Eric downed the shot and asked for another and said. " Keep the change. Now what about that room?"

" Ten blocks west, "The Mayfair Hotel" the best and the safest room if their not filled up. You can get a cabby at the corner, he'll bring you right to the hotel."

Eric took a few sips of his beer and looked around the room at the action at hand with most any woman he'd desire. He downed his shot of whiskey and began to finish his beer when a fine looking young red head with big blue eyes and a great body asked if he was looking for some company. Eric asked, "What's your name?"

" Amy, Amy Carthright."

Eric call over the bartender and said. "Do you know this beautiful looking red head?"

" I guess I should, she's my niece. She works as a waitress by day and at night, what she does is strictly her own business."

" So miss Amy what would you like to drink?"

" I'll have what ever your having."

" Actually I was going to finish my beer and try to get a room at the "Mayfair Hotel." What I really wanted was some dinner besides a room."

" The restaurant at the "Mayfair" is very good, but a room will coast a small fortune. You could stay at my place, and for the right price have me in bed with you all night, I'll even throw in some dinner."

" Lets finish our drinks and talk. I'll consider your offer, but with all that's going on aren't you a little afraid I might be the ripper guy in your newspaper?"

" I can take care of myself and besides you don't look like a killer to me."

" How far do we have to walk to get to your place, sounds to me like the streets are a little dangerous at night around here."

" Not to worry I carry a small gun and I can shoot the eyes out of a snake at fifty feet."

" Maybe I should be more scared of you?"

After a few more drinks Eric figured what ever the vortex had in store for him, it was time to go with the flow. He told Amy. "Lets go to the " Mayfair Hotel" and eat, afterwards we'll talk about that room and your warm body in my bed all night.

She agreed and they left the pub and took a carriage ride to the hotel. Eric keep a close eye on the landmarks and street signs. When they got to the hotel he could not pay for their ride because of the money exchange, the cabby couldn't break a twenty so Amy paid for the ride. As they entered the hotel Amy said.

" You better check with the front desk before we order food in the restaurant."

Eric immediately talked to the front desk manager and explained he was from America and had not exchanged his dollars into English currency. The hotel manger told him there would not be a problem with American money in the hotel or restaurant. Then Eric checked the price of a room for one night, the manger told him it would be ten dollars American for a large room which included a private bathroom. Eric told him to hold that room for tonight, then he slipped him a twenty dollar bill and said. " Keep the change". They entered the King Arthur Room and after being seated, Eric ordered the best steak dinner in the house.

"You do like a good steak?" He asked Amy.

" Of coarse, but who could afford it. Not in this place."

" Then consider this your lucky night, How would like a bubble bath in your own tub?"

" My own tub, in my own bathroom?"

" Yes, a lady of grandeur for the night. Now lets eat."

When dinner was over Eric went to the front desk to get his key, the manager said. "I'm giving you and your lady friend the grand Suite for your ten dollar tip. I'm sure you'll both like the accommodations."

Eric signed the registration book and quietly ask the manger.

" Do you have a hotel safe for your guest?"

" Yes! We allow our guest to deposit their valuables in our vault, just fill out this form and place what ever you'd like in this numbered pouch that has a lock with a key. In the morning you can get your valuables just by showing your numbered key and signing the form. If the signatures match your done."

Eric asked Amy for her gun and said. "Lets put that little pea shooter away for the night and we can go up to the room."

Amy was a little taken aback, but handed her gun over to Eric to be placed in the vault with his money and jewelry. Then they both went up to the room, Amy could not believe her eyes when Eric opened the door to the suite. This was something she had only heard of, or read about in magazines. The first thing she checked out was the bathroom.

" Oh my God! This is bigger than my apartment. Would you look at that tub and all the toiletries."

She was like a kid in a candy store with enough money to buy anything she desired.

"I'm going to run a hot bath, and get cleaned up for you. Why don't you look around the rest of the suite, maybe you'll find something interesting."

Eric shook his head in silent laughter, it amazed him how unspoiled the women of that era were. When a hot bath or a good meal could excite them. As Eric explored his suite he found two bedrooms and a second smaller bathroom. Feeling more relaxed knowing he was in a secured room and Amy's gun was in the hotel safe he began to think this could be an interesting night, Then he thought about Kristy, James, Carol and the good spirits he left behind on the ship.

Back at the ship Kristy and Carol were still anxiously waiting for Eric's return. They were unaware of the events that had taken place on the pool deck between the good and the evil spirits. Carol would check on James from time to time to see that he was still asleep never knowing his spirit was in the middle of a fight for the control of the ship. For Carol and Kristy were living in real time where every second hung like minutes and every minute hung like hours. Kristy began pacing back and forth in the parlor nervously crunching her hands in anticipation of Eric's return. Then she told Carol the truth about her relationship with Eric, saying how they meet only a few days ago in Las Vegas. That he picked her up at the bar in Caesars Palace and that they hit it off right away. After a few drinks and a couple of slow dancers he ask her to have dinner with him in his suite, of course I was desert. After a very hot steamy night he ask me to come on an adventure with him. I must admit he paid me well for my company so I figured what the hell was the harm. I never signed on for anything like this, I thought all his ghost stories were just that, stories. He told me if he didn't return by the time the first tour begins on the pool deck go to the suite and find a hidden panel in his carry-on case. There on the right side I will find five thousand dollars, take the money and start over, away from prostitution.

"If your going back to the suite for the money, you better take all your clothes and if I were you I'd take all his clothes too. Express check-out and get off the ship as fast as you can and never look back."

" I have to tell you I'm scared to death to go back in the suite alone, especially after what happened to me in room B.340. Fighting for my life in the pool as Eric just watched me almost drown."

" We still have several hours before the early morning tours begin. Lets just wait and hope for the best, but I will tell you this. I'll go with you when the time is right and then we will all leave together."

Kristy hugged and thanked Carol for being her friend and understanding her fear, and so the waiting game continued. At the same time Michelle came to James to show him a different side to being a spirit on the ship. She walked him around the ship and explained why it was so important to keep the evil vortex off the ship. The spirits who stay here on board can move at night between the dimensions of the days of grandeur and the nights of today. The spirit world is a place of time and space, some spirits choose to be seen briefly and disappear. Kind of a cat and mouse game they like to play, others find their long lost loves and choose to stay with them in their time period or move back and forth in different time dimensions. Every vortex is a time dimension, but every vortex is not evil. When an evil vortex appears the master is looking to consume more souls and spirits to strengthen themselves so they can move on to a demonic state which they have not yet achieved. Will we be able to keep that vortex on the pool deck from coming back or reopening remains to be seen, for now we are safe.

" What about Eric?"

The question Michelle knew James would ask.

" Eric has been taken into a time dimension that will answer all the questions he is looking to know. Who he is, and where did he come from. How long will it take, or will we ever see him again. I cannot answer."

"Explain to me the difference between a demonic evil spirit and evil spirit?"

Michelle thought for a while and then, she said. " Demonic spirits have been roaming the earth from the dawn of man. They came down from the heavens to battle the angels sent here from God to help man make a better world and to watch over God's chosen leaders. The Devil sent his army to end the dawn of man. Good has been fighting evil for a thousand centuries, it will continue for another thousand centuries. God against Lucifer, Angels against Demons. History always repeats it's self, and God's church must fight a disciple of the Devil. Every so often he rears his ugly head. Genghis Kahn, Caesars, Napoleon Bonaparte and the most evil of them all Adolf Hitler. When man was drawn out of the darkness and stopped believing in pagan idols, that's when the devil start to lose his foot hold on the world. In the beginning man had to fight on his faith until the Son of God came to show us the way. The struggle still continues today, but lets not worry about that now let me show you all we could look forward too."

As Michelle walked James around the ship showing him some of the aspects of her world, Eric was enjoying his night with Amy. Just watching her take a hot bubble bath that in her mine, was meant for someone of high society. After all she was just a prostitute from the East end of London. When she revealed her newly cleaned body as she stepped out of the tub her milk white skin against her auburn red hair produced a vision only Eric could imagine. She didn't have the gorgeous shaped body Kristy has, yet there was something mesmerizing about her blue eyes against her pink blush skin. She was well versed in her craft, she knew how to please a man in every way possible. Sex was an art to her, maybe it was her surroundings that brought out her vixen ways. Maybe it was Eric and his muscular body that turned her on. What ever the reason she was at the top of her game, a cornucopia of sexual delights. In a strange way Eric began to enjoy his time in his new time dimension, at first light he started to think about weather or not he'd be able to return to his own time. Having over two thousand dollars on his person gave him a great advantage considering the prices things cost in the late eighteen hundreds, he would be among the wealthiest of men. He gently started to wake Amy from her sleep.

" Wake up sleepy head. It's time for some breakfast."

Then he kissed her on her neck and rolled her over on her back pulled her covers back and began to caress her left breast. Her nipples got hard and grew in his mouth as he sucked ever so gently between his lips. Looking up at her she smiled back saying.

" Don't stop, feel how wet I am."

Suddenly breakfast was the last thing on Eric's mind. He began to get an erection and as he mounted her his penis slipped into her moist hot vagina. With every inch he got bigger and harder until she began to scream, " Harder, give it to me harder!"

She wrapped her legs around his lower back and with every stroke forward she pulled in with her legs to get the deepest penetration she could get. Then she held him there as she climaxed with orgasm after orgasm. Then she tightened her vaginal muscles again and again until he ejaculated inside her, when she finally released her gripe on Eric they were both in a pool of sweat.

"I think we're both going to need a shower after that," Eric said.

Amy just smiled her vixen smile in complete satisfaction of her performance.

After showering they both went down to the hotel restaurant and had breakfast. During breakfast they both had many question for each other. Eric was interested in finding out why he was here in this time period. While Amy was interested in who was this American stranger and why would he come to the East end of London? Eric asked Amy to show him the sights and tell him where the nearest bank would be to the hotel. She agreed and after they finished their breakfast they took a leisurely walk to the better part of London, the financial district and the closest bank to the hotel. Eric went into the bank and asked for the branch manger. He was directed by the front door security guard to the office of Mr. Fredrick Goldsmith, Eric knocked on the office door and waited to hear a response. A voice said. "You may enter." As Eric opened the door he could see a well dressed man sitting behind a very elegant desk, he looked up and said. "What can I do for you sir?"

Eric walked over and extended his hand in a gesture of friendship.

" Hello Mr. Goldsmith, I'm Eric Von Ellstein from America. I'd like to open an account with your bank and establish myself as a business man here in London."

" Fine, how large an account would you like to open?"

" I need some walking around money, I'm presently living in the Mayfair Hotel. I have a suite at a very reasonable price, so how about Eighteen hundred dollars to start with."

Eighteen hundred was a very large sum of money, when most business men carried three or four pounds on their person. (The equal of six dollars American.) To the lower class working stiff that was a weeks salary. The bank manger smiled and said.

" Very good, very good indeed sir. I have the papers right here just fill in all the required information and sign your name at the bottom."

" Can I take the paper work with me and return tomorrow as I was just walking by and my money is in the hotel safe. Also I hope you can direct me on some business investments."

" Gladly sir." He handed Eric the papers and extended his hand with a big smile on his face. Eighteen hundred dollars deposit was considered a very large sum of money in that era of time. Eric extended his hand assuring him he would return tomorrow, then he left to a waiting Amy. They continued their walk around the London streets. As they were window shopping, Eric suggested to Amy she needed a new outfit if she was going to stay with him. If he was to meet important men and new business associates she would have to look the part. They walked into a very fashionable ladies boutique. Amy was completely in awe of her new surroundings. She could never afford the price tags that accompanied such personal attention. The salesperson outfitted her from head to toe. When she finally came out of the dressing room, she was a new woman. Eric gave his nod of approval. These would be her clothes when he needed her to attend, his upper class dinner meetings. They returned to the Mayfair and got ready for the evening. Later that night they returned to "The Wild Boar" for a few drinks and some local conversation before returning to the Mayfair for a late night dinner.

Walking in they noticed it was three deep at the bar. Had it not been Amy's connection with her bartender uncle they might have never gotten a drink. Two boilermakers she called out and pointed to the end of the bar where they were delivered. They sat at a table in the rear of the bar were it was less noisy. Everyone had an opinion on the early events of another murder in the Chapel Hill district `of London. Some of the ladies of the night covered their fears by joking around saying, "I hope he has a big winkie and gives me a right good one before he slits me throat."

After finishing her drinks Amy told Eric she was going to her apartment which was two flights above the bar for her best clean fresh clothes, before they go to dinner. When she left Eric was still drinking his beer. That's when a strange man asked if he could join him at his table. Eric looked up and said. " Do I know you?"

The man answered back, "No, but I know you!"

Eric had a bewildered look on his face but immediately offered a chair, the man sat down Eric asked, " Just how do you know me? I'm not from here."

" That's true but then who do you think brought you here?"

" Are you the gatekeeper?"

" I never thought of myself as such, that's a fair description of what I do."

" Why did you bring me here?"

" To find out who you truly are and why you were chosen."

Then the man excused himself and left leaving Eric to wonder who he really was. When Amy returned, Eric quickly rushed her out of the pup and into a carriage telling the driver he wanted to go to the "Mayfair Hotel."

He didn't tell Amy about the strange man. He couldn't figure out how to explain his encounter, how could he when even he wasn't sure what it was about. The one think he was sure of, he'd see him again. He knew trying to explain the vortex and coming from the future would only freak her out. Especially with all the murders of recent times. Eric was very quite during the ride back to the "Mayfair Hotel." Even Amy noticed the change in him, saying. "Is everything okay, have I done something wrong?" Eric just smiled and said. "No." Then, she only saw the rich American who had popped into her life and was showing her a side of grandeur she only dreamed about. When they got to the hotel Eric paid the cabby and they went directly to the restaurant. After being seated, Eric ordered a bottle of wine and looked over the menu for the evening. As usual he ordered for the two of them. He selected lamb chops cooked medium well, mashed potatoes with gravy, and a side order of mixed vegetables. He looked over to Amy and said." Is that okay for you, or would you like to order something different?"

" Anything that comes out of this kitchen is far better than what I would be eating at the Wild Boar." Was her reply.

" I love lamb gravy on mashed potatoes." Said Eric as the waiter proceeded to open the wine. After he popped the cork, he handed it to Eric to smell and give his satisfaction of approval. They were almost finished with the first bottle of wine when their dinner came out. The waiter poured the rest and placed the dinner on the table. Eric ordered a second bottle of wine, and began to eat his meal. Everything was cooked perfectly, each cut of lamb was dipped in the gravy and a scoop of mash potatoes was added too each fork full.

" How are you enjoying your dinner?" Said the waiter as he poured the wine.

" Excellent, my compliments to your chef."

When they finished with dinner, the waiter ask if he could bring the desert menu. Then he said." Our special this evening is triple layer chocolate fudge cake with fresh whipped creme, topped with Cherries."

Eric smiled and said. " One slice two spoons."

" Very well sir."

" I could have had a whole slice just for me." Said Amy.

" All I want is a taste, so the rest will be for you."

The waiter brought over the most delicious looking slice of chocolate delight Amy had ever seen. Eric was a man of his word and just tasted the corner and left the rest to her.

" Wow that is very excellent!"

Amy began to tease Eric by saying. " Would you like some more, we could take the rest up to the room and have some fun with it."

" I could order another slice and take it up to the room, all for myself."

Then they both laughed, and Amy ate her cake, and Eric drank his wine. After dinner was over they made their way back to Eric's suite. Only this time the extra wine Eric drank, had taken it's toll, and he passed out on the bed. Amy thought to herself he can't hold his wine. Guess it's time for a bubble bath. When she was finished with her bath she went into the bedroom and Eric was still in the same position. She made him more comfortable by removing his shoes, pants, and jacket. She threw a blanket over him and closed the lights, any chance of a sexual romp was over. She'd have to save it for a morning delight. The next morning Eric was very eager to return to the bank. He filled out the papers the bank manger had given to him, and was fully dressed by the time Amy woke. She rubbed her eyes and gave out a big stretch, and yarn. Then she said.

"Your all dressed. What's the rush? I thought you'd like a little morning delight to make up for last night."

" What I'd like is breakfast, mostly coffee. I drank to much wine last night. I haven't had a headache like this in years." Said Eric.

" Maybe it was the boiler makers you had before the wine?"

" Beer, whiskey, wine doesn't sound to good the next morning, does it?"

" No, it doesn't. Give me ten minutes to wash up and get dressed and we can go eat. I'm a little hungry myself." Amy said.

" Sounds very good to me."

Ten minutes later they were on their way to the restaurant in the lobby of the hotel. The hotel offered a buffet special for their guess. All you can eat for a dollar a person, every variety of food you could imagine. From freshly made eggs, to waffles, and pancakes. Breakfast sausages, to slice beef to oatmeal, slice fruits fresh baked breads and rolls. The smell of hot cinnamon danishes filled the air, while cheese, apple and peaches complimented the dessert table. After breakfast was over Eric felt much better saying.

" I knew a good breakfast would settle my stomach, and a couple of cups of coffee would get rid of my headache. I really think I ate to much"

Amy smiled and said. " I'm glad to hear your feeling better, I think we both ate to much. That had to be the most impressive display of food I've ever seen for breakfast."

Eric made motion to the waiter for the check. When he brought the check, he also brought a note in a small envelope. Eric opened the envelope and read the note.

See you tonight, 10:00 p.m. at the "Wild Boar."

Don't be late, we need to talk.

Gatekeeper!

Amy said. " All of a sudden you look grey. Bad news?"

"No, not really. Just business."

Eric began to think. Maybe going to the bank with most of his money, is not a good idea.

He decided to wait until he heard what this so called gatekeeper had to say. He began to think he was going to get good news that he was being sent back to the Queen Mary in his own time. Amy asked. " Are we going back to the bank?"

"No, not today. I have to meet a man tonight at the "Wild Boar" about ten o'clock. We can spend the rest of the day in the suite. Later a nice dinner and then on to my meeting."

" Sounds very encouraging to me, an afternoon of sex can open anyone's appetite."

Eric smiled and took Amy by the hand and lead her up to the suite. She always seemed to know what was on his mind, even before he spoke a word. He knew a hot bath and a very sex filled afternoon was just what he needed to get his mind off of his encounter later that night. When they got to the suite, Amy lead Eric to the bedroom and began to undress him. She began by removing his jacket, then his shirt, after she open his pants she pushed him on the bed and pulled off his pants. She began to dance around him removing her own clothes, trying to sexually arouse him. When she was naked, she crawled up the bed like a tiger ready to devour her prey. She rubbed her breasts on his body until he was fully erected, then she continued up his chest until her fingers ran through his hair. She kissed him, and in one motion he was totally inside her. Once again

Amy did not disappoint Eric, she was in total control of her sexual powers. Their sexual frolic continued all afternoon until the light of day turned into the darkness of night. Eric commented on Amy's sexual appetite saying, " Don't you ever get enough to satisfy your desire?"

" Not when it comes to you." She replied.

" I think it's time to get dressed and have dinner, if we're going to get to the "Wild Boar" in time for my meeting."

" I could be washed and dressed in a flash, if need be."

" I'm to exhausted to move that fast. Some of us are not as young as others." They both laughed, Amy went into her bathroom and ran a hot bath while Eric took a hot shower in his. Later they both got ready to go to dinner. After another wonderful meal they hailed a cabby to take them back to the pub. On the ride over Eric again began to think about Kristy, James and Carol. Would he ever get back to "Queen Mary" and his own time dimension. They entered the " Wild Boar" as usual the pub was packed with the locals deep in conversation, while enjoying their nightly brew. Eric and Amy walked to the back looking for an empty table with two chairs. When no tables were available they stood at the end of the bar, and ordered two boiler makers. A short while later a table became available, Eric immediately walked over and placed his drink down, to hold the table. Then he signaled Amy to come over from the bar. They both sat down in anticipation of Eric's mysterious meeting. About ten o'clock Eric saw his new found friend walking towards the back of the pub. He leaned over to Amy and said, " Can you give me fifteen minutes alone to talk business?"

Amy replied," Sure." As she left the table and walked back to the bar.

Eric's mysterious friend sat down at Eric's table. Eric signaled the bartender for another round, which was delivered to the table by Amy. After placing the drinks on the table she gave Eric a wink and a head nod, her expressions kept changing until she walked back to the bar. Eric took a sip of beer, and downed his whiskey in one gulp. Trying to fine the courage to ask, the questions, he knew he had to ask. "What is it you want from me? When am I going home?"

" I thought you liked it here. Hasn't Amy been treating you right?"

" What does this have to do with Amy?"

" Did you think it was just a chance meeting with her. I had her long before you entered my realm."

" Is she under your power? Is she one of your disciples?

" Let's say she helps me when I need her. For that I let her live, and reap the benefits like meeting you."

" You haven't really answered my questions. What should I call you. Does JACK fit the calling."

" Your smarter than I thought. I can see I have to approach this in a different manner. We'll talk another day."

As the stranger left the table, Eric screamed out, " When do I get back to my ship and my friends?"

The man disappeared in the crowd as he made his way to the front door. When Amy came back to the table Eric was really upset with her, saying. " Why didn't you tell me you knew that man?"

" I meet a lot of different men in my profession. Mostly I try to forget them."

" He said you help him whenever he needs you. Does that mean you know how to contact him?"

" He contacts me. He told me you would be coming into the pub. He wanted me to be nice to you. He said you were a long lost relative, he was trying to reconnect with. So I did, but I liked you right from the start."

" I think I'm going to go back to the hotel alone. I need time to think this through. I have to know your not playing me."

" I'm not! I really liked the time we spent together. I thought it was going to be a casual drink together and invite you up to my room for a quick lay. I never dreamed you were going to treat me like a lady of grandeur. This has been a couple of days women like me only dream about. You know where to find me if you want to spend time with me again."

As she starts to walk away towards the front door she looks back and smiles a very devious and evil grin, as if to say your right Jack and I just played you.

Eric leaves the pub, and hails a cabby back to the hotel. On the ride back he begins to think about Kristy and the ship again. When he gets to the hotel, he pays the cabby and exits the coach. The cabby starts to drive away, and as Eric turns to enter the hotel he is back in the vortex. In what seemed a split second, he was back on the ship in the same place he left. No time passed and no one knew he was ever gone. He was headed to James' suite in the hopes Kristy was still with Carol. In his mind he had just left the pool deck and the evil spirits were sucked in the vortex, and it was closed behind them. As the perception of time got clearer, he started to remember the days he spent in old London. Did Amy tell him the truth? Was he a direct descendent of "Jack the Ripper" if so how could he ever break the bonds between them. When he finally got to James' suite he knocked on the door, and waited until Carol opened it. Walking in he saw a frantic Kristy, who greeted him with a big hug and kiss " I was so scared for you." Kristy said.

" I have news for you, I was scared shitless myself. No one will believe what just happened on the pool deck. Where is James?"

Then Carol said, " He's sleeping in the bedroom. Do you want me to wake him?"

" No. Let him sleep, we still have a few hours until the ship starts to get active with tours and breakfast. I still have to sort out a couple of things that are bouncing around in my head. One thing is for sure we all have to get off this ship before it's to late."

" What do you mean, before it's to late?" Said Carol.

Then he gave Kristy a hug and kiss and said. "Remember where the money is in my bag. If I'm not back by ten leave the ship, take the money and start over."

After he left the suite. Carol looked at Kristy and shook her head and said. " If I were you I'd leave now. Take the money and run while you can."

Eric proceeded to the pool deck looking for Michelle. When he got there it was dark and empty. He looked around hoping to find something that could help with the answers he really didn't get when he was transported back in time. He started to call out for Michelle, but there was no answer. He yelled louder and louder saying. " Michelle were are you. I need answers. You know I was sent back in time, help me."

" Why should I help you." Michelle's spirit answered." Your on the side of evil."

" No. I don't want to be. I'm not a bad person."

" Search your soul. The answers are there inside you. Go back, and confront the evil there. Only you can close the vortex here forever. The souls that are here will stay here, and the evil souls will not be able to return."

" How do I go back?

" You must will it, with all your heart and soul. Think of Amy, she is now a part of you. I won't lie to you, a very tough task lies before you." With that Michelle's spirit was gone from the pool deck.

Eric was still not sure how or if he wanted to go back in time again. Although he did miss Amy. Facing his so called adversity "Jack" did not appeal to his nature. Was he a long lost relative? Did he have plans in turning Eric into the next gatekeeper? Did Eric have enough good qualities to over come the evil men do? These were all the questions whirling around in his mind. He decided to return, he had to close that chapter of his life one way or another. He knelt down on one knee, placing his right elbow on his right knee and bending his head supported by his right hand. He began to think with all his might about Amy and London. Then all of a sudden the vortex open and he was whirling around and dropped back in the East end of London. Only this time it was not the time he left, but two months later. November,8th,1888. The first thing he did was to look for Amy. Returning to the "Wild Boar" only to find it closed. He remembered Amy had a small apartment up stairs from the pub. Entering the side door he walked up the stairs and stopped at the door he remembered as Amy's. He knocked and he knocked, just as he was about to leave. The door opened slightly. Amy peaked out of the cracked door only to see Eric standing there. When she opened the door fully, he did not get the reception he was hoping for. Amy was quite taken aback, and still upset he left her, without a word, so suddenly. Eric said. " Aren't you going to invite me in?"

" Why should I? You left me without a word, I didn't know if you were coming back. If you went back to America, if you were dead."

" I'm sorry about that, I can explain. Maybe."

She turns and walks away leaving the door wide open. Eric follows her into the apartment. Amy is still in her night slip. Eric says, " There's something different about you. Have you put on weight?"

" What makes you say that?"

" First of all, your breasts are much fuller than I remember. You never had a cleavage that pronounced, and your rounder in the middle."

" Maybe it's because I'm with child."

" Child! Who's child?"

"Your child. I wasn't pregnant before you, and I haven't been with anyone after you. When I waited and waited for you to return, I began to feel a change in my body. My breasts began to hurt and feel larger."

" I'm in shock. I came back for you but I never expected this."

" What do you mean this? Is it, you don't believe me? Or are you sorry you came back?"

" No, nothing like that. It's just, wow. Let's start over, don't be upset."

Eric walked over to her and pulled her close and kissed her in a very romantic way. It was his way of letting her know he approved. As Eric held Amy in his arm he began to think what in the world has he gotten himself into. Not that he didn't care for Amy, he did, but did this news mean he could never return to his own time. This was a very complex situation, that had to be handled with kid gloves. He told Amy to get washed and dressed so they could go out and get some lunch. During lunch Eric asked Amy what she planned to do. Amy looked down and said. " I know I'm not the kind of woman a man wants to take as his wife. Heaven knows I've made mistakes, but that doesn't mean I won't be a good mother to my child."

" I think you'll be a good mother. You have to get out of the East end of London, out of this environment. Let me help with your finances. Let me get you a new apartment, new clothes, a good doctor."

" Is that all you intend on doing? Let me know now, so I won't be disappointed later."

" I'm not going to make you promises I may not be able to keep. This is a start, it's a good start."

" Okay you win, I have no leverage. I know who I am and where I come from. What ever you do to help me is more than I could ever hope for."

Amy gets dressed and they both go out to have lunch. Amy suggests a little cafe out of the East end of London. Eric hails a cabby and Amy says, " Cafe Livingston."

The cabby turns and looks at Amy and says.

" Are you sure you want to go there?"

" Why am I not dressed properly?"

" No mum. It's just a very expensive place to have lunch."

Eric interjects," Thanks for the heads up. I'm sure it will be no problem."

The cabby turns and continues on without saying another word. When they got to the cafe Eric pays the fare and they go on in. After being seated they look over the menu.

The cabby was right, their prices for that period in time were far more than anyone from the East end of London could afford. All the ladies were looking down on Amy. Even wearing her best attire did not compete with all the fine dresses worn in the cafe. Eric reassured her not to worry, " They all wish they were as pretty as you."

When the waiter came back to take their order he said. "How long are you with child?"

"What makes you say, I'm with child?"

" You have a certain glow about you. Having four daughters myself, I can tell that look. My wife had it with each girl she delivered. You have a girl on the way."

Eric then said. "We'll have two lunch special."

" Anything to drink sir."

" Yes. I'll have a beer and the lady will have cold milk."

Amy gave Eric a look that would stop a horse dead in it's tracks and said. " I don't want milk. I'd like a beer with my lunch."

" From now on you are eating healthy. Vitamins, calcium, protein, no booze."

After lunch they walked aways when Eric spotted a sign in the window of a dress store.

The sign read apartment for rent. Inquire inside. So Eric took Amy by the hand and they walk into the store to inquire about the sign. Eric asked the woman behind the counter,

" I'd like to ask about the apartment. Where is it and how much is the rent?"

The woman replied. " It's just above the store, Three an a half rooms fully furnished. The rent is twenty dollars a month. Can you afford that?"

" Yes, no problem, but I'd like to see it first. I'm Eric and this is Amy."

The woman then introduced herself saying. " I'm Mrs Kirkland owner of the store and landlord of the building. Right this way we can take the side steps up to the second floor. I live in the smaller flat in the back. Since my husband died I have no need for the larger flat in front."

As they climbed the stairs to the second floor Mrs Kirkland said, " Of course you have your own entrance in front of the building."

At the top of the stairs she unlocked the door and they entered. Eric and Amy looked around and couldn't believe their eyes or their luck to find a very clean and well furnished apartment. The second bedroom was small but Eric thought he could use it as an office. What sealed the deal for Eric was it had it's own bathroom inside the apartment. Eric looked at Amy and said," What do you think?"

" I love it." Said Amy.

" We'll take it. I'll give you five months rent in advance. I have to tell you we're having a baby. Is that a deal breaker or a problem?"

" Not for me, I love children. Especially babies. By the way I knew she was with child the minute you walked into my store. If you hadn't said anything about it up front I would not have rented to you."

" Does that mean we have the apartment?"

" Yes, and you can call me Margret.

" Margret, I'd like you to take Amy down stairs and fit her for a couple of nice dresses, bras, panties and socks. Will thirty dollars cover it?"

" That will do nicely. Thank you very much."

Then Eric said, " Amy while you are getting your new clothes, I will go back to the Mayfair Hotel and get the rest of my money out of the safe."

" Okay, I'll just wait here, or maybe I'll bring my new clothes up to the apartment."

" Either way I'll find you after I've completed my business."

Eric left and found a cabby to return to the Mayfair. When he got there he paid his fare and walked into the hotel. Immediately he looked for the manger who was at his usual post behind the large reception desk. The manager recognized him immediately and said, " Mr. Von Ellstein, so nice, to see you again. Do you need a room?"

" No not at this time. What I need is to get into your safe and get my money."

"Just sign the release card, show me your key, and I'll open the safe. Then you can get what ever belongs to you inside."

Eric signed the card and retrieved his locked pouch. When he opened it and turned it over his money slipped out along with Amy's gun. He placed the money in his pocket and the gun in his jacket. He thanked the manager with a hand shake and returned to Amy at the dress store. On the cab ride back he thought to himself maybe I'll just shoot Jack and be done with it. Then he realized maybe that's what he wants, so I would be a murderer just like him and the rest of the souls in the vortex. When he entered the dress shop Amy was not there. Margret told him she when up to the flat to rest and put her new clothes away. Then she reminded him, when your having a baby you need extra rest time. He went up stairs found her sleeping on the bed. He gently woke her up saying,

" Amy wake up, I've got my money. We have to go to the bank and open an account."

Amy woke up rubbing her eyes and yarned. She washed her face and they both walked to the nearest bank which was only two blocks away. Entering they walked to the managers desk and told him they wanted to open a joint account. The bank manager introduced himself and handed Eric his business card which read,

Charles Goodly
Amalgamated Bank- Manager
1800 Miller Court
London, England

Then Mr. Goodly opened his desk draw and handed Eric and Amy the papers to be filled out and signed. Then he asked, " Just how much money did you want to open this account with?"

Eric reached into his breast pocket and pulled out his envelope filled with money and said,"I think eighteen hundred is a good number to start."

Mr Goodly checked the paper work and made sure both signatures were in there proper place, and said, " Everything looks right. Lets get you both over to the teller and make your deposit, and get your bank book. Right this way."

When there business in the bank was over. Eric said," Now if I have to leave on business you can withdraw money as you need it."

" You mean I can take money out without you being here?"

" Yes, your name is on the account. Remember this is your nest egg to pay for bills, doctors for the baby, food, medicine, and anything else I can't think of right now."

Amy hugged and kissed Eric saying. " No one ever worried about me before like this."

" Later on tonight, after dinner we'll go back to "Wild Boar" you can gather some of your personal things while I take care of some business downstairs."

After dinner Eric followed through with his plan to return to the East end and finalize his business. When they got there Amy went upstairs to her flat and gathered her pictures, shoes and underwear. Then she looked around to see if there was anything she might have missed. She went to her closet and pulled out some of her better outfits. She place them in the sack and waited for Eric to return.

Downstairs Eric waited patently for Jack to show up, when he did they took the last table at the end of the bar to talk. Walking past the bar Eric ordered two beers, but Jack waved off his drink indicating he was not drinking. When they sat down the bartender brought over Eric's beer. Then Jack said." Where is Amy?"

Eric immediately got defensive. " Why is Amy so important to you? Are you looking to have sex with her again?"

" Sex with her again, what are you talking about?"

" You said you had her long before I arrived on the scene."

" I meant under my power. You took that away from me, when she was with you."

" I've taken her out of the East end, and given her a chance at a new life."

" What will happen to her when I send you back. Where is she?"

Eric gets up without saying a word and walks out the front door. He looks back into the pup to see if Jack is following him. When the cost is clear he runs up the side stairs to Amy's flat and grabs everything she has thrown in the sack and pulls her out of the apartment and down the back stairs. On the way back to their apartment across town, he tells her about the conversation he had with Jack.

" He is going to be one pissed off pit bull," says Amy.

" I think we better stay close to the apartment tonight, and not even think about going out. Tomorrow I'll go get some breakfast food and we can eat in."

That night Amy starts to get very sexual with Eric, after all it's been months since she has had any sexual pleasure. Eric is very taken aback saying to her. " Wait, I've never had sex with a pregnant woman before."

" Just be gentle, and let me do the rest."

Eric followed her lead and they had very passionate but gentle sex. Amy's appetite for sex had not diminished at all. When they were finished Eric said I never knew a pregnant woman could still have an orgasm. "Tell me what's going to happen when you stomach gets so big that I can't get inside you?" Amy thought for a second and then she said.

" If I get up on my knees at the edge of the bed, lower my shoulders as far down as I can and your gentle not to push yourself all the way in, we can still have very enjoyable sex."

" Wow I guess your never to old to learn something new."

The next morning while Amy was still sleeping Eric got dressed and went out for some food. As he approached the corner the newsboy was shouting as loud as he could. "

EXTRA, EXTRA, READ ALL ABOUT IT!

When Eric stopped and reached for some coin in his pocket the newsboy said.

" Paper Governor!"

Eric hands the newsboy a nickel and looks at the front page of the newspaper.

NIGHT MOVES

London Times:November 9, 1888

" JACK THE RIPPER STRIKES AGAIN"

Mary Jane Kelly found on Miller Court in the East end of London was mutilated with her throat cut from ear to ear. This time the Ripper removed her heart and took it with him. Police are saying this is the worst mutilation of all.

What the newspaper failed to report or thought to gruesome and to frightening was to print what the police really found at the scene of the crime. Mary Jane Kelly's body brutally mutilated. Both her breasts were cut off and placed under each arm. Her heart totally removed. Her intestines were cut out and place at her knees.

Eric folded the newspaper under his arm and continued to the bakery. There he purchased two buttered rolls, two pastries and a cup of coffee for him and a cup of tea for Amy. Then he rushed back to the apartment to show Amy the bad news. She was right the pit bull took his insane anger out on the next poor soul he in counted. Amy said she didn't think she had any appetite for food. She was starting to experience morning sickness. Something Eric had never seen before. She ran to the bathroom and closed the door behind her. Eric could hear her as she hugged the bowel to vomit her last meal. When she came out of the bathroom she was wiping her face with a damp towel. Eric handed her the tea saying." Drink this it will settle you stomach."

As Eric sat at the kitchen table watching Amy sip her tea, he realized he had to get her out of London. Jack would never stop looking for her on the London streets. He also realized the money he had put in the bank and the few hundred dollars he had in his pocket would not last her long. He had to get back to the ship and get the five thousand dollars hidden in his suitcase before Kristy disappeared with it. His biggest problem would be how to tell Amy he was going to be gone for several months again, and why. The last time he left seemed only like a few hours, but by the time he returned the vortex moved three months ahead. How much time will pass this time, it could be years. There was no way of being sure or if he would ever get back to the same place. How much control did Jack have over the vortex time.

Eric began to eat his roll trying to find a way to explain to Amy what was about to happen. Then he said, " We need more money! The only place for me to get enough money to get you out of London and take care of the baby is New York. I have to go back to America and sell my holdings and stock on wall street. If I leave tomorrow I can be back in two months. The money in the bank won't last forever, but it will last longer than two months.

" I don't want you to leave me again. Why can't I go with you?"

" The sea voyage is rough enough for a woman. I can't imagine what it would be like for a pregnant woman. If we encounter, one bad storm you'll be sicker than you could ever think. That little display you had earlier would be nothing compared to the sea sickness you'll have. It's too dangerous. The ocean is treacherous this time of the year. Besides they'll never allow you to leave the country without all your passport documents. Amy began to think this was all bull shit on Eric's part. There was no way he'd ever marry a prostitute, no way he'd ever believe this was his baby. She finished her tea and went back to the bedroom to lie down again. Locking the door behind her. Eric began to think and wish for his return to the " Grey Ghost" as he preyed the vortex opened, and he was swept away. In a matter of minutes he was back on the pool deck calling for Michelle. Over and over he called until she finally appeared saying. " Did you find what you were looking for?"

" No, not really. Now there's even a bigger problem."

" You mean the pregnant girl you left behind."

" You know about that?"

" I can see the past as well as any spirit. You did not just happen into the vortex, you were meant to be there. You could never have stopped what the evil one set into motion."

" I have to get the money in my suitcase and bring it back. I have to get Amy out of London."

" If you go back again, you'll never return to this ship. Do you really think he'd let you take Amy out of London. You've done all that you could to help her and her unborn baby. The money you left her will go far, and she'll be forever in your debt."

" I still don't know why she means so much to him."

" She's his youngest daughter, and you've given him a grand daughter. Who will grow up to be just like his oldest daughter, Lizzy Borden the axe murderer. Evil blood always finds a way to evolve. Your grandfather will be the son of Lizzy Borden. The blood line will never end, your father, you. If there's any real goodness in you, leave the ship with Kristy and never come back. The vortex is closed for now, lets hope it stays closed for ever."

" So what is going to happen to you and James?"

" James is now in the after life with me. His wife will find him dead when she tries to wake him and will assume the trip was just to much for his old heart. She can take his body home to be buried in their family plot, but his soul will be forever with me on this ship. Free to move about in different time warps from the first ocean crossing to the last. I have waited fifty years for the only man I have ever loved with all my heart and soul."

When Eric returned to his suite he found Kristy packing to leave the ship. She turned around towards the open door way and couldn't believe her eyes. She thought Eric was gone forever, but there he was alive and well. She stopped what she was doing and rushed into his arms.

" Oh my God I though you were lost forever! What happened, where did you go?

" You wouldn't believe it. Even I'm not sure it was real. This ship has ways of playing tricks on your mind. The things you believe to be true are just fleeting memories of visions in your head. The person you think you are, you're not. The places it sends you, who knows. But, the person it makes you want to be, that is the important question."

"I don't really know what your trying to say here. The only thing I do know is lets get off this ship. I don't want to hear about ghost, I don't want to go looking for ghost. Lets leave the sprit world to the sprits"

" Do you want to go back to Vegas with me?"

" Are you offering me a ride back, or are you asking me to go back and be with you?"

" I guess I'm offering you a ride back and saying lets see where it goes from there. Maybe on the way back to Vegas you can help get all this craziness out of my head and we can just enjoy each others company."

"Okay your on, lets give it another go and see where the chips fall."

Kristy then went back to finish her packing. When she was done she told Eric he was all packed.

" Did you take the five thousand dollars out of my carry on case?"

" No. It's still there. I guess I want you to come back more than I wanted the money. I've always been able to make money."

Eric opened his case a took the five thousand out of the secret compartment and put all but one hundred dollars into his pocket. Then he went to the writing desk in the parlor and sat reaching for an envelope. He then took the one dollar bill and wrapped it around the master key to room B.340, and placed it into the envelope. After he sealed it he wrote on the outside. For "bellman" and placed it in the do not disturb pouch at the back of the door. Eric then called for his limousine. His driver was ordered to stay close to the area in case Eric decided to leave at a moments notice. The driver responded and said. " I'll be there at the ship's dock within a half hour! It was just enough time for a quick cup of coffee and danish or two. Kristy then asked if they should let Carol and James know they were leaving the ship. Eric responded by saying. " I think we should let Carol and James make their own exit from the ship."

After all how in the world could he tell Kristy he knew James had already passed on, and that he was with Michelle in the sprit world. Knowing how close Kristy had gotten to Carol she would never have left her to face James' death alone. His main concern was to get off the ship as quickly as possible. He even ordered their coffees to go, along with a bag full of breakfast donuts and cheese danishes. As they exited the ship they could see it was going to be a beauty southern California day. Their timing could not have been more perfect as they reached the dock, their limousine was turning onto the pick up area. The driver stopped and immediately open the door and placed the luggage in the trunk. Kristy stopped and took one last look at the "Queen" and said.

"I really feel bad about leaving without saying good by to Carol. While you were gone, if it wasn't for her help I would have lost my mind. I have her number in my cell phone, but my phone is dead and my charger is in my car. I want to go back to the ship."

Eric knew this was not going to happen, there was no way he would enter the ship in fear the vortex would bring him back in time to London. He told Kristy he thought this was a bad idea. She understood and agreed to leave. As they entered the limousine Eric took a deep sigh of relief. The limo driver closed the car door and entered the drivers seat. Then he turned and asked. " Where are we going sir."

" Back to "Vegas" Eric replied.

Back at the ship Carol was still unaware that James had passed on. It was still quite early so she looked in on him and decided to let him sleep a little longer. She thought a quiet breakfast in the suite would be a nice way to start the day. She picked up the phone and called room service and ordered, two egg omelets, coffee and hot muffins. When the voice on the other end of the order told Carol it would take forty-five minutes to deliver Carol thought for a second and said. " That's fine, just make sure the muffins are hot and bring extra jelly."

With plenty of time to spare before waking James she decided to go back and relaxing on the couch. She began to read a magazine, Carol was so engrossed in her article, she couldn't believe forty-five minutes had past until she heard a knock at the door. A voice on the other side rang out. " Room Service"

Carol answered the door and told the waiter to set up the table in the living room. The she tipped the waiter and called out for James to get up. She set the food out and poured two cups of coffee. She called out again to James and started to butter her hot muffin. A few minutes went by, when James didn't come out she began to think there was a problem. She called one last time. " James the hot muffins are getting cold, and so is the coffee I poured. Then she put down her coffee and went into the bedroom.

" James honey, wake up Iv'e been calling you."

As she got closer to the bed she let out a scream. James! Fainting to the floor. When she came to she was on the floor. She sat there for a few seconds trying to come to her senses. She was still dizzy and foggy as to what had just happened. Then she slowly rose to her feet and slowly walked to the bed and sat at it's edge. She put her hand on James' cheek, it was ice cold. With tears running down her face she threw herself at James' lifeless body. Hugging him as tightly as she could saying over and over. " Please God don't let this be. Wake up James, wake up."

Carol knew in her heart as well as her mind, her James had left her forever. How could she explain to the boys their dream vacation had turned into a complete nightmare. When she finally got the courage to call the front desk, she asked for the ship's doctor to come to her suite. Explaining she thought her husband of fifty years had a heart attack and died in his sleep. When the doctor came and examined James, he pronounced him dead and said it looks like he had a heart attack. He told Carol that usually in this situation an autopsy has to be performed to determine the cause of death. Under the circumstance, because of his age and medical condition with all the prescribed medicine he takes he would talk to the coroner about waving the autopsy so Carol could ship James' body home. When the coroner arrived he examined James' body and found no evidence of any physical trauma what so ever. He told Carol she could take James' body home as soon as the paper work was cleared. That would take about twenty-four hours. The doctor saw how shook up Carol was and he gave some medication to calm her down. The day manager of " Queen Mary" Mr. Collins arrived and told Carol not to worry they would take care of James' body as if he were family and see to it he gets home to his family. Carol explained there would be a car waiting for her on the dock to take her back to LAX for her flight home. The manager explained it was going to take more time to make all the necessary arrangements, but her husbands body would follow in a few days. The hotel manager called for a housekeeper to help Carol with her packing while she showered and dressed before leaving the ship. When she was ready the housekeeper said. " The front desk would look for her car and let her know when to leave her suite." Carol told her to tell the front desk her drivers name was Wilson. They sent a bellman out to the dock to find Wilson and inform him of the passing of James De Marco. The bellman knocked on every waiting car window until he found Wilson. He told him of the sad news about Mr. De Marco. He also explained that management was handling returning the body home. All the arrangements were being made and he was to take Mrs. De Marco back to LAX to catch her flight home. When Carol finally walked out of the elevator and onto the dock Wilson immediately went over to her and expressed his condolences. He placed her in the car and waited for her luggage to be brought from the ship. The limousine had full bar so he asked her if she like a glass of whiskey to take the edge off. Carol explained the doctor had given her something to calm her down, but it wasn't helping and she was afraid a drink would make her pass out. Wilson replied. " That's not a bad thing. It's still a long ride to the airport and a little libation may just be the thing you need." When the luggage arrived Wilson opened the trunk and placed all the luggage in the trunk. When he closed the trunk he found Carol standing outside the car just looking at the old "Queen." Wilson walked over to her and said. " Don't worry " Queen Mary" will make sure your husband gets home safely."

     " I BELIEVE HE'S ALREADY HOME!"

GHOST HUNTER !

On the ride back to LAX Carol rested her head back on the cool leather seat of the limousine, closed her eyes and began to drift off in her memories of the days events. The ride back was longer than she remembered. The freeway was at a complete stall due to what was assumed by Wilson as a car accident. Considering the time of day the traffic should be moving quite freely. His experience driving the California Freeway brought him to that conclusion. There was nothing he could do to expedite the ride back. Then he turned to Carol and said. " Looks like we're in a real pickle here, no way to get off and try to find an alternate route back to the airport. Where just going to have to wait it out and hope for the best. It's a good thing you have a late afternoon flight, no need to worry about the delay. I'm sure we have plenty of time to make your flight."

Carol just stared out the window, and thought about some of the situations that lead up to this tragedy. Was James' reluctance to come on this trip a premonition that he would die on the ship? What were the signs she never saw concerning his health? Was it her fault insisting he come back to the Grey Ghost where he relived all his bad memories.

Were those war time memories to much of a strain on his heart? Maybe if she hadn't insisted on the trip he'd still be alive. Her grief keep making her think she was to blame. Then it hit her how could she tell the boys without making them think possibly it was their fault. Her mind just went around and around until she said to Wilson. " I think I need that drink."

With the traffic at a complete halt Wilson offered to make her a drink. Carol replied,

" I think I can make my own drink, maybe I'll make a double we may be here for a while."

She poured herself a double vodka and added a little coffee liquor. To her it tasted like a warm cup of coffee with a smooth kick. The more she drank the calmer she got, until she was totally relaxed. Without her realizing it the combination of her drink and the medication the doctor had given her on the ship, put her in a complete euphoria.

Then before she was finished with her drink the traffic slowly started to move and before long they were up to speed heading north to LAX. The double vodka seemed to take the edge off Carol's blame. Then she started to put all that had happen on board in it's proper perspective. All the craziness started the afternoon she met the mysterious Eric Von Ellstein and his so called mistress girlfriend Kristy. Had he cast, some kind of a spell over them with all his ghost, and spirits, and stories of a haunted room. Was it true that in room B340 Kristy was taken by some evil spirit and sucked into a mirror only to find herself fighting for her life in a filled pool that has been empty for years. Why was James so taken in by the evil vortex story about the good spirits fight against the bad spirits for possession of the ship? Did he know more than he lead Carol to believe? Why didn't Kristy ever say good bye before leaving the ship, and did Eric ever return to the ship? So many unanswered question that just rolled around in Carol's head. Then she said to Wilson. "Turn around, get off the freeway and go back to the ship."

" What, you want to go back?"

"Yes turn around,"

" Do you think that's good idea. I mean if your still worried about Mr. De Marco's body don't be."

" You don't understand, I want to go back. I have to go back."

" There's an exit about two miles ahead with an under pass where I can turn around and head back south."

Carol immediately took out her cell phone and called the ship. The person on the other end of the line answered.

" Good morning Queen Mary, how may I help you."

" Hello is this hotel reservations at the front desk?"

" Yes, how can I help you?

" This is Carol De Marco I was just there for the weekend and my husband had a heart attack and died this morning."

" Yes I know, very sorry for your loss."

" Has the suite I was in been rented?"

" No it's still available."

" Good. You have my credit card still on file?"

" Hold on please. Yes, I have it right here."

" I'm coming back, Run my card for two nights, but I want suite M101."

" I'll have housekeeping clean the suite immediately."

" Thank you," Carol hangs up and call the airline and tells them she need to change her return flight home because of James' passing. The operator on the other end was quite understanding and had it cleared with her supervisor. Whenever she was ready to return home just let them know in advance. Then she thought about the boys, how was she going to tell her son's their father was dead. The right way was to tell them all together, but that was almost impossible. Their jobs always kept them apart, who was out of town on business, who was working the night shift, who had to be with his in-laws. It was always a fight to get them all together. That's why planning our fiftieth anniversary party was such a big deal for them. By rights Jimmy was the oldest and he should be told first, but he was never able to handle bad news with a clear mind. The only one was Joe, even thought he was the youngest he was always able to handle adversity and bad news and still take charge. Maybe because he had to fight his older brothers for everything he got. He was never the baby brother, he was always the little brother hanging on their coat tails chasing after them. So they strengthen his character by boys being boys. She decided it would be Joe she would call first when the time was right. First she had to get back to the ship and set her mind at ease. She didn't know what she would find and she wasn't quite sure what she was looking for. When Wilson finally reached the exit where he could make his u-turn and head back south he ask one last time. " Are you sure you want to go back to the ship."

Again Carol answered with even more conviction. " Yes. Get me back to the ship."

After that brief conversation they didn't talk to each other until they reached the " Queen Mary." When Wilson reached the arrivals area he stopped the limousine, popped the trunk, got out and opened the door for Carol. As she got out of the limo she looked at the ship and thought what was she getting herself into. Wilson took the luggage out of the trunk and signaled for the bellman. Then he gave Carol his card and said. " Here's my card. Call me when your ready to be picked up. Just remember it will take me time to get here from Los Angles, call me the night before and if I don't answer just leave a message." He waited until the bellman brought Carol's luggage on board and she was out of sight. Then he got back into the car and drove away. In his mind he had fulfilled, his end of the contract he was paid for by the boys.

Carol went directly to the registration desk and reregistered. After handing over her credit card the clerk swapped it and she signed for incidentals. Then she reminded the clerk they were holding suite M101. He said. " Just as you requested." Then he rang for the bellman and said. " Please take Mrs De Marco's luggage to suite M101."

Carol followed the bellman to her suite. He opened the door and said. " I'll put your luggage in the bedroom." Then he asked." Is there anything I can do for you just let me know." Was he just being polite or did he really mean what he had just said. Carol held out a twenty dollar bill as his tip and said. "There is something you can do for me. She looked at his name tag so that her request would be a little more personal. Juan is it, can you get me the key to room B.340."

" We don't rent out that room. Can I ask why in the world would you want to get into room B.340?"

" I have my reasons. There's a hundred dollars for you, if you can get me the key. I just want to be in it for a couple of minutes, and look around."

The look on his face and the shake of his head said no.

" I'll make it two hundred!"

" I'll see what I can do, but it has to be later when my shift is over and the hallways are mostly empty."

" I have all night. I'm not going anywhere. As a matter of fact, I'll have my dinner brought to the suite. I'll be here waiting."

" If I can't get the key, I'll let you know. If I can I'll bring a flash light as I'm not sure if there is any electric lights that work in that room."

With that Carol thanked him and he left the suite. She sat on the couch and decided to call home. With the three hour time difference she was sure Joe would be home from work. She was quite nervous and went over and over in her head just how she was going to tell Joe about his father's passing. She dialed Joe's home phone number, as it rang she got even more upset. She almost hung up when Joe finally answered.

" Hello."

" Hi Joe it's mom.

" Hey mom, how's the trip we were all waiting to hear from you guys."

" Joe, I have bad news dad has passed away."

" What. Oh my GOD! What happened.

" His heart gave out. He passed in his sleep, God was very good to him, at least he didn't suffer. Joe he was so happy to be back on the ship. He couldn't believe how beautiful they had restored her. This was a wonderful ending for him. I'm going to stay out here and come home when they release his body."

" Mom do you want me and the boys come out there and stay with you until then?"

" No, by the time you come out here I'll be coming home. Besides do you know how expense it would be for all of you. Just tell your brothers and don't worry I'll be fine. We all knew it was just a matter of time with your father's heart condition."

" Mom maybe if we didn't give him that trip he'd still be alive. Maybe it was just to much for him, with the traveling and all."

" Stop it Joe. Don't you go blaming yourself for this. It was a wonder and exciting trip for both of us. Your father was so happy reliving his younger days as a young Lieutenant. I'm still on the ship and I'll let you know when I'm coming home. Please call your brothers and tell them of the situation out here. Love you Joe."

" Love you too Mom."

Ten minutes later Carol's cell phone rings. Carol looks at the pager and it's her oldest son James. She takes a deep breath as she knows she must repeat what has happened to his father. She answers the phone.

" Hi James."

" Mom, I'm coming out there. You can't be alone at a time like this."

" James please don't come, by the time you get a flight I maybe on my way home. You'll be coming west and I'll be coming east with your father's body. I've been told they may release him as early as nine A.M. I've already made provisions with the airline to get on the first flight east into Newark Airport. I'll be fine, really."

" Okay mom, sounds like you've got everything under control. I'll see you tomorrow when you land. Love you."

No sooner than she hands up, her phone rings again. This time it's John. She answers.

" Hi John."

" Mom."

John was always the most sensitive of her three boys. So it was only natural he'd take the news of his father's passing the hardest. All Carol could hear on the other end of the phone was uncontrollable crying, John was trying to collect his emotion.

" John it's okay. Please stop crying I know how you feel."

Instead of John comforting his mother, It was Carol comforting her son.

" I'm sorry mom. (collecting his emotions and thoughts) I'm so upset over the fact that your out west alone without our support."

" I'm fine I have everything under control. Please don't worry, I'll be home before you know it."

Carol hangs up the phone and sits quietly on the couch. Then she picks up the phone and calls room service. She orders a pot of tea and a couple of muffins as she didn't have any breakfast and she was getting light headed. Within fifteen minutes there was a knock at the door. She got up and answered, it was her breakfast order. The waiter rolled in a table with a white cloth covered by a tea pot, a plate with three different muffins, a cup and saucer and two small bowls one filled with butter and jellies the other with sugar. There was also a serving cup filled with milk. The waiter set the table, placed the knife and fork and poured the tea. Then he asked.

" Is there anything else I can get you at this time?"

Carol smiled and said. " No, everything is fine. Thank you." She tipped him and signed the bill. He left thanking her for her generous tip. Carol took her tea over to the couch and placed it on the coffee table. Then she opened a corn muffin and buttered it and placed it next to her tea. Sipping her tea and eating small bites of her muffin she looked around the room and realized she was alone. Then she thought this is the way it's going to be until it's my time to leave this world. She began reflecting on her life with James and reminiscing all the good times they had together the pass fifty years. Their life together growing up the boys, and what a fine job James did building their character into men. She could see him playing football with them in the yard, helping them with homework and teaching them to drive the old station wagon. She thought how did fifty years go by so quickly. As determined as she was about finding the truth in all the stories told to her and James this pass weekend. Her memory kept going back to happier times in her life. She began to think about the Christmas' when the boys were young and still believed in Santa. How they had to put out three cookies with milk before the boys would go to bed. The next morning after all the presents were opened James would have to explain why a bite was missing from all three cookies. James would say that's Santa's way to let you know he was here, and that each of the boys left him a cookie. Every year Jimmy would ask why didn't he eat all the cookies? James would explain if Santa eats a whole cookie left for him by all the good little boys and girls around the world, well that's a lot of cookies, even for Santa. Her thoughts keep flashing all over the place, who was going to take out the garbage or shovel the snow, help bring in the groceries. Then she thought it's amazing how the little things are taken for granted until their not there any more. Life without James was certainly going to be different, his presence was going to be surely missed. Looking around to her surroundings she was quickly brought back to reality and the mission before her. Taking a larger bite of her muffin she was able to wash it down with her tea that had now cooled as she swallowed a larger gulp. Finishing her muffin and tea Carol decided to unpack her clothes. Then she laid on the bed holding tightly to the very pillow James rested his head on. Tears began to roll down her checks as she remembered finding James only a few short hours ago, and how she held on to him until he was taken away. Before she knew it she was fast asleep from nervous exhaustion. Carol had slept away most of the day, by the time she woke it was late afternoon. It took her a while to get her bearing hoping it was all a dream. When she realized the days events had happened she went back to the reason she returned. Carol call the front desk to check on the scheduling and if she could still get on the tour. The person at the front desk informed her the last tour had already started. Checking the time she was told they had left the wheel house or (bridge) and were on there way to the Lady Di part of the tour. If she wanted to take a half tour she could meet with the tour in an hour. At that point she would see the hospital, prison and the pool deck tour. It was only the back end of that particular tour she was interested in. What clues she might find to help better understand the past weekend stories of ghost and spirits remained to be seen. An hour later she was tagging along listening to the history of the hospital and how many soldiers were saved while coming back to America. The hardship the doctors and nurses had to endure during surgery in the rough ocean of the North Atlantic. Carol focused on the manikins in the hopes she would see what ever James saw to get him so upset when they first saw that part of the tour. She found no evidence of spirits or ghost and was quite concern that the rest of the tour would result in the same conclusion. When they reached the prison tour, she felt no signs of evil spirits or that anyone had been murdered or simply died while being held there. The pool deck was the same, the tour guide explained how the empty pool was used as a morgue. How the men and women lockers had to be walled up to keep what most people claimed was the area they most heard or seen ghost. Carol found no evidence of an evil vortex that Eric and Kristy said was there. As the tour was ending and everyone was leaving the pool deck a strange chill came over Carol. It was as if a spirit had touched her. Then she remembered James saying spirits are only seen late at night when few if anyone are around. Had she just wasted time and energy on a tour that produced no physical evidence at all. Carol realized she would have to wait for a later time, maybe when she was delivered the key to room B.340. She was sure that room would be the place she would get the answers she was looking for. After all, why would the ship's captain give orders, that room is to be closed and off limits for registration. What really was the big mystery behind the door to that room and why was it so important for Eric to get in there. Even more important if true why did he need to bring Kristy into that room. What exactly did he expect to find there? Was the tall tail she told Carol about being suck into a mirror by spirits only to be fighting for her life in a pool filled with water just that? Yet everyone knows that very pool has not been filled for years, Who was the mysterious Eric Von Ellstein? She decided a walk around the outside deck would help to clear her mind. Then she remembered how chilly it gets at night at the waters edge. She walked into the bedroom and found the winter sweater she had brought with her. She folded it over her arm and left the suite. The hallways were still quite warm so she didn't put on her sweater until she was outside walking to the bow of the ship. The skyline of Long Beach was most impressive from the back of the ship. The city lights were fully illuminated and reflected off the water. Carol began to think how beautiful and peaceful it was standing there and how much she was going to miss James to share these moments. How different everything was going to be from now on without James. Michelle was very aware of the emotions Carol was feeling so she keep James' spirit in an other time dimension. In her thinking she waited long enough for the man she loved. Carol had James for fifty years filled with wonderful memories and three sons to hold onto. There was no way she was going to let James' spirit off the ship. After a while Carol began to feel cold even with a heavy sweater because a breeze kicked up and made her think better of staying out any longer. She decided to returned to her suite but on the way there she stopped at the ships cafe and pick up a hot cup of tea to bring back with her. As she walked

the hallways the heat from the hot cup of tea warmed her
cold hands. Entering her suite she placed the tea on the
table removed her sweater and sipped her tea. Once again
she felt alone, yet the warm tea was comforting her in her
loneliness. Kicking off her shoes and placing her feet on
the couch she covered them with her sweater and stared at
the emptiness of the room. She started thinking again
about the boys and how they were taking the news. Then
she realized she hadn't had any thing to eat since her muffin earlier this morning. She was fighting within herself as
weather to order room service or go to one of the restaurants. Which was the lesser of two evils, sitting alone in the
suite looking at four walls. Or sitting alone in the restaurant at a table for two, feeling very uncomfortable. She
started feeling sorry for herself and decided to stay in the
suite. Carol did not want any one seeing her cry, her pride
would not allow it. Besides she didn't really know what time
her bellman friend would show up with the key to room
B.340. That was top priority as far as she was concern.
Picking up the phone she call room service and ordered a
Caesar's Salad with grill chicken, a pot of tea and of course
a slice of their famous Apple Pie. The voice at the other
end of the phone line said. "The wait time would be forty
minutes."

Carol walked over to the television and turned on the
news. Then she calmly waited for her food order to be delivered. She started to doze off when she heard a knock at the
door. She was hoping it would be the key she so anxiously
waited for. When she answered the door it was her food
order. The waiter rolled in a table with a white table cloth
and a complete setup. A pot of tea with all condiments as

well as milk, honey and sliced lemons. Then he took her salad out of the warmer, removed the cover and placed it in the center of the table. He then told her. " I'll leave the apple pie in the warmer."

He handed Carol the bill and she signed it and included his tip. Thanking her he left the suite and once again, Carol was alone. Picking up a folk and her salad she sat on the couch and watched the news as she ate her dinner. When she was finished with her salad she placed it on the table and poured her tea, open the warmer and took out her apple pie. Carol placed her tea on the coffee table and sat back down with her pie. Taking her first bite she knew why it was their signature dessert. She thought to herself this is even better than my own homemade apple pie, though she could not quite put a handle on why. A second fork full told her it had to be the apples. Sometimes a tree or orchard will bear a better tasting apple, what ever the reason this was the best ever.

Several hours later Carol received the knock on her door she was waiting for. It was her bellman friend bringing her the key to room B.340. When she open the door the bellman came in. He showed her the key and Carol went to her purse and took out two one hundred dollar bills. She handed them to Juan and he handed her the key and a flash light. Then Carol said.

"Are you still coming with me?"

"I must be nuts for doing this, but yes I won't let you go in that room alone."

With that they both left the suite and took the elevator down to the old B- level of the ship. When the elevator reached that deck they proceeded with great caution not to be seen. When they reached room B.340 Juan looked around at the empty hallway and said.

" The coast is clear, hurry open the door."

Carol fitted the key into the lock and turned it with no extra effort. The lock was loosened somewhat, when Eric opened the door only a day earlier. Entering the room Carol immediately open the flash light to get her bearing. Then she found a light switch on the wall and turned it on. A lamp sitting on a small night stand next to the bed lit illuminating a dim light near the bed. Carol would have to keep her flash light on if she wanted to clearly see the other side of the room. She walked over to the bed where it is said a man was found with an axe buried in his head even though the door was locked from the inside. Carol slowly sat down on the end of the bed. The room was cold and musty, when she looked back at Juan he making the sign of the cross, shaking in his shoes. Carol said.

" If your that scared just leave."

" No. I'll just stay here near the door, just in case I need a quick exit."

Then Carol walked towards the center of the room, that is where Kristy said she was when she saw the ghost of the murdered man lying in the bed. She looked back and saw nothing but an empty old bed. She proceeded, to the infamous mirror that some how reached out and sucked Kristy into it only to find herself in a pool fighting for her life. She flashed her light on to the mirror hoping to see something. All she saw was her own reflection. Getting closer she reached out and touched the mirror, closed her eyes and waited. Again nothing happened, she was starting to believe the stories Eric and Kristy told were just bull shit.

Just trying to scare two old people, real practical jokers. Then Carol turned to Juan and said.

" There's nothing here, but and old dirty disgusting, cold room filled with cobwebs. Let's get out of here, it stinks in here."

" Those are the best words I could hear you say."

Just then the lights started to flicker and the room got colder. Before she could turn the light off Juan was gone. She ran out into the hallway only to find Juan leaning against the wall bent over holding his knees talking in Spanish. Carol walked over to Juan and said.

" Are you all right?"

" Did you see it, did you see it?" He repeated.

" See what?"

" The man in the bed, with an axe in his head."

" I didn't see anything, lets go back inside."

" Not with me. I'm not going back in there. There's not enough money in the world to get me to go back in there."

With that Carol opened her flashlight and walked back inside. Before she could get the lamp lit at the bed, the door slammed shut behind her. Juan knew immediately this was not a good sign. He took a deep breath and composed himself enough to open the door while standing out in the hall. The room was still dark with no evidence of any light, not even the flashlight. He leaned into the room and called out.

" Mrs De Marco are you there. Hello, where are you? Please answer me, I'm not coming in. Just call out."

Then he began to panic. "Oh my God! I'm going to lose my job. How in the world am I going to tell them I gave her the key, and let her in. Now she's disappeared. Who's going to believe me."

He sat on the floor in the hallway brought his knees up to his chest and buried his head against his legs. He was screwed and he knew it. His job, the future of his family destroyed for a few hundred bucks. What was he thinking? He keep thinking what to do, what to do, what to do. Then it hit him, who's going to believe me when I tell them. All I have to do is return the key and say nothing. No one has seen it, all I have to do is put it in my mind it never happened. Juan looked around no one was in the hallway so he locked the door and returned to the front desk and secretly returned the key. Michelle knew Carol had been taken to a paradox dimension. Kind of like purgatory, a state between heaven and hell. In her wildest dreams did she ever think Carol would venture into room B.340. It was now up to Michelle, to try and get Carol out of there, but how. She knew she would have to tell James what had just happened to Carol and how she tried to help her in that room as she was being taken. She just didn't have the power by herself to combat the evil spirits within. It was going to take more that the power of two spirits to bring her back. Once again, she would have to call upon the good spirits within the "Queen Mary" for their support and strength. When she got back to James she told him Carol had been taken. James said.

" I thought the vortex was closed and all the evil spirits had left the ship."

" Not in room B.340, that's why that room is off limits to all passengers."

" Why in the world would Carol venture into that room? Doesn't make sense, she should be off the ship and half way home."

" James she was obviously looking for answers to what ever is running through her brain. I'm sure it has something to do with you, Eric and Kristy. First things first, we have to get her out of the paradox dimension. I have to find some of the spirits that helped us close the vortex. Strength in numbers is the only way to get her out of the paradox. If we can bring her back to the exact time in room B.340 just before she was taken her memory of the paradox would be erased."

Michelle and James went down to the boiler room deck in search of some of the men who helped her to close the vortex. When she found some of the men and told them what had happened most were reluctant to help saying. "We all know the spirits in that room do not look to harm us, as long as they are left alone. Everyone knows not to enter that room. Why should we risk ourselves for a foolish woman."

James explained the woman in question was his wife of fifty years. He told them as far as he knew she would never do anything like this. Maybe his passing has confused her mind because of the events that had taken place this past weekend. Michelle pleaded, it's as much our fault as anyone else, we put her husband in harms way to help us fight the evil that was before us. Together we beat all the evil that was trying to take over the ship. Then the spirit of the sailor said. " This is different, the spirits in room B.340 never wanted to take over the ship. They were happy in their own little realm. We didn't bother them and they didn't bother us.

It was only when the two strangers entered the room this passed weekend that everything was disrupted. The vortex was able to open, souls were retrieved from the pool morgue and the fight began. I say let it lie, leave the woman where she is. All will calm down again and we will have peace."

Michelle shouted back. " We would be as evil as those in the vortex. I for one cannot do that. James would not do that! Who is with us."

A voice from the back of the room said. " I am with you." Then another and another. Before long most of the spirits joined Michelle and James. They again had a group strong enough to enter the paradox dimension and bring back Carol. What they needed now was a plan. A course of action that would work without alerting the vortex. Michelle presented her idea to the others saying. " I believe we should enter quietly and just find Carol and bring her back before any of the spirits there realize what we are doing."

"A group this size enters and goes unnoticed, impossible." Said another sailor.

Another sailor said. "What about charging in grab the woman and charge out. If anyone gets in our way we just knock them down and keep going until were out."

"That's a stupid plan," yelled one sailor. Then they all started shouting and yelling at each other. Each spirit screaming his idea that would work. Then James took charge like the lieutenant he was, and their commanding officer in World War II. " Pipe down, I out rank all of you and let me think, without all this yelling back and forth." Said James.

Michelle took him aside and asked if he had a plan. James answered." No, not yet."

Then he walked away from the group, trying to collect his thoughts. Then he went back to the group and said. " I'm new to this spirit world, so after I tell you my plan if anyone has a better thought I want to hear it. In an orderly manner. No one knows me in the paradox dimension so if we all go back to room B.340 I will slip inside and cross over.

Quietly I'll find Carol and bring her back. She will trust me more than anyone else to follow my lead. What I think all of you should do is wait outside the paradox in case I need your collective strength to help us get back."

" Sounds like a plan to me." shouted one of the sailors.

Michelle grabbed James by the arm and pulled him to the side saying. " Do you think it's wise to go in alone?"

" Knowing Carol the way I do, she will be more understanding to follow my lead. Once I get her and start to bring her back you can tell everyone to return to their deck of choice. You can stay and help me to pull her out of the paradox passed the room and into the hallway at the exact time she entered. Carol and Juan will be out in the hallway together as if nothing had ever happened."

" And if your plan doesn't work, what then?"

" You better come in with the boys like the cavalry, and rescue us."

Michelle shook her head and shrugged her shoulders and said. " Lets do this."

Then they all followed James back to room B.340. When they entered all the spirits stayed against the wall without touching anything inside the room. Michelle stood against the door, and only James went in and started to sit on the bed and touch the mirror. He was tracing the foot steps Carol took just before she was taken. Then as he felt the paradox open he stepped in. Once inside he was out of his league. He never imagined what he was seeing. Spirits were passing by in their own time warp. It was like seeing a motion picture in slow motion. There were spirits flashing by like white sheets of light. While other were fully clothed and walking by as if they knew him. One minute he was in the medieval times the next he was back in the war. It seem to him the time the person entered the paradox was the time they stayed in. Their spirit roamed the time zone they lived in. So what he had to do was find the present day time zone. What he thought was going to be any easy fix to the situation Carol got herself into was now turning into a real problem. Was it he didn't have enough time himself in the spirit world or was he to inexperienced to figure out how to navigate in the paradox dimension. He continued his search to no avail. No matter what he tried he could not find the right entrance to the present time. He decided to return to room B.340 and explain to Michelle what he had experienced there. As he returned to the waiting group of spirits, he explained his frustration. It was obvious they need a new plan if they were going to find and bring back Carol. Then Michelle said, " Let me try to bring her back. If I locate her I can always say I was a friend of yours in the war and hope she follows me out."

" What if she won't follow you out for fear, she doesn't know you?"

" I can always come back and bring you in with me. The most important thing is finding a way to the present time zone."

James agreed to let Michelle give it a go by herself. In hopes she could navigate the paradox better than he knew how to. After all she had years of experience moving from one time zone to another. She understood the paradox and what went on inside it. Then in a flash Michelle was gone. James and all the other spirits began the waiting vigil. For James it was harder to be outside the paradox then it was inside. At least inside his mind was filled with what he was seeing and thinking how to move from one time zone to another. When your on a mission you don't have time to worry and think the worst. He could only wait and hope for the best. The longer Michelle took the more the other spirits began to mumble, about how much longer were they supposed to wait. Being in that room was quite uncomfortable, they were all looking to return to their own haunts. James began to plead for them to stay strong a little while longer by saying.

" Please give Michelle more time. We started this together lets stay together. Don't let the time I wasted facing the unknown take away from Michelle's quest."

One of the sailors said. " We own Michelle more time, she has always been there for us whenever we had to fight the vortex for this ship." An other yelled out. " Okay we stay."

James realized if Michelle wasn't back with Carol soon there was no way he was going to hold the spirits together. Meanwhile Michelle was having her own problems, she was able to find the nineteen forties and world war II zone but was having a hard time passing through. She needed to get to the present day time zone to find Carol and it just wasn't happening. Someone or something was holding her back. She began to fear that one of the evil spirits from the vortex was there and remembered her from their encounter on the ship. Michelle kept up her search, finally she was moving forward in paradox time warp. She began to see all the progress the world had made since the end of World War II. The age of nuclear power had brought huge changes in the the world. Technology she could never have dreamed of living in the nineteen thirties and early forties. Life was so simple then and people lived without stress, their word was their bond, and greed had not taken over the world. She didn't know she had lived in the "Greatest Generation" of all. When she found Carol helplessly wandering in her time zone she took her by the hand and said.

" Have no fear, I'm here to help you get back to the ship."

" I know you." Carol replied.

Michelle was taken aback, and she said.

" How do you know me?"

" I saw you and my James as young lovers on board the " Queen Mary." Your the reason he didn't want to come back to the ship. I saw all the dark secrets he kept from me all the years we were married."

" It was years before he met you. Don't think about old haunts just come with me to safety. When you get back to the ship you will have no memory of what you saw in the time warp."

" I don't believe you. I can't go back knowing he never really loved me."

" How can you say that when he was a perfect husband, and father to you and your boys."

" Yes! He was a perfect father. I wish he loved me as much as he loved his son's."

" After fifty years of marriage if you really think he really didn't love you, your a fool. Enough of this, we have to get out of here before we met with a different kind of evil spirit that could hold us here forever."

A stubborn Carol refuses to hear any words Michelle is saying. Her pride is more than hurt and her heart is broken. To think her life was built on a lie, as far as she was concerned she could stay right where she was. The exit warp was the closest it was going to be Michelle decided to grab Carol and make a quantum leap back to the present time. As the two passed through the paradox Michelle's spirit stopped at the door way to the room where James and the other spirits waited. While Carol found herself in the hallway where Juan was having breathing attack. All bent over he saw Carol and rushed to her aid. As Michelle predicted Carol had no recollection of what happened in the paradox. When Carol looked back into room B.340 the light was off, so she immediately closed the door behind her. By that time Michelle, James and the others had left the room and returned to their own haunts. Juan quickly locked the door saying. " I'll never venture into that room again." Then he made the sign of the cross and blessed himself. Carol having no memory said.

" What are you so scared of? I told you it was all lies, nothing but bull crap just to get people excited about ghost stories. The "Queen Mary" legend has lasted for years because people who come here want to believe it's true. It's time for you to go home to your family and for me to go back to my suite and order a hot cup of tea."

With that they both went their separate ways. James and Michelle were quite happy with the out come of the nights events. When Carol got back to her suite she picked up the phone and ordered from room service, a pot of hot tea and a pastry. Comfort food to satisfy her night of dismay. She thought to herself a well deserved cup of tea can always calm the nerves. As she sat on the couch and waited for her order. She became very pleased with herself, she faced her fears head on and proved what she knew in her heart was true. Ghost stories belong to children at "Halloween." A short while later there was a knock at the door, and her order was delivered. She prepared her tea the way she like it, sugar and lemon. Sipping her hot tea Carol began to think there was no reason to stay an extra night. She had accomplished what she set out to do, and if Wilson was available she'd make her arrangements to return home.

Carol picked up the phone and called the airline and told the person answering her situation. Explaining her husband's body may be released tomorrow late morning or early afternoon. Was there an available seat for her with her husband's casket in the belly of the plane. The airline representative checked her computer and assured her there would be no problem. Then Carol asked for a twenty-four hour hold on a seat back to Newark Airport. Again the reply was no problem, and she took all the additional infor-mation needed. Then Carol called Wilson's cell phone and left a message, whether he would be able to pick her up in the late morning hour. The only thing left to do was to contact the coroner's office to see if all the paper work was ready to release James' body. She knew she had plenty of time to call the boys once she was sure of all her plans.

The only thing left was to try and get a good nights sleep. She was hoping watching television would make her sleepy. She closed her eyes and never left the couch. James told Michelle he never had a chance to say good by to Carol and wanted to see her one more time. Michelle asked.

" How important is it for you to say your good byes?"

" I feel it's something I have to do, after all we were together for fifty years."

" If I don't help you to do that you'll never be full happy here in the spirit world."

" How can you help me?"

" Would you like to visit her in her dream world?"

" Very much so, I feel it will bring closure to our life together."

Michelle was still a little unsure about helping James enter Carol's dream world. She knew it could be dangerous as well as fruitless. The subconscious world is made up of millions of memories the older a person is. Every thought pattern is in there and one can get lost among the many flashback that are thrown their way. There was also the worry that Carol would not remember James' visit with her. They shared so many memories together that James' spirit could get caught in the vacuum of space which is absolute energy. He could get caught in there and never get back to Michelle. Was that a chance she wanted to take after waiting so many years for him to return to her. The more she thought about it the less she wanted to do it, then she told James.

" I've thought it over, it's much to dangerous. You could get caught in a dream and never come out."

" It's a risk I'm willing to take."

" I'm not. I've waited for you fifty plus years and now you want me to help you. No I can't do it, I won't do it. I'm sorry I ever mention the dream world to you."

James was very upset as he walked away from Michelle, then he said.

" I'll find my own way to say good bye.

Michelle knew that would be impossible for a new spirit. There would be no way James could navigate and pull Carol into the spirit world the way she did with James. He didn't have enough time or experience. She didn't want James to be mad at her and start their time together on a sour note. Michelle ran and caught up to James, then she said.

" There is another way, but I must warn you if I help you pull Carol into our realm when she comes through I will be standing next to you. Then you will have to explain who I am, and why I'm with you."

" Why can't I be there alone when she comes through?"

" You don't have the power to hold her there. Also you must know when she see me there is a chance her memory of what she saw when she was in room B.340 may return."

" You mean if she went back to the time we first crossed on the Grey Ghost during the war?"

"Yes. Right now she has no real memory of what happened in that room. Do you want to jar her memory and have to face the consequences of knowing the secret you've been carrying in you heart and mind all these years?"

" Your confusing me, first you say you can help, then you say it's too dangerous."

" I'm just trying to tell you all that could happen. It's always dangerous when you bring someone into the spirit world. You never experienced this because you were totally committed to me. I can't say the same for Carol. I have no previous connection to her when I was alive in the real world. She has found her closure, believing all the ghost stories were just that stories. She truly believes you were happy coming back to see how the old Grey Ghost was restored and that you were at peace when you passed on. I think your just feeling guilty because you're here with me on board this ship in my realm."

" Maybe your right! Maybe it's because I'm happy here with you, and she's so sad with the worse yet to come."

" Your thinking of your boys, and their reaction when they finally see her back home."

" Yes."

" That's something they all have to face, whether or not you are with me on this ship."

" I have one question to ask. What will happen when Carol passes on, will she see us together and then know the truth."

This was a question thrown from left field. One that Michelle never thought James would ask. She thought about it for a while and then tried to answer the best she could.

" When her time comes, to pass on and she is on the East coast, her realm will probably stay close to her children. Where she can look in on them from time to time and watch her grand children grow. Only if her will is strong enough to want to sacrifice that realm to find you can she leave. Then she would have to know exactly where to find you. Even if she comes back to the ship knowing it was the last place you were when you passed. It doesn't mean we can't move to a different dimension, until she leaves. It will be sort of a cat and mouse game, but I don't see Carol's passing for many years to come."

James excepted Michelle's answer, and was much relieved and feeling less guilty about being back together with her aboard the Queen Mary. He decided not to try to contact Carol. He felt there was no reason to possibly hurt her after fifty years of loyalty and love. The bond he formed with Carol was quite different from the one he had with Michelle. Even though he knew Michelle didn't understand it, he respected her truthfulness. That night he stayed with Carol and held her hand even though she was unaware of his touch, he hoped she could feel his presents in her dream world.

The next day as Carol awoke she though about her life with James. Although she was unaware he had held her hand all night, she did feel he was with her and she knew it was time to bring James home. Her first order of business was to call for a hot pot of tea, an egg and cheese on a roll, and a bran muffin. Then she called Wilson and left an other message on his answering service to call her back. She knew her breakfast would take twenty minutes which gave her time to take a hot shower and get dressed. Twenty minutes later her breakfast was delivered, and she preceded to pour her tea and eat her egg sandwich while it was hot. Carol put on the television to watch the early morning news mostly for company, then she went back to her breakfast. Ten minutes later she received a call from Wilson who told her he could be there to pick her up about noon. It gave Carol enough time to contact the ships manager, to find out from the city coroner's office on the release status of James' body. He told her, he would get all the information she needed and get back to her as soon as possible. She had set all the wheels in motion, now it was time to return to her tea and wait. An hour later her nerves were getting the best of her so she decided to pack her clothes just to take her mind off of her worries. When her cell phone rang she was sure it was one of the boys calling to find out when she was coming home. Much to her surprise when she heard Kristy's voice.

" Hello Carol is that you?"

" Kristy, yes it's me."

" I'm so sorry I left without saying goodbye. Eric wanted to leave the ship immediately, and if I wanted a ride back to Las Vegas his car was waiting and we had to leave now. I tried to call you from the car, but I forgot to charge my phone and I had no service."

" Are you still in Las Vegas with Eric?"

" No, I'm back in L.A. he gave me some extra money and said he had to go on a business trip. He took my cell number and said he'd call when he got back. I guess it was a nice way of blowing me off to getting rid of me. I just want to thank you for being so kind and understanding to me while we were on the ship."

" I really could have used your friendship the morning you left. James passed away in his sleep. When I tried to wake him he was already gone."

" Oh my God, Carol. I'm so sorry. If I had known I would never have left with Eric."

" It's okay, I believe you."

" Is there anything I can do for you?"

" No, I'm just waiting to hear when they are releasing James' body so I can take him home.

" Again please except my deepest condolences. I'm so sorry for your loss."

Carol began to cry as Kristy hung up the phone. After a good cry she though to herself that was one phone call I never expected, a strange ending to an even stranger weekend. Just then the phone in her bedroom rang, it was the front desk manager Mr. Collins informing Carol the city coroner's office had told him James was released and was being shipped to L.A.X. Airport to be placed on American Airline flight 602 east bound to Newark Int' Airport. The flight is at five o'clock and a first class seat was being held for her. The only thing left was to wait for Wilson's arrival. She called the airline to confirm all that Mr. Collins had told her, but she had one question to ask. What should she do with the small suitcase of James' clothes. The agent explained not to worry, just show the return ticket in James' name and they will wave it as a second bag and place it to accompany the casket when it is picked up from the funeral home. Carol thanked the agent and said. " That is a load off my mind. Thank you again."

The agent replied. " American Airline is very sorry for your loss. If there is anything else we can do to comfort your return home please feel free to call again."

Carol hangs up and call the bellman to pick up the two bags of luggage. Explaining she will be leaving the ship as soon as her ride back to L.A.X arrives. An hour later Wilson calls and tells Carol he is about fifteen minutes away from the pick up area. With that Carol proceeds to the front desk to check out and pay her bill. When she is there she asks for

Mr. Collins wanting to thank him one last time. The person at check out explains he is in a meeting, but will be sure to give him her message of thanks. Carol was hoping to deliver her message in person but under the circumstances with Wilson waiting at the dock she just smiled and said. " Please don't forget, thank you again."

When Carol got down to the pick up area her luggage was waiting for her and so was Wilson. She handed the bellman her ticket and he brought her luggage to the curb as Wilson pulled up, stopped and popped the trunk. He immediately got out to open the door for Carol. When she got in he put the bags in the trunk, closed it and began to drive back to L.A.X. Then he said,

"Same as before. American Airline back to Newark?"

" Yes, same as before."

" Hope your return yesterday was fruitful, and you found what ever you were looking for."

" Pretty much."

Wilson could tell Carol wasn't in the mood for conversation. He couldn't tell if the whole ordeal had taken it's toll on her. He figured she would talk when she was ready. He pulled away from curb and proceeded, to leave the dock and Queen Mary behind. Traffic was light and getting on the freeway heading north was no problem, Carol was still very quiet as she looked out the window. Wilson could only imagine what might being going on in her head, after the tragic death of her husband of more than fifty years. Then he said. " If the traffic keeps moving this way you'll have more than three hours to flight time. I know a nice cafe just off the airport exit, we could stop and get some lunch. It's a long flight home even for first class."

" Maybe a sandwich and a cup of tea would be good, but where are you going to park this car?" Said Carol.

" No problem, I know the valet he lets me park right out front."

" Okay, let me know when we get to the exit."

Carol got very quiet the rest of the ride north. Wilson's was hoping his idea about having lunch together would open her up to conversation. Just before they reached the off ramp to the airport Wilson reminded Carol about lunch saying.

" A quarter mile to the exit with plenty of time to spare. Would you like to make that stop and have lunch together?"

" On second thought I think I'll skip lunch, first of all I'm not really hungry, second I'm not good company right now. Although I appreciate your kindness, and thoughtfulness."

Wilson continued to the airport and stopped at the departure ramp for American Air Line.

The ramp was backed up with the afternoon traffic as each car or van took it's turn to get close to the curb to unload. It took almost twenty minutes for Wilson to reach the drop off curb. Then he said.

" Good thing we didn't stop for lunch, later this afternoon the traffic to get close to the curb will be even heavier."

When he finally stopped he popped the trunk and open the door for Carol. Then he got out the two bags and signaled for a skycap. The skycap placed the two bags on his trolly and checked Carol's tickets. Then he told her she would have to check-in at the first class counter as her tickets were for a different date. Wilson said.

" I'm sure your all right, so I'll say my goodbyes, and again I'm very sorry for your loss."

Then he gave her a hug and a soft pat on her back. When Carol tried to tip him he would not except her money, saying.

" That's quite alright, you don't have to do this."

" Nonsense, you made a special return trip that wasn't part of the original contract. I hope two hundred is enough to cover it?"

Then she placed the money in his hand and closed it, and gave him a kiss on his check whispering in his ear. Thank you so much."

Carol smiled and followed the skycap to the reservation desk. There were no lines at first class as Carol was very early to check-in. The skycap placed James' bag first as Carol explained her husband casket would be returning on the same flight with her. Then he placed Carol bag on the weight scale. Carol tipped him as he said." Sorry for your loss."

The agent then assured Carol both bags would be placed in the belly of the plane next to the casket and both would accompany the casket to it final destination so she didn't have to worry about lugging the bags home. When out of the blue a voice said. " Carol."

She knew in an instant it was Kristy, she turned and said. " What in Gods name are you doing here?"

" I remembered you said it was American Air Line, so I had to come and say goodbye in person. You were too good to me on that ship not to. I'm so sorry for your loss. Maybe we can have a cup of coffee and talk."

" I'd like that, lets go find a diner or something."

The agent over hearing them talk, and told Carol. " There's a first class club up stairs where you both can have coffee and something to eat, until they call your flight for departure."

Carol thanked the agent and they both continued to the fIrst class club. They were greeted at the door by another agent who checked Carol's ticket and politely invited them both in saying. " Welcome to American Airline V.I.P. Club, please make yourself comfortable, we have coffee, soft drinks, tea and hot and cold food. When you hear your flight being called you may go right to your gate for boarding."

Carol and Kristy helped themselves to a tea, coffee and some hot snacks. They found a table at the end of the room, where it was private with less noise. After a few sips of tea Carol asked.

" Why in the world did you come out here? It had to be quite a ride from Los Angeles."

" I did want to give you my condolences in person, but I really needed someone to help understand what happened this weekend."

" I guess it was a little weird."

" Talk about weird, the drive back to Las Vegas really freaked me out. About half way there, I fell asleep on the bench seat, and when I got up I heard Eric in conversation. At first I thought he was on his cell phone, then I realized he was just talking out loud. No cell phone, no bluetooth, nothing. I pretended to be asleep, he was fighting with somebody named Jack that wasn't there. All he keep repeating was, Why do I have to be like the rest of the family. It's not in me to be evil. I never wanted to drown her and I don't want to go back to London. As soon as he realized I was awake he stopped talking to who ever, and became very quiet. When I questioned him about who was he talking to, he became very upset. Later he started to make small talk about seeing me again after he returned from some business trip. I just don't know what to do, I really like him, and not just as a client."

" I really don't know what to tell you, he spooked me out when we were on the ship. Every time I mention it to James he would just say, Eric was not a bad guy. How did you leave off with him?"

" When we got back to Vegas, I left him at the front door of the hotel. He made some lame excuse about getting his money out of the casino cage and having to leave on a trip to England. Then he got my bag out of the trunk of the car, handed me an envelope of money, and said he would call me when he got back. So I high tailed it out of there and headed straight back to Los Angeles."

" If I were you, I'd get a new number, and get out of your business before some nut really hurts you. Go get a job in a men's clothing store on Rodeo Drive. With your looks and body you have to be a hit with the customers."

" I know your right. It's just hard when you get use to big money. L.A. is an expensive town if you want to live right. A twenty dollar an hour job after taxes doesn't cut it. Even when they give you commission on your sales."

" You rather take a chance on loosing you life meeting up with a weird crazy. Work a normal job meet normal people, meet a man who can appreciate you for who you are. I got to see the other side of you back on the ship. Give yourself a chance, you got lucky this time, you may not be so lucky the next time. What's the worse that can happen, you try it and if doesn't work you go back to being a prostitute."

" It's not going to be easy, but I'll give it a try, I promise."

" That a girl, remember the image you project is the person that they see. Carry yourself with class, your an educated college graduate. Be that person again. There's my flight call, I have to leave. Here's my home phone number and cell. Call me any time you want to talk, heaven knows I have the time. Oh, stay away from Eric!"

Carol and Kristy get up from their table and hug, like a mom leaving her daughter behind. Carol walks away and Kristy decides to sit back down and finish her coffee. Pondering all the good advice Carol had given her. A few minutes later a very well dressed middle aged man approaches her and asks.

" Excuse me for saying, are you all right you seem very upset."

Kristy looks up and says. " What!"

" I asked if you were okay. You look very upset. Was that your mother leaving? Very attractive and classy looking woman. Hi I'm Jason Roberts, my friends call me Jack, may I join you?"

Kristy begins to think maybe this is a former client, that she can't remember. Then she says. " Sure have a seat."

" Are you flying out today?"

" No, actually, I was seeing my aunt off. She heading back home to New York."

" Are you from back east?"

" No, I live here in L.A. Came out here to attend UCLA. Met my husband, got married, five years later got divorced, went back to school and got my degree. Now I can't find a job. Are you flying out today?"

" No I'm just coming in from a business trip. My plane got in early and I figured I could kill some time over a good cup of coffee, while I wait for my car to arrive. What type of degree did you get at UCLA."

" Business. I majored in business with an associates degree in accounting. It seems every high paying firm wants a masters degree. Every job out there pays peanuts. Today a college degree is like a high school degree years ago. Well, it was nice talking to you but I have to get a cab back to the city."

" Why a cab? Don't you have a car?"

" I do, but did you ever try to find a parking spot in this airport? Insane, and if you do find one you have to walk a mile to the terminal. It's easy to just pay a cab and get dropped off at the terminal door. The problem is leaving you have to wait some times an hour on the cab line."

" I'd be glad to give you a ride back to where ever you want to go. My car should be here, (Checking his watch) in about ten minutes."

" Really, I wouldn't want to put you out of your way."

" No bother at all. I'm free all day, no business appointments, and I'd love the company."

" Okay, sure that would be great."

They both get up from their chairs and proceed to the pickup area in front of the terminal. Walking out Kristy realizes her new friend Jack has no luggage, not even a carry-on bag. Then she comments. " Traveling light, are you?"

" Yes it was a short flight, Vegas and back. Had to meet up with a long lost acquaintance of mine. Walking through the double doors to the outside, Kristy looks to her left and says. " Oh my God! Look at that cab line, it would have taken forever to get out of here."

Just then a midnight blue sedan pulls up to the curb. The driver gets out and opens the rear door. Just as she is about to enter she says. " Wow, is this a Rolls Royce?"

" No. This is a Bentley!"

" Very impressive." Says Kristy.

Entering the car, she feels the seat before she sits. Doe skin leather, way softer than any limousine she has ever been in. Kristy is now like a kid in a candy shop, totally over whelmed. Jack gets in and his driver closes the door. Then he gets in the driver seat and pulls away. Kristy thinks to herself I wonder how much he'd pay for a good blow job. Then Carol's words rang true in her ear. Give up that life and take pride in yourself before you meet up with the wrong man.

" Kristy you never gave me your last name." Says Jack.

" To tell you the truth, most men never ask for my last name. Anderson, Kristy Anderson. I think the last time I gave my last name was in a job interview twelve months ago."

" What have you been doing for the last twelve months to earn a living?"

" You know odd jobs. If you saw me in a Las Vegas Hotel Casino Bar all dressed sitting alone, what would you ask?"

" Can I buy you a drink?"

" Okay, then what?"

" Are you alone?" Are you looking for company?"

" Continue."

" After some conversation, maybe would you like to have dinner? I always find that to be a good way to know someone."

" Well you've got the line down pretty good. I guess you've been around the block a few times, but your missing the last piece of the puzzle. Which is would you like to come up to my room. Which I would answer, sure a thousand dollars for the night."

" I guess I was reading you all wrong."

" Maybe. I promised my aunt just before she got on her plane I'd leave the business and give it the old college try, and get a real job."

" I was going to give you an opportunity for a real job with one of my many companies, but now that I know there's a different side to you. Maybe I'd like to met the sexy side of you."

" Your a little to late. I made a promise and I'm going to stick with it for as long as I can. I have a few dollars saved to carry me until the right job comes along. So just drop me off at any bus stop, and thanks for the ride. A Bentley can't wait to tell my friends."

After a few minutes Kristy could see Jack was pondering in deep thought. When he reached in his suit jacket pocket and pulled out a business card and wrote on the back of it. Then he handed it to Kristy and said. " It's to late for an interview, but tomorrow go to the Bridgewater Towers. Take the elevator to the fifth floor, ask for Mr. Spencer. Give him my card and he'll give you and interview for a job. Fill out the application, take the test and someone from the company will get back to you. The higher you score on the test, with a college degree, the better your position and pay scale."

Then he told his driver to stop at the nearest bus stop. He let Kristy out and wished her good luck. Kristy stood at the curb and watched the Bentley drive away. She looked at the card and read the back that said. This is a good friend, of mind, treat her well, and he signed his named. Kristy figured what the hell, a job interview is exactly what she needed. Now it was all up to her to score as high as she could and impress the so called Mr. Spencer. It turned out to be a really good day. She got to talk with Carol, gave her condolences and got a job interview. Not to mention a ride in a Bentley. She was very proud of herself for sticking to her guns and not giving into Jack's proposal.

A NEW LEASE ON LIFE

The next day Kristy got up bright an early, went to the kitchen and made a pot of coffee. While the coffee was brewing she took a hot shower, shampooed her hair wrapped herself in a bath towel and dried herself. Then she put on her robe, blew dried her hair and put on her makeup. She then went into her bedroom and picked out a business type outfit. Checked herself out in her full length mirror, and decided she was ready for the corporate world. After a well needed cup of coffee, she made sure she had her card for Mr. Spencer and left for her interview. Traffic was moving quite well so she knew she had plenty of time to spare. She was real happy finding a public parking garage across the street from the Bridgewater towers building. After leaving her car and collecting her parking ticket she thought to herself this may very well be my lucky day. When she got to the fifth floor she told the receptionist she was there to see Mr. Spencer for a job interview. The reception-ist was very taken aback saying at this level you usually all ready have the job. Then she showed the card Mr. Roberts gave her. Kristy was told to have a seat and wait for Mr. Spencer who had not yet arrived for the day. Twenty min-utes later the receptionist told Kristy she could go thru the doors at the end of the hall where Mr. Spencer was waiting. Then she handed her back her card. Kristy's nerves were starting to get the best of her. It was a long time since she went down that long corporate road. At the double doors she took a deep breath, collected her thoughts and entered the room. Mr. Spencer was seating behind a large desk sipping a cup of coffee. He gave her a smile and pointed to take a seat. Kristy sat and took the card out of her purse. This was like no interview she had ever been on before.

" My receptionist has informed me your here for an interview."

"Yes. I was told to come here and see you by Mr. Roberts. He gave me his card to give to you."

Then she got up and handed him the card, and sat back down. Just then the phone rang and he answered it turning his swivel chair around as not to let her see his expressions, or hear what ever he was saying. When he was finished he turned back to her and said. " That was Mr. Roberts confirming you may be in today for an interview. He was very glad to hear you were here. I told him I read his card and would give her, every consideration, for the job." Then he handed her an application to be filled out, and told her she could sit at the side desk in his office. Kristy took the application went to the small desk on the side wall and proceeded, to fill out every line. When she was finished she gave it back to him and sat down. Mr. Spencer looked it over and commented about her education saying.

" I see here your a graduate of UCLA. Have a degree in business but no real corporate experience. You do understand that this interview is for an executive associate position."

" I wasn't aware of that. I only followed Mr. Roberts recommendation to come in and see you."

" Why did it take you so long to get your degree?"

" I met my ex-husband in my junior year got married. Five years late got divorced, went back to school when the money ran out. I got a job in retail as an accountant/ saleswoman while I went back to night school. Every corporate interview never panned out. Every one is looking for a masters degree. I have no shot at this job, right. I'm just wasting my time and yours."

" We'll get back to you in a day or two. Don't be discouraged, you have the backing of Mr. Roberts a man who sits on the board of directors of this company, and carries a lot of weight as to what goes on."

Kristy gets up extends her hand and thanks Mr. Spencer for his help. Leaving the building she believes Mr. Spencer was just being gracious because of the card she had from her friend Jack Roberts. Then she thought maybe she should have showed him the sexy side he had asked for. When she got to the parking garage she asked the attendant where the nearest diner or luncheonette was, as she realized she had not eaten all day. He told her two blocks down was a good diner type eatery, with really good burgers and shakes. She followed his direction, entering the diner she could not believe how busy it was for that hour of the afternoon. When she returned to the garage she told the attendant he was right. The hamburger, french fries and milk shake were A, one. Then she handed him the ticket for her car and paid her bill. The drive back home on the freeway was slower as she was in the middle of evening rush hour. As traffic snarled she began to think about her passed weekend on the Queen Mary. How could one week-end have so many highs and lows. If it wasn't for the friend-ship she made with Carol, who really got her through the low times, she would have gone crazy. Why did Eric have such a hold over James with all his ghost stories. One thing she was sure of her fight to stay alive in that pool was no dream. When the traffic opened up her concentration was back on driving. Two days later she was pounding the street of Rodeo Drive leaving her resume with every store man-ager she felt could use her talents, looks or education for a job. When out of the blue her cell phone rang and it was Mr. Spencer asking her to come in tomorrow about eleven o'clock for a second interview. Thinking to herself, wow I thought that job opportunity was long gone. I guess Mr. Roberts does carry a lot of weight, in the company.

The next day at eleven o'clock she was sitting in front of Mr. Spencer's desk. He was looking over her application when he asked. " Would you be interested in going back to school to get your masters degree in business?" Kristy thought for a minute and then she said. "Sure, but I can't afford to go back to school without a job, and I can't get a real job without a masters degree. Catch twenty-two."

" This is the situation, we would give you a job as a trainee at a lower pay scale. Pay for your schooling to get your masters, and then when you do, raise your salary to the level of an executive associate.

" That's a very good offer. Can I live on a trainee's sal-ary? I mean I do have a college degree."

" We're well aware of that. The starting salary is $34,000 dollars a year. That's a little more than $650 a week."

Kristy takes a deep breath and lets out a sigh, thinking out loud as she says.

" That's about the same salary I was making working in the retail industries. After taxes it does not cut living in L.A. The schooling does make it an attractive offer. I could never pay for school on that salary. Okay if I'm going to give this corporate world a chance, I guess this is the best offer I could get. When do I start?"

" I'll take you down to human resources department, and they can start your paper work. Personnel will give you a form signed by us. Acknowledging that we will be paying for your tuition upon registration for your required classes needed for your masters degree. Monday will be your first official day of work."

Eight months later she had completed her first semester of night and on-line classes at UCLA. Between work and night school plus extra classes on the weekends she was starting to burn out. There was no time for herself, even though she passed all her classes with straight As. There was going to be a few weeks before classes began again, so she thought this would be a perfect time for a Las Vegas weekend. She packed a small bag with just enough clothes for a weekend, then she thought about a swim suit. Although Vegas was still a little cool this time of the year for the pool. Taking the sun would feel like heaven. Making a reservation at a twenty dollar a night off the strip hotel was no problem. She could choose any one she wanted. This was the off season. They were all clean and safe, but her favorite was the Orleans. Only because they had the best seafood restaurant, with inexpensive prices. Caesars was still her favorite hangout, but the Oysters Rockefeller at Orleans were the best. After reserving a room for two nights she headed straight east over the mountains to the Vegas strip. When she got to Las Vegas blvd and Tropicana she make a left hand turn straight to the Orleans Hotel.

After checking in she dropped her bag off in her room and went down stairs to the casino floor. Passed the gaming tables and stopped at the seafood restaurant for her favorite, New England Clam Chowder and Oysters Rockefeller. The long drive and a full belly told Kristy it was time for a nap, besides she wasn't about to loose, her hard earned money gambling. After a three hour nap and hot shower she was ready for a full night she felt she had earned. The outfit she picked was not as sexy or provocative as she would have worn if she was out to score a John. It was some where between corporate and evening. When she was fully dressed and ready to go, she gave herself one last look in a full length mirror. Checking herself out one last time to make sure her hair, makeup and clothes were perfect. They say a woman always knows when she going to get laid. A man has to get lucky, unless of course he's paying for her services. That was not Kristy's intention at all, she just couldn't break old habits of looking her best. Waiting for valet to bring her car to the front door, she decided to visit her old digs at Caesars Palace. The music at Cleopatra Bar was always the choice of the evening. She preferred slow dance and easy listening to hard rock and techno music. When she reached the front door of Caesars she valeted her car and walked in the direction of the Cleopatra Bar. In the old days she would have turned left to check out the rotunda lobby, where every high roller or big shot would be checking in. That was the best place to get noticed. This time she turned right and followed the music. At the far end of the bar there's five small tables with chairs where you could sit have a drink and listen to the live band playing on the barge. That area is dimly lit because the barge forms a wall on one side, and the people sitting and standing block the light from the bar. Kind of a hide away when you don't want to be seen. Kristy in her former business would have been sitting at the other end of the bar. A well lighted area where any man coming off the elevator on his way to the casino would see her sitting. She sat at a table in the back relaxed, this was a first for her. Usually when she sat back there it was with a married man not wanting to be seen, but looking for a little extra excitement while his wife played the slots or was shopping at the mall. When the waitress came over to take her drink order she commented. " Hey! I haven't seen you here in a long time. What are you having."

" Grey Goose and soda with a twist of lemon." Said Kristy.

" Coming right up." As she placed a napkin and a small bowl of chips on the table.

It was more than eight months since she was last here. The weekend she met Eric, and all his crazy talk about ghost hunting. The only good thing that came out of that weekend was making friends with Carol, and the envelope filled with money Eric gave her. Almost losing her life in that pool, and James dying were imbedded in her subconscious mind and there they would stay. The waitress brought over her drink and left. A young good looking man in his late twenties came over and said. " Hi I'm Steve. I see your alone would you like to dance?"

Kristy thought for a second and said. " Sure. I'd love to."

The band was just starting a slow dance set, and the dance floor was quite crowded. Holding her close was not an option, and Steve had every step down pat. His movements were as smooth as silk, the tighter he held her the more she enjoyed it. Never saying a word, just letting his body do the talking. He started to get aroused because Kristy could feel him getting an erection. His placement was perfect between her legs, He moved one hand under her hair and tickled her neck. Then he slowly moved his other hand down her back until he reached the check of he butt, pushing her as tight as he could to his erection. He looked into her eyes and smiled, Kristy placed her head on his chest and let herself be engulfed in the strength of his arms, and the magic of the music. When the band stopped playing he walked her back to her table and asked. " I'd like to sit with you and buy you a drink."

Kristy made a hand gesture to sit. Steve took a chair from another table and pulled it over and sat. Then the small talk began, he said. " What's your name?"

" Kristy Anderson. Where did you learn to dance like that?"

" Ballet. I took Ballet to strength my legs. I'm a minor league pitcher for the San Diego Padres. Been kicking around the minors for six years trying to make it in the big league. Don't get me wrong it's good money, but it's not big money. Where are you from?"

" L.A. I'm working in the day and going to school at night, trying to get my master degree at UCLA. That's where I graduated from."

" I graduated from USC. Went there on a baseball scholarship. Got drafted by the Dodgers right out of school."

" So what happened?"

" Hurt my knee, needed an operation. loss the strength in my leg, couldn't push off the mound. nine months later they traded me to San Diego. Do you come to Vegas often?"

" Not like I use to. Haven't been here in eight maybe nine months. Once I started school there was no time."

" Are you staying here in the hotel?"

" No, I can't afford the prices that they charge here. I have a room at the Orleans. It's off the strip, but it's clean and safe and they have the best seafood in Vegas. What about you?"

" I'm staying here. My agent is in the middle of working on a new contract, so I have a few days off. Have to report back by Monday afternoon. Are you hungry? Would you like to join me for some dinner?"

Kristy thought to herself, here it comes. The famous final scene before he tries to get me in bed. " Where are you eating?"

" I like the food at Spargo's off the back casino."

" To tell you the truth, I ate when I checked into the Orleans but that was five hours ago. I could eat something light."

" Great, lets go."

Spargo's is an indoor Alfresco Dining Restaurant. When they got there Kristy was surprised there were no lines and they were seated immediately. Steve looked over the menu and said. " Would you like to share a pizza, and pasta?"

" Pizza is fine but no pasta for me."

When the waiter came over, Steve ordered a pizza, a dish of pasta for himself and a bottle of water with lime. When the pizza came out it was smoking hot right out of the brick oven. The waiter placed it on the table and opened the bottle of water and poured two glasses. Steve separated the slices place one in a dish for Kristy, then he did the same for himself. Only on his he put plenty of grated cheese, oregano, and a little crushed red pepper. Then he said. " This is the New York Italian way to eat pizza. He folded the crust in half, picked up the slice and held it in his hands when he took his first bite. " Are you Italian?" Asked Kristy

" Half, on my mother side. As a kid I was raised in New York. Staten Island really, but most people don't know where Staten Island is. So you get use to saying New York."

" Wow, I have a very dear friend that lives in Staten Island. Carol DeMarco."

" You know that name sounds familiar. Maybe I played baseball with or against a kid named DeMarco back in the day."

" If you did it will come back to you."

When they were finished with their dinner, Steve suggested they walk the strip and take in the sights. This was also a first for Kristy who usually followed dinner with a roll in the hay for a thousand bucks. Walking the strip was always a good way to digest a late night meal. They stopped along the way and took in all the attraction each hotel offered the sidewalk crowds. Kristy thought this was almost like a date with a normal guy. She hadn't been on one of these since she was dating her ex-husband back in her college days. Most of the men she attracted were older and just looking for sex, at any price.

She started to feel good about herself. Just like Carol had said. " Give yourself a chance, let someone see you for who you are." Just then Steve ask. " Do you have any plans for tomorrow, would you like to come and hang out with me at the pool at Caesars?"

" I have no plans for tomorrow. That would be nice."

Steve took out a card from his pocket and wrote his cell number and room number. He handed it to Kristy and said. " When you get up in the morning call me, we can meet at the Venus pool."

They walked back to Caesars and he waited with her after she gave the valet her ticket for her car. When the valet brought her car to the front door he walked her to the car and kissed her whispering in her ear. " I had a really good time tonight with you, I hope I see you tomorrow." Then he kissed her again. Kristy got in her car and drove out the long fountain driveway. Just before she turned right onto Las Vegas Blvd, she looked in her rear view mirror and he was still standing there. Driving back to the Orleans she thought, I don't get it, this guy didn't even try to put a move on me, and invite me to his room. Maybe Iv'e lost my charm, to much work and no play. What a difference from the last time she was here with Eric, and that crazy weekend on the ship. All of a sudden all the memories she suppressed all these months started to come back to her. She wondered if James' spirit was really there with Michelle just like Eric had told her. Does things like this really happen when you find your one true love. Is the power of love that eternal? Turning into the driveway of the Orleans Hotel she valeted her car and went up to her room, thinking about spending the next day with Steve. She was as excited as a teenage school girl. The next morning she woke up about nine o'clock, took a hot shower, shampooed her hair and blew it dry. Then she shaved her legs, under arms and her bikini line. Making sure every part of her was ready for what ever the day or night may bring. She moisturized her skin until it felt like satin, then she put on her bikini swim suit under the outfit she decided to wear. Putting an extra bra, panties and sweater top in her large black beach bag. Stopping at the cafe, she got a coffee and muffin, sat a table and called Steve's cell.

" Hi Steve, this is Kristy are we still on for today?"

" Hey you, I didn't think you were going to call, It's almost noon."

" A girl has to prepare you know. You just can't hop out of bed and go."

" Okay I guess I'm around to many guys all the time. How soon can you get here?"

" In about a half hour, hoping the traffic on the blvd isn't crazy."

" Great meet me at the Venus pool, Just ask one of the attendants where it is and give him my room number. If you have a problem page me on a house phone."

"Wait I don't know your last name."

" Jensen, Steve Jensen! I changed it from Steven Jenkowski, I got tired of hearing dumb Polish jokes or being call Pol-wop, or Jew-wop because my father is half Jewish.

" I like the name Steven, it's more fitting for a professional ball player.

An hour later she arrived because of the heavy traffic on Las Vegas Blvd. When she reached the pool entrance she asked for a towel walked pass the large doors and turned left walking down the stairs to the next podium. Where she had to give Steve's name and room number, because the Venus pool is topless for adults only. Finding Steve relaxing on a canopy bed, He immediately got up and greeted her with a hug and a kiss. She warmly excepted both, then she slipped out of her shoes, unbuttoned her blouse and took off her pants. After she folded her pants and her blouse, she, neatly placed them in her large black bag. This was the first time Steve saw what he could only dream about. The perfect body in a string bikini. Wow was all he could think of, he looked her over from top to bottom, and couldn't take his eyes off her breasts. Then the vixen came out of her when she smiled and said." See anything that turns you on."

He looked her in the face and said. "Babe, you are amazing, I knew you had a body when we were dancing last night. Seeing you in the light of day, you've taken my breath away. I better order a couple of cold drinks to calm down." Just then he signaled the cocktail waitress and ordered two "Grey Goose Frosty" Then she continued to tease him by saying. "Guess I better not take off my top. I wouldn't want to give you a heart attack."

" Please do, I could always call for the paramedics." They both laughed and Kristy said. " I'm sorry I'm breaking your chops. I just couldn't resist."

She leaned over and gave Steve a kiss. The waitress delivered the two drinks and Steve signed for them saying. " You can get stoned and have brain freeze at the same time on one of these."

" I've had that happen to me a few time, what an experience." Said Kristy.

She sat on the corner of the bed, with her back to the entrance. When suddenly a cold feeling came over her. It wasn't the Frosty, it was a feeling she had when she was on the ship. Two men walked passed her on there way to the back bar. Kristy knew one of them was Eric. Even though she never saw his face, she knew she had to get out of there. Finishing her drink a fast as she could, she grabbed her black bag and excused herself saying she needed to use the ladies room. Only she didn't go to the one next to the Venus Bar, but walk out of the pool area and across to the opposite side of the hotel to the outdoor restaurant. Entering the ladies bathroom she tried to compose herself. Fifteen minutes later she called Steve on his cell, saying she didn't feel good and was going back to her hotel to lay down. Then she apologized for ruining his afternoon. Steve told her to wait there for him, and he would walk her out to the valet or better yet drive her back. Kristy's response was. " That's crazy, then you have to take a cab back."

" That's no problem, what's the big deal a cab ride. Just wait, I'll be right there."

Steve rushed right over to Kristy asking how she felt. Kristy answered. " A little dizzy. I don't know if it's the sun or the booze or maybe both."

" Here's the key to my room. Go up lay down and when you feel better call me on my cell. I can come up or you can come down, or we could just talk and figure something out."

" Why are you being so good to me?"

" What are you talking about. I like you, we're friends. That's what friends do for each other, they help when needed."

" Okay fine, I'll call you when I feeling better."

She takes the key and kisses him and leaves. Walking back into the hotel she's still not sure if this is the right move. Her feelings for Steve are clouding her judgement. Kristy knows getting out of the hotel and going to the Orleans was what she had to do. Walking directly to the lobby she left Steve's key with the front desk, continued on to the front door valet and handed him her ticket. In a couple of minutes her car was brought to the front door. She tipped the valet entered her car and pulled to the side away from the crowded cars. Calling Steve she told him she left his key with the front desk and was going back to the Orleans. Using the lame excuse if she got sick she'd feel better in her own room. Then she added, I'll call you later if you have no plans maybe you'd like to come over here. Steve's reply was " Okay call me." Then he hung up. Kristy felt her friendship with Steve was never going to get off the ground, but she also felt there was no way Eric would come to the Orleans. He'd stick to Caesars where he was known and treated like the high roller he was. Why pay for anything when you could get it for free as a guest of the casino. When she got back to the hotel she went to the box office to see if there were any seats available for tonights show. The ticket agent asked if she was a guest of the hotel. She said she was and showed him her room key. Then he said. " We're only selling tickets to hotel guest, other wise the show is completely sold out. How many tickets would you like?"

" Just two, can I charge them to my room?" Answered Kristy.

" No problem. I need two forms of identification" Then he picked up the phone to verify if Kristy was guest of the hotel. " I have two seats center stage, Ten rows back for thirty five dollars each."

" That will be great, I'll take them."

Kristy got her tickets and walked out to the pool area behind the hotel, found a lounge chair and took the sun. Because of her fair skin she applied plenty of sun block. About five o'clock she called Steve and told him she was feeling much better and to make it up to him if he was free she had two tickets to see " Air Supply" it was her way to get him to come to the Orleans and say she was sorry for the afternoons events. She told him the show started at 8:30 pm and she would meet him in front of the showroom. He told her if that was the only way he could see her, he excepted her invitation and would be there on time. Kristy got dressed went back into the hotel. Stopped at the cafe and ordered a burger, French fries and a coke. After she ate she went up to her room took a shower and picked out her best outfit. By eight o'clock she was ready to leave the room and go down to the showroom and wait for Steve. At eight twenty, she began to think he wasn't going to show. Everyone was already in the showroom and she was the last person still outside pacing back and forth. When she saw Steve her heart started pounding as he gave her a kiss and said. " I'm not late, right."

" No, your not but lets go in and find our seats."

Two hours later they walk out of the showroom. Steve said. " Wow I forgot how many hit songs those guys had. It was really a very good concert."

" I'm so glad you liked it. I just love their music. I could listen to them all night."

Then Steve handed her a concert T-shirt and a CD saying I got these for you when you went to the bathroom after the show." Kristy was like a kid at Christmas. So excited she hugged and kissed Steve saying. "I'll play this all the way back to California."

" Where do we get some food around here, I'm starved."

" I told you they have the best seafood in all Las Vegas."

" Take me by the hand and lead the way." After dinner Steve remarked that was the best ever, but you only had a bowl of soup and a roll. Then she said. "I'm saving my self for dessert. " There's an Italian restaurant here that will let you sit at a table outside the restaurant for the best Cappuccino and Cannoli in town.

" Be still my waiting heart. Lead the way, my darling."

Outside the restaurant they found a table, sat down and looked over the dessert menu.

Kristy knew exactly what she wanted so she didn't even open the menu. After a few minutes Steve said. " Cannoli and Cappuccino it is!"

Steve ordered two, Cappuccino and Cannoli. They continued there small talk, when Steve said. "I know were both leaving to go back to our jobs, but I really want to see you again. Can you come down to San Diego on the weekends and watch me pitch? After the game I'm free and we could have dinner or just take in a movie. When we play up north I'll be close by to do the same."

" I think we could work something out." Said Kristy.

When the waiter delivered their dessert, the talking turned to satisfying hums. Steve called over the waiter and ordered two shots of Kahlua. Kristy asked why he needed the Kahlua, Steve said. "The Cappuccino is good, but it's not New York great. Wait until you taste it when you add the Kahlua." Kristy did and took a sip and said." Wow. Your right what a difference. That extra flavor with a little kick. You learn something new all the time." Steve smiled. " I'd love to show you what I could do with the Cannoli filling."

" Okay order one to go. Here's the key to my room, we can take it up stairs and you could show me."

Out of no where a voice said. " Hey Steve, what's going on dude." Without looking up Kristy knew it was Eric. Thinking to herself what the fuck is he doing here in this hotel. Coming closer he said. " How did you like the show? I love those guys what a voice. Oh hi Kristy I see you're with a client, I'll leave you both to talk business. See you around Steve." As he walked away into the casino crowd.

" You know that guy?" Asked Kristy.

" Not really. After you left last night I stopped for a drink at the Cleopatra Bar. He was there talking to an older distinguished looking man named Jack who recognized me as a baseball pitcher. They insisted on buying me a drink. We talked for a while and then I went up to my room. What did he mean you're with a client Talking business?"

" That guy is evil. Stay as far away from him as you can."

" Answer the question Kristy. Tell me the truth."

Kristy put her head down and starts to get up from her chair. Steve grabs her by the arm and pulls her back into her chair. " Tell me the truth!"

" Everything I told you about working in a company and going to school at night is all true. I haven't had sex with any body in nine months. That was the last time, and the first time I met Eric. He was a high roller at Caesars. Pick me up at the bar, bought me a drink, took me to dinner and wanted me bad. I was down on my luck and almost broke. I told him it would cost him a thousand dollars up front. He offered me five thousand to stay with him for the weekend. Then he takes me on a crazy trip to an old ship on a ghost hunt and almost gets me killed. The man is crazy, you wouldn't believe what happened to me. I don't believe what happened to me and I was there."

" So what were you going to wait until we got up to your room and ask for a thousand dollars."

" If I was looking for money from you. I would have told you last night, forget the walk. For a thousand dollars take me up to your room and I'll fuck your brains out."

Steve got real quiet and Kristy could see his wheels turning in his head.

" It was nice while it lasted, forget you ever met me."

Getting up from her chair, she reached for her key and her bag. Steve said. " Wait! Give me a chance to digest everything you just told me."

" There's nothing to digest. What did you think I was a virgin. Everyone has a skeleton or two in their closets. There's always going to be an Eric or Bill lurking around, you either handle it like a man or just move on."

Walking away as fast as she could not to let him see she was crying. On the elevator she began cursing Eric, wishing she had never met him. Inside her room she kicked off her shoes, took off her blouse and went into the bathroom to wash off her makeup. Unexpectedly there was a knock at the door. She answered it without opening the door.

" Who is it." She asked.

" Kristy it's me. I just want to say I'm sorry. Can you open the door? Please."

" Go away Steve. There's nothing to apologize for."

" Please open the door."

Kristy gave in and opened the door. Holding a bath towel in front of her, because she was still only in her bra, she said.

" Say what you want to say and please leave."

" I'm sorry, I acted like an immature stupid fool. All I know is I want to be with you tonight, tomorrow and maybe forever. We could have something special if we work at it.

We could." Kristy put her hand over his mouth.

" Shut up, before you put your foot in your mouth and kiss me."

As Steve got closer she dropped the towel. Steve kissed her first very softly, hoping for the response that would tell him, they were having the same feelings. When Kristy held him tightly he kissed her with more passion. Then he walked her to the bed and sat her down on the edge. Caressing her face and hair with the most passionate touch Kristy had ever felt. She felt herself getting wet without him even having sex with her. This was something she hadn't experienced since she was still a virgin. She began to unbutton his shirt, standing up to allow him to unhook her bra. Opening his belt buckle and unzipped his pants, she laid back down on the bed and removed her own pants waiting for him to remove her black lace panties. When he was naked he got on top of her kissing her neck, working his way down to her breast. Sucking ever so gently on each nipple until they stood out as far as they could. Licking her belly, while holding her breasts until he reached her panties. Removing them he climbed on top of her and slowly penetrated her hot wet vagina. This was not a man just looking to get laid and Kristy knew it. She had been with enough different men to know the difference. Steve was making love and she wanted more. She waited for him to have the best orgasim, just as he was coming inside her. After several hours of love making they both fell asleep in each others arms. In the morning as the sun beamed into the bedroom, Steve woke and started to touch Kristy's face, waking her she said.

" You have the most gentle touch. Do you handle all your woman like fine cut crystal?"

" Only you."

He started to hold her and kiss her, running his hand up and down her naked body. The more he felt her the more excited he got until he was fully erected. Then he rolled her over on her back and mounted her until he penetrated her fully. They didn't stop until they were both in a pool of sweat reaching a climatic finish. Steve said. " Lets take a shower, get dressed and have breakfast together, before I have to leave to get back to Caesars."

After they showered and dressed, they went down to the outdoor pool cafe. Steve ordered the usual breakfast fair. Coffee, juice, eggs, bacon and toast. The pool area was a very pleasant, relaxing finish to a very sexual night. During breakfast Steve asked Kristy. "Do you still have my cell phone number?" He told her he would call her during the week to let her know how his contract negotiations were going, and when they could plan on seeing each other again. Kristy smiled and said.

" Sounds good to me, and yes I have your number in my phone."

" What time are you planning to leave the hotel?" Asked Steve.

" Check-out is at eleven, so around that time."

" Same at Caesars."

Finishing his food he signaled the waiter for the bill. When he brought it over, Steve looked at it handed the waiter two twenty dollar bills and said. " Keep the change."

Getting up from his chair he kissed Kristy good-by and whispered in her ear. " This was the best weekend ever. I'm going to find a way to make this work for us. I'm not letting you go, just be patient until I get my career squared way."

Kristy watched him walk away, and just before he entered the hotel he turned a threw he a kiss. She sat for a couple of minutes finishing her coffee and pondering where was this all going to go. Was Steve for real or was this just a Vegas wham, bam thank you mam weekend. Like the old saying goes, treat a whore like a lady, and a lady like a whore. Only time will tell. The drive back to California was long and boring. Kristy couldn't get Steve out of her head. Monday morning it was back to the old grind, work in the day, school at night. By friday she thought, well it was a nice weekend being treated like a lady. At noon she was quite surprised when her cell phone rang and it was Steve. He told her the contract took a little longer that he thought, but he got the contract he wanted. He also said he was off Saturday and Sunday didn't have to report until Monday. He was very excited hoping she was free and hadn't made any commitments.

Kristy reminded him she still had school that night but she was free all weekend. Steve suggested they meet in the middle. He would drive north from San Diego and Kristy would drive south from Los Angeles. He said. "He knew a great restaurant in Santa Ana that was right on the water. Take the freeway south and get off to route 5 south, it will lead you to the "Outrigger" Santa Ana. I'll met you there about one o'clock, oh don't forget to pack a bag and a swim suit."

Kristy agreed and the next morning she was driving south to Santa Ana. It was a little over an hours drive, but it was a beautiful morning with blue skies and white puff clouds. The best part of the drive was no traffic on the freeway. Saturday morning no working people to jam the freeway with cars. No start and stop, no parking lot of cars. An hour later she was taking the exit to route 5 south. Following the signs within fifteen minutes she was parking in the lot and looking for Steve who was waiting outside the front door.

Seeing her walk across the parking lot he ran to her picking her up and whirling her in the air. As he put her down, he kissed her like two long lost lovers. Taking her by the hand they walked to the front door. " I'm starved, I can eat a horse. Make that a lobster or two." Said Steve.

He tipped the Hostess and asked for a table by the window, with a beautiful view of the ocean and the sail boats passing by. They looked over the menu and made their decision on what they were going to have. Steve ordered a bottle of wine and said. "He wanted the broiled sea food platter, the one with the lobster tail. The lady will have the stuff shrimp with a bake potato, make that two and don't forget the sour cream."

The waiter came back open the white wine and poured two glasses. They tapped glasses and said, " Salute" an Italian expression of good fortune. Kristy said. " Tell me all about you new contract. Are you rich?"

" Not rich, no. It's a two year with a third option year. There giving me a chance to make the majors. I'm to report to camp next week, with a chance to make the starting rotation."

" So how much are you going to make?"

" $400,000 with incentives that can reach $550,000 the first year. $650,000 the second, and $1,000,000 the third.

" Wow, no wonder your excited. I'm very happy for you. Now that you've made it to the big league, are you sure you still want to be with someone like me."

" Why do you keep selling yourself short. I told you we can have something special. I knew it on the dance floor in Caesars. Here comes our food, stop being foolish and lets eat."

After a great meal, Steve got up from the table and walked to the reception desk and asked if there were any rooms available on the second floor for the night. The person at the desk answered. "Sorry we all booked up for the weekend."

" Do you know any other place a room might be available for the night?" Asked Steve.

" Not on a Saturday night. The only place you maybe able to get a room is in Long Beach, on the "Queen Mary" hotel. It may be expensive but there are always a suite available. Would you like to have me check?"

" Sure, that will be great. I'll be sitting at my table having dessert, let me know."

Steve returns to Kristy and orders two Cappuccinos with Kahlua and one slice of cheese cake topped with cherries. While they were having dessert the desk manager comes to the table and whispered in Steve's ear telling him. " I got in touch with reservations at "Queen Mary" they do have a suite available for the night at a cost of $ 175.00 they are extending me a courtesy save for an hour. Let me know what you want to do, and I'll be happy to make that reservation."

Kristy asked. " What was that all about?"

" Just trying to get a room for the night. I should have called ahead to stay here, but I thought it would not be a problem. Should have realized Saturday night at the shore, big problem. The desk manager can get us a suite on the "Queen Mary" for the night.

" Oh no. The last time I was on that ship crazy things happened. You do know that that ship is haunted. That's why they called it the Grey Ghost.

" You don't really believe all that bull shit stories?"

" All I know the last time I was there, Eric scared the living shit out of me. I thought I was going to die. I thought I was never going to get off that ship alive."

" Kristy do you really think I'd let anything happen to you?"

" Please Steve, don't make me go. I really like you a lot. You make me feel like a woman being loved by her man. Maybe we can make something special come from it."

Suddenly Michele tells James, I feel a ripple in our dimension. We have to return to modern times before something bad happens on the ship. James doesn't understand it but as always he agrees to go along, with what ever Michele is feeling. Michele grabs James' hand and says. "Hurry there's no time to waste, We have to get back as soon as we can. Evil forces are about to invade our ship. When Michele and James finally return to the ship, her first order of business is to alert all the good spirits they are about to face a new evil. James inquires." How do you know evil is coming?"

" When your on this ship as long as I have been, you'll know. Don't forget I been here for fifty years waiting for you. You are a young spirit just learning the ropes, as they use to say in life. In time you'll understand not to ignore certain feelings."

" Guess I have a lot to learn about this spirit world."

In the mean time Steve is being very acertive about spending the night on the ship. He keeps promising Kristy nothing will happen to her as long as she is with him. After a few more drinks she give in, saying to herself. It's never going to work out anyway, if he get famous, sooner or later someone will recognize me for who I am. Then he'll dump my ass under the pressure. Steve leaves the table to call the reservations desk at "Queen Mary" himself. Kristy decides to call Carol for advice on what to do. When Carol answers the phone she is very happy to hear from Kristy. She can tell by her voice that something is troubling her, so she asks. " What's the matter, I can hear in your voice you don't sound right."

" I'm really upset. Iv'e met a wonderful guy named Steve Jensen. He's a future big league baseball pitcher. This is only our third date and he wants to celebrate the signing of his new contract on the "Queen Mary". I have to tell you I'm scared to death to go back on that ship. He keeps telling me not to worry, he'll keep me safe. I'm so afraid if I say no, I might lose his friendship. I really like this guy, he treats me like a woman wants to be treated. The best is he doesn't care about my past, he keeps telling me we can have something special. Please tell me what to do?"

" If your afraid of all the ghost stories Eric was spinning, don't be. I went into room B340 after James passed and found nothing, but a dirty musty smelling old room. I sat on the bed, touched the mirror, felt the walls and nothing happened. Eric was just a con artist and a bad person to be around."

" You got that right."

" Go with your heart. If you believe in him, give it a chance. Just be careful and keep an open mind and stay away from the pool deck, room B.340 and any place you feel uncomfortable. Listen to the voice in your head, sometimes it's an angel talking to us from heaven. I wish I could tell you more. I'll keep my cell phone on all night call me if you think there's any chance of danger. I'll call the front desk immediately and have security sent wherever you are. Good luck honey, and be careful."

" Thanks Carol, I knew talking to you would help"

Kristy hangs up just as Steve is returning to the table. He informs her that he has reserved a suite for the night and they can check-in any time they like. The front desk is available all night. " I'm really excited about this. The desk manager went on line and showed me pictures of the ship while I was making the reservation. Wow, I never expected to see anything so beautiful. I love that art deco nostalgic stuff. Did you know they have different tours through out the ship? I was looking at them on-line, if we leave now we can still make all the tours."

" I'll go on the Lady Di, and the wheel house tour. Anything below the cabin decks are out for me. There's no way I'm going down there again, especially the pool deck. You couldn't get me down there with a gun to my head!"

" Okay no lower deck tours. I promise. Can we leave now?"

Kristy agrees to follow Steve with her car, after he pays the lunch bill. Driving behind him she begins to think, it's a good idea for me to have my car. If anything gets scary bad, I can bug out any time I please. On the way there all she can think of was her last experiences aboard the ship. Remembering what Carol told her about not finding any evidence of ghosts. She starts to doubt herself. Was she dreaming, to much booze, did Eric brainwash her into believing his ghost stories? At least one good thing did happen, her friendship with Carol was true. When they reached the ship they parked in the guest lot and walked to the ship pulling their overnight bags. Steve was in awe of the massive size of "Queen Mary." In his mind ships from that era were much smaller. He really had no knowledge of " Queen Mary or the legend that she was haunted, until Kristy told him.

Stepping off the elevator at the reservation deck, Steve could not believe his eyes. The opulent splendor recreating a by gone era was mind boggling. Of course this was old hat to Kristy, so she let him enjoy the moment. After checking in they went to their suite before joining the last tour of the day. The bellman opened the door to suite M131 down the hall and on the opposite side of the ship. There was no way she wanted to be the same suite she shared with Eric. The bellman placed the bags in the bedroom, Steve tipped him and they all left together. The tour started in the Wheel House as it was called back then. Kristy was find with that but after they went their separate ways. Kristy joined the women on the Lady Di tour and Steve went to the lower decks and on to the hospital, prison, and the morgue which was on the pool deck. Kristy told Steve he could find her in the cafe, reading a book over a cup of coffee. Kristy found the Lady Di tour absolutely wonderful. The elegant gowns she wore and the matching shoes, handbags and jewelry were fit for the Princess she was. When that part of the tour was over she went to the cafe, ordered a cup of coffee and continued the novel " Where Evil Lurks" that Carol loved. Telling her the story had nothing to do with evil ghost. Finding a table in the far corner, she sat and began to read, sipping her coffee with each page. About a half hour later Steve found her exactly where she said she would be. He sat down next to her and asked. " Are you enjoying your book and would you like a second cup of coffee?"

" Yes, and yes." Answered Kristy.

" Are you getting hungry?

" Not really, we had that big lunch."

" Well we have to eat something or we'll be starving later. I over heard some of the men talking about the Observation Bar, how elegant it is and what a great time they had last night. We have to go there."

" The're right it is quite elegant, the art deco on the walls, the columns. You have to see it to believe it. It's like stepping back in time. I'll tell you what we should do. Lets finish our coffees go up to our suite, get dressed and come back here for a light supper. Maybe a bowl of soup and a salad, then we can go to the Observation Bar for some drinks."

" Sounds like a plan to me, lets do it."

A short while later they were both sitting on the bed in their suite talking when Steve said. " Last week I was almost broke and a week later I'm holding a check for $ 250,000 dollars as a signing bonus. A three year contract worth over $3,000,000 dollars with incentives, how lucky am I. Not to mention lying on a bed with the most beautiful girl in the world, I must have an angel on my shoulder."

He pulls her on top of him and starts to kiss her with all the passion he could express. Then he whispers in her ear. " You're my Angel!"

They proceeded to make love unaware that night fall was about to change the exuberant joy they both were feeling. While the sun still shone on the ship no evil spirit would surface. Michele knew the feeling she was having was getting stronger as the sun went down and evening emerged. Michele knew she was going to have to stay close to Kristy the rest of the night. James went to the lower decks to warn the other good spirits they may be needed at a moments notice. If Eric or the vortex were going to try to take Kristy, they would all have to work together as a team to prevent it. James went from deck to deck reminding the spirits the vortex was last seen on the pool deck, and that's where they all needed to be. Then he went back looking for Michele to be with her when she needed him. Staying as close to Kristy as she could would give her a good opportunity to look inside Steve's spirit world. She was starting to have her doubts about him. It was almost like he was to good to be true. Unless he was an old soul with the values you just don't see today. Making sure he wasn't part of Eric or Jack's scheme to entice Kristy back on the ship. Michele went to the suite to look in on Kristy and Steve what she found was the two of them making love under the sheets. Although she could only see from their shoulder to their heads, the movement was unmistakable. Then a though popped into her head, they make love just like James and I did when we were young. Unless Steve was a master of deception, to her his love was the real thing. When they finished with their love making, Kristy emerged from the bed first. Making her way into the bathroom to take a hot shower. Steve rolled over and drifted into a quite sleep. This was just what Michele was hoping for, a chance to be inside his spirit world. She looked into his family back ground and found nothing that would indicate he or any of his ancestor were linked to Eric or to Jack. Other than the chance meeting they had together in Las Vegas, where they spent time together at the bar. Michele felt Steve seemed to be pure in heart and soul. If this was a grand plan to get Kristy back on the ship, it was way over Eric's head. Only Jack could manipulate such a cleaver plan. Only time would tell the out come. Kristy came out of the bathroom and woke Steve telling him. " It's your turn to go freshen up, so we can go an eat."

" Guess I dosed off for a few minutes. You wore me out woman."

" It was a lot longer than a few minutes. I showered shampooed and blew dry my hair and with all the noise from the dryer you were sleeping like a baby."

With that Steve made his way into the bathroom while Kristy got dressed. A quick shower and shave and he was ready to dress and start the evening. As they were leaving the suite Steve turned to Kristy and said. " I think that work out you put me through has opened my appetite for more than soup and a salad. Why don't we go to Sir Winston's Restaurant and get a real meal."

" Do you really think were going to get seated without a reservation?"

" What's the most they can say, sorry not without a reservation. So we go eat at the cafe."

" Okay by me, lead the way."

When they reached the restaurant, it wasn't overly crowded. A twenty dollar tip got them a table for two by the window with a view. Kristy was quite impressed for a ballplayer acting like a high roller in Vegas. After being seated, a waiter came over and handed them each a menu. Then he introduced himself as "Michael" he handed Steve a wine list and walked away. Steve said. " I'm going to pass on the wine, if you want a glass with dinner just say so."

" I'm fine with a glass of sparking water." Replied Kristy.

When the waiter returned to ask about the wine, Steve answered. " A bottle of sparking water will be fine." As he handed the wine list back to Michael. Then he picked up the menu and started to look for an inviting entree. Kristy did the same but for some strange reason she looked up and saw Eric walking across the room. Steve had his back to that part of the room, so she immediately raised her menu to cover her face. What she did not know was Michele was running interference from Eric. There was no way she was going to allow him to get close to Kristy.

Peeking over her menu she saw Eric leaving the restaurant. She sighed a relief as she gasped for a breath of air. Michael returned to take their food order, they decided on Beef Wellington for two. Steve handed him the menus and said. " Tell the chef medium, but not bloody. Pink make the beef pink."

" Very good sir." Was Michael's reply.

All during dinner Kristy was on edge constantly looking to see if Eric was returning. Even though the beef was cooked perfectly she was not enjoying her meal. Steve sensed something was wrong, but had no idea what was troubling Kristy. Then he asked. " What's wrong? Is it the food? You seem to be upset."

" No nothing like that. My stomach is a little queasy, maybe after dinner I'll go back to the suite and lay down."

She was looking for a safe place to be so she didn't crash into Eric. She knew how much Steve wanted to see the "Observation Bar" so she told him to go ahead and have a drink and if she was feeling better she would join him there. Steve insisted on walking her back to the suite. After entering he said. " I really don't have to go to the Observation Bar, I can order some drinks and hang out here until you feel better."

" Nonsense, you've been talking about wanting to go all afternoon. Maybe I need some bathroom time alone, I'm not use to all that heavy rich food we enjoyed today.

A girl needs a little privacy sometimes."

" Okay, I get it, but if you feel better you promise to come and meet me."

" Absolutely. Cross my heart and swear to spit."

" Now you sound like an old time baseball fan."

They both got a chuckle from it as Kristy lead Steve to the door, gave him a kiss and waved goodbye. Knowing there would be no way she would go to the bar for fear of seeing Eric she went into her bedroom and sat on the edge of the bed. Kicking off her shoes and removed her pants and blouse. After hanging them up in the closet she turned on the television not because she was interested in watching a show. It was the sound she needed not to feel completely alone. Turning down her bedding she fell asleep cuddling the pillow. Things were quite different at the bar, as they say. " The joint was jumping" the music was swinging, the drinks were flowing and the conversation was loud. Steve found a slot at the bar where he could squeeze in an order a drink. The bartender asked. " What will you have"?

" Vodka and soda with a twist of lemon." Replied Steve.

Then he looked around the room at the magnificent Art Deco work on the walls and behind the bar. It was like stepping back in time, to an era only seen in the movies. Looking up at the mural behind the bar Steve feels a tap on his shoulder, as he turns it's Eric.

" Hey Steve. How's it hanging dude? I thought that was you. How did you get so close to the bar?"

" Just lucky I guess. How's it going Eric? Seems every time I turn around it's you. Are you from the bloodhound family or is it just coincidence, your always in the same place I'm in?"

" Be a pal, and order three drinks for me."

" What are you having?"

" Three Dewars and water." I'm sitting at a table with a couple of real hot numbers, why don't you join us. Easy score, pick either one I could care less. They'll both rock your world."

" Thanks, but no thanks. I'll pass."

" Please don't tell me your here with that chick from Las Vegas, Kristy."

" Matter of fact I am."

" So where is she?"

" Back in my room, she wasn't feeling well."

" Well go get her. We can have a gang bang orgy back at my suite."

" Your drinks are here. Just pay for them and go back to your table."

Eric pays for his drinks and brings them back to his female friends at his table. Steve watches as he places the drinks down and talks to one of the girl pointing to Steve standing at the bar. A few minutes later the girl comes over to Steve and says.

" Hi I'm Nancy, Eric tells me your here with Kristy. Were old friends from Vegas, we worked the same client list. Different side of the street of course, but we became friends. Tell me what room she's in and I'll go get her, I'm sure once she knows we're all here she come and join us."

" Listen Nancy, first of all she not feeling well, and second she not traveling in the same circles as you and your friends any more. She has a real job and she's back in school working for her masters degree. She putting her life back together one step at a time. So go back to your table and tell Eric to stay away from me and Kristy."

Nancy goes back to her friends and informs Eric what Steve has told her, then she says.

" This guy is in love with Kristy. I can see it in his eyes, you're never going to get the room number from him. He's trying to turn her life around."

" A few more drinks and I'll get him to change his tune."

Keeping a close eye on Steve from afar he sees him having more drinks as he keeps looking at his watch wondering if Kristy is going to show. Eric decides enough time has passed and he leaves the table and walks over to the bar to talk to Steve.

" Hey Steve, have you changed your mind yet?"

" About what?"

" Getting Kristy and joining us in an orgy."

" Your really starting to piss me off, I told your friend to tell you to stay away from me and Kristy. So get the fuck out of my face before I knock you on your ass."

Then Eric gets real loud for everyone at the bar to hear. " You want to knock me on my ass, because I told you the truth. Your girl friend is nothing more than a hooker from Las Vegas. I banged the ass off that Bitch."

With that Steve punches Eric sending into the crowd and knocking over a table. Eric get up and charges Steve throwing his own punches as the two of them really get into it. The bartender calls for security as the fight escalates. Both men are pulled apart and held back by hotel security. Eric waves it off as a misunderstanding and offers to pay for any damages and is willing to buy anyone close to the fight a drink on him. When security found out that Steve threw the first punch and initiated the fight. They wanted to know if Eric wanted to press charges. If so they would call the local police and have him arrested. Eric told them it was a simple case of to much to drink and a misunderstanding of words. He did not want to press charges as it was as much his fault for saying hurtful and improper words about his girl friend. He was only protecting her honor, as any man should. With that security allowed Steve to return to his suite. When he got there he tried to cover up the fight by entering the bathroom and removing his torn shirt, and washed the dry blood from his face. Although there was not much he could do about the black eye and the fat lip he received in the fight. Coming out of the bathroom Kristy was ready to ask how he enjoyed the art deco of the Observation Bar. That though quickly vanished when she saw Steve face.

" Oh my God, what happened to you?"

Steve tried to explain the fight without mentioning Eric's name. He just said it was a misunderstanding with too many drinks clouding good judgement. Kristy got a face towel and ran it under cold water. Then she rang out the excess water and went to the ice bucket and place ice cubes in the middle forming an ice pack and placed it on Steve's face. Kristy began to question Steve's story saying. " Did anyone notify the ship's security? Did they get the name of the man you had the fight with? Should we call the police? Is there something your not telling me? I'm sensing something not right."

Steve decided to come clean, and tell the whole truth about the fight.

" I don't want you to get upset. The fight was with Eric. First he just wanted to talk and get a few drinks for himself and a couple of girls he was with. Then he wanted me to join the group, one of the girl even said she knew you from Vegas. They wanted us to join in on an orgy. When I said no Eric got loud and started to say some things I didn't like and that's went I belted him in the face. From there all hell broke loose."

" Was the things he was saying about me?"

" What's the difference, the guy's an evil jerk."

" We have to get off the ship."

" I'm not in any shape to drive, right now. Iv'e had to much to drink and Iv'e got a splitting headache."

What Steve didn't know when he first left Kristy to go to the bar was, she cuddled up with her pillow and feel asleep. That's when Michele came to her to tell her Steve was a good guy and his love for her was real. She showed Kristy all the family qualities he brought with him from back east. She let her know whenever she was facing the evil forces that surrounded Eric she would be close by to help. Michele also told her not to leave the suite until day light. No evil forces would penetrate the suite as long as she and James were there. She took Kristy back in time, showing her how strong James' love was for her when they were young. Michele said she was very wild and had many sexual partners before meeting James. She knew the first time she saw him, the first time they danced together she knew she had found her real true love. It didn't matter to James that she wasn't a virgin, he loved her and that was it. As long as they were honest with each other, it was easy to keep skeletons in a closet. No one cared to look, not like today. Today you must work harder and not give up on yourself. Then Kristy remembered Michele's words about not leaving the suite until daylight. Michele's words about her being safe as long as they stayed in the suite, keep coming back to her.

Suddenly there was a knock on the door, Steve went to see who it could be. When he looked through the door eye he could see it was Eric. He told Kristy. " It's Eric, what balls on that guy."

" Don't answer him, maybe he'll just leave."

" Come on Kristy come out and join the party. Your girl friend Nancy is here. You remember Nancy we had a three way romp together. As I remember you were very turned on by Nancy's tricks."

" Steve it's not true. I know Nancy from Vegas, but we never had a three-way. He's making up stories to get you to open the door."

" That's it I'm going to knock this guy out."

" Stop Steve, that's what he wants. He wants to get under your skin so you'll open the door and he can come in. If you do he'll bring his evil force with him. He doesn't want to have a sex party, he wants my spirit to satisfy the vortex of evil."

" Your starting to freak me out with all this evil spirit stuff. Your starting to sound as crazy as Eric."

" Believe me as beautiful as this ship is, the legend of it being haunted is true."

" Don't tell me you believe in ghost."

" I witnessed things on this ship the first time I was here, even I can't explain. All I know is, I almost drowned in a pool that hasn't been filled with water in sixty years. If I wasn't a champion swimmer, I'd be dead right now. It was Eric who tricked me to come here and it was Eric who just stood there and watched as I fought for my life. That's why I will not go near that guy, he has some kind if mean, evil aura about him."

" Come out Kristy, you can't hide from me forever. Sooner or later, I'll find you and bring you back." Yelled Eric in the outer hallway Kristy picked up the house phone and called the front desk. She explained " The man who had a fist fight with my boyfriend is banging on our door, suite M131. Please send security to remove him before there is another fight."

The front desk manager informed Kristy that security was on there way. When they got there they asked Eric to please leave, and return to his own suite. Eric got very indignant saying.

" I'm just trying to apologize to my old girl friend for having a fight with her new boy friend, but she's all high and mighty calling security. (banging on the door) Kristy."

" You've had a little to much to drink, lets go back to your suite where you can sleep it off." Said one of the security men.

Steve opens the door, against Kristy's wishes. In the hallway with security in the middle they start to shout at each other. Kristy immediately closes the door and locks it. Other passengers start coming out of their suites to find out what is the commotion all about.

" What the hell is going on out here." Asked one passenger. Trying to keep Eric and Steve apart, they now have another problem, asking the other passengers to stay calm, and go back in the suites. A few minutes later Eric is back in his suite, Kristy has let Steve back in their suite and life on board " Queen Mary" is back to normal. Or so it would seem. Eric is alone in his suite, his two gal pals are still at the bar. Michele decided this is a good time to confront Eric.

A NEW LEASE ON LIFE

Entering the suite Eric is pacing back and forth because he has not for filled his obligation to Jack. Michele brings Eric into the spirit world where she can find out why Eric is so adamant about Kristy. Michele knows Eric can not lie to her in the spirit world. Why is Kristy so important to you, and why are you on such a quest to deliver her into the spirit world from this ship?"

" I should have known it was you protecting Kristy when I couldn't enter the suite.

She is a direct descendant of " Jack the Ripper" after he left London and came to America searching for her great-grandmother whom he fell madly in love with, after a brief affair. When he found out she was pregnant. He searched and killed her boyfriend, who was not the father of her unborn child. She left him after she started to suspect he was the killer. She returned to her roots, a Catholic convent where she grew up in Boston. Jack could never enter holly grounds nor could he feel her presences. There she stayed until after she gave birth to their child a baby girl. Always moving from one convent to another, until the little girl grew up to be a beautiful woman. Because she was baptized and received her sacraments the angels of God protected her. It was by chance that he was in Las Vegas the same time as Kristy. In sin city there were no angels to protect her yet he could not bring himself to kill her. That's when he ordered me to bring her to the ship. He knew the best way to get her in his fold was through the vortex. He'll never stop trying to get her into the vortex."

"If he needs the vortex to bring her into his dimension, then we need to see that she never returns to the ship."

" He'll find a way to get Steve to bring her back."

" As long as I'm on this ship and have the backing of all the other spirits on board then we can stand united against him."

Then as fast as she entered Eric's suite she was gone, leaving him with no real memory of their conversation. She now was aware of Jack's plan and she had to convince Steve that as long as Kristy is aboard she is in grave danger. She went back and told James all that Eric had told her. He agreed the best course of action was to inform Steve. Later that night when Steve and Kristy finally turned in for the night. She entered Steve's dream world and showed him what really happened to Kristy on the pool deck. Hoping what he had seen would be embedded into his subconscious mind, and that he would listen to the voice in his head.

The next morning Steve and Kristy were lying in bed getting romantically frisky as Steve started running his hand up and down Kristy's body. When he reached inside her panties she pulled away saying. " If you want me, I have to go to the bathroom and tinkle."

Then she slipped out from under the covers and left Steve panting and moaning he was losing his erection. When she finally came out of the bathroom Steve was sitting on the edge of the bed. " What took you so long?" Asked Steve.

" Well I needed to tinkle, brush my teeth, and freshen up.

You didn't want me all smelly and dirty now did you?"

Steve pulled back the covers and showed Kristy his thrill was gone. " Don't worry I can get him back up for

" Kristy has been taken back in time to London in the late 1800s. There her great ancestor Jack wants to control her soul."

She did not mention that it was "Jack the Ripper" as her ancestor. She didn't want to scare Steve off his quest to bring Kristy back. She told Steve. " If Kristy is truly your soul mate than only you could rescue her. Look deep into your heart to find the answer, if your not sure then there is no way I can bring you back."

Steve thought for a while and said. " Yes I'm sure, Kristy is the one I want to be with the rest of my life. What do I have to do?"

" First your going to need money to live."

" I have about five hundred dollars on me."

" That amount will go far, next you need to find the Wild Boar Pub. That's Jack favorite hangout. There are rooms above it for rent, so try to get one. You need a cover story like your a newspaper journalist from America. Do not ask for Kristy right away that will only arouse suspicion. When you locate her make sure Jack is not around. If she seems like she does not know you it's because Jack has her under his spell. I will let you know what to do next when the time is right."

The next thing Steve knew he was in a different place, in a different time. He began to wonder the streets asking where he might find the Wild Boar Pub. Finally a man gave him direction as to where the pub was. He followed the direction the man told him, and there he was standing under the sign for the Wild Boar. He looked inside from the glass window, it didn't seem to busy so he entered the pub and walked up to the bar.

" Hi, can I get a beer."

" American ah." As he drew a draft beer.

" Guess you can't mistake the accent."

" Had an American here nine or ten months ago. Claimed he was a businessman, but after he got my niece Amy pregnant he disappeared. Ran back to America like a scared rabbit. So what's your business here?"

" I'm a journalist for the New York Times. I'm here to write a story on what's been going on here the pass year."

" So your doing a "Jack the Ripper" story."

Steve was very slow to answer, as he tried to absorb the fact that his Jack could very well be Jack the Ripper.

"Yes, America is very interested in that story."

" Good luck, hope you don't end up with a slit throat."

Steve reached for his throat, shallowed hard and said, " Me too. I think I need a shot of whiskey, maybe two."

" Coming right up, governor."

Steve downed his whiskey and thought to himself, what the hell did I get myself into. Finding Kristy and get her home is one thing, facing a cold hearted killer like Jack the Ripper is a whole new ball game. He had no idea how he would react if he had to face Jack. " I need a room for a couple of weeks. Do you know of any near by?"

" I rent a one bedroom flat furnished for five dollars American, one week. A second floor walk up."

" Can I see it first?"

" I can't leave the bar, but I'll give you the key and you can take a look."

" Perfect."

The bartender gives Steve the key and shows him the door to the hallway from the bar.

" Second floor, end of the hall, flat number 201."

Steve takes the key and follows the instruction the bartender has given him. When he reaches the door that has the number 201, he places the key in the door takes a deep breath and slowly opens the door. Quite to his surprise the flat as they call it in England is clean and well kept. Not at all what he expected. After giving the rooms a through inspection he decides to take it. Returning to the bar he informs the bartender of his intensions.

Then he asks. " Where can I find a mens clothing store, I need a change of clothes, the ship lost my luggage."

" More like you were robbed. Especially if it was a fine piece of leather, that could bring a handsome price. You never told me your name."

" Steve Jensen. Who cleans the room and brings in fresh towels?"

" Cleaning service, will coast extra."

Steve hands him a twenty dollar bill and says. " Let me know when that runs out. Now about that clothing store."

" Out the door turn left, three blocks cross over to the other side and you'll see the sign, Lebowitz and Son!

Steve leaves the bar, finding the store in question. He buys under wear, socks, a shirt and a jacket. The climate is very different from southern California. After paying he looks for a stationary store and finds one a few blocks away. A journalist without a pad and pencil makes for a weak cover story. Walking back to his flat he realizes this is not the area one visits in London. He begins to think about Kristy and hopes it doesn't take long for him to locate her. His best bet is to stay close to the Wild Boar in the hope Jack shows up with her. That night he brings his pad and pencil to the bar and listens to the chatter as he writes in his pad taking notes. He stayed until closing but Kristy never showed. He didn't know how long it would take so he tried a different approach on the second night. He started to ask question about Jack in the hopes it might flush him out.

By the third night he began to get frustrated, playing his cat and mouse game. About midnight the bar started to empty when Jack and Kristy walked in and sat at a back table. Steve got as close as he could, asking question loud enough for Jack to hear. He never approached their table until Jack called him over.

" What's all the question about mate?"

" I'm a journalist from America, trying to write a story on Jack the Ripper.

Extending his hand. " Hi I'm Steve. Can you give me any information about the murders?"

" Sorry only know what I read in the papers, like everyone else."

" What about the young lady?"

Kristy looked up from her drink and just smiled.

" She doesn't have anything to say."

" Well enjoy the rest of your night, sorry to have troubled you."

Steve moved to the front of the bar an began interviewing other patrons. He hoped he could follow Jack to were ever he was staying, but when he turned back to see if they were still there. They were gone, how they passed him without him seeing them leave was boggling his mind. It was as if they just vanished as they appeared. How in God's name was he going to get Kristy alone to bring her home. Once they were gone he went up stairs to his room and laid on the bed reviewing all that Michele had told him.

Back on the ship Michele and James were keeping a close eye on Steve. Knowing if they entered Jack's ora would weaken them. In that dimension he is at his strongest. When he leaves that time dimension he is still stronger than any one spirit, but not as strong as Michele, James and the other spirits on the ship when they ban together against him. Michele had all the good spirits on high alert, just in case Jack followed them across when she pulled Steve and Kristy out. After a good night sleep Steve took a carriage ride to the Mayfair Hotel for breakfast. The dining room was very busy as many of the business men were preparing for their day of work. The hostess informed him it would be a wait unless he wouldn't mind sharing a table with another couple. Steve replied." It's okay by me, if the other couple doesn't mind."

" Not at all." As she escorted him to the table. The man and woman seated had their backs to Steve, as he pulled out his chair he said.

" Hi, I'm Steve from America." Then he saw it was Jack and Kristy. " Well hello again."

Without speaking Jack just made a hand gesture to sit down, while Kristy just smiled.

" Thank you for letting me share your table. I see you still have your menus in front of you. Have you ordered yet?"

" No were still waiting for our waiter to return. Quite busy this morning."

" Good. Then I insist on buying breakfast."

" Quite good of you old chap, but I'm quite capable of buying my own breakfast."

" Nonsense, it's the least I could do for not waiting on that line. In God's name I would be there until lunch."

Steve could see Jack's facial expression change when the word GOD was said. It was like he touched a nerve that Jack did not care to hear.

" By the way, I never did get your names last night. Once again I'm Steve, and you are?"

" Jack and this is my niece Kristy."

" Excuse me for saying, but she doesn't say much."

" She's extremely shy around people she does not know. Here's our waiter lets order. I'll have a three egg with cheese omelette, well done bacon, toast with butter and jam, and a pot of tea. The lady will have the same."

The waiter then said. " And for you sir."

" I'll have the same. Only make mine coffee instead of tea."

" Very good sir, coffee and tea will be out right away." Said the waiter.

When the food arrived Steve kept the conversion to how good the food was, and how glad he was that one of the patrons at the bar told him about the Mayfair Hotel.

" This is the best breakfast I've had in days, I have to make this my every morning visit. With a good breakfast I don't mine pounding the streets to do my job."

" Good luck with that." Replied Jack.

When the bill came Steve immediately reached for it, and paid including a service tip.

Twenty percent of the bill as a tip was unheard of in those days. The waiter came back to the table and thanked

Steve for his very generous tip. Then they all left together, at the hotel entrance Jack and Kristy went their separate ways. Steve watch until they were out of sight. Then he walked in the same direction hoping to catch a glimpse of where they were going. They must have turned into one of the buildings because he never caught up to them, or could he find them. So he decided to walk back to the Wild Boar. He needed the exercise, and on such a beautiful day what else did he have to do. His only hope was that Jack would show up at the pub that night. Later that night Steve began to drink a little to much. His nerves were wearing thin, so when Jack and Kristy finally showed up he was much to drunk to play the part of an investigating journalist. It was actually the best thing that could have happened. It completely threw Jack off his suspicion about Steve. When he walk up to the bar and put his arm around Steve and said. " What are you drinking mate, let me buy you a round."

" Hey Jack, what the fuck are you doing here. What a trip, seems were always running into each other."

The bartender placed another beer and whiskey chaser in front of Steve. Picking up the whiskey he said. " Cheers mate." He downed the shot in one gulp, then he fell flat on his ass. When the bartender said. " I think he's had enough. Anybody want to help him to his room, there's a free beer here for you."

" I got him." Said Jack. " What room is he in?"

" Room 201" Said the bartender.

Jack helped him up from the floor, and practically carried him up the stairs. Then he took the key from Steve, opened the door and placed him on the bed. On the way out Jack looked around and found the notes Steve had written down about the Jack the Ripper story. To him he was very satisfied Steve was who he said he was. Placing the key on the table, Jack locked the door behind him and left. The next morning with a splitting head ache Steve couldn't remember much of anything from the night before. He sat on the edge of the bed holding his head, then his stomach. Most people say when you wake up like this, the hair of the dog that bite you is what you need. The thought of a shot of whiskey just upset him more. He had never had a hangover from cheap booze before. A pub in the East end of London is not serving premium whiskey. After changing the clothes he slept in, washing his face and combing his hair. He settled on a cup of coffee and a plain roll at the nearest cafe. After a second cup of coffee, he began to feel much better. His stomach calmed down and his headache went away. He began to remember bits and pieces from the night before, but none of Jack putting him in bed. The rest of the day he spent stopping people on the street, asking question and taking notes. He was playing the role of journalist, hoping to see Jack and Kristy on the street. That day and night proved to be uneventful. The next morning feeling like his old self because of a booze free night, he decided to have breakfast at the Mayfair Hotel. When he got there most of the business men crowd had already left for work. There was no waiting lines and plenty of empty tables. The hostess, walked him to a table were he sat down and got immediate service from the waiter he generously tip a few day ago.

" Welcome back sir." Said the waiter. As he handed him a menu, and poured a cup of coffee, placing a small amount of milk next to the cup. Steve handed the menu back to the waiter saying. "I know what I like to eat. Two scrambled eggs over waffles, bacon on the side well done. A few minutes later his food came out and Steve was enjoying his meal. When out of nowhere came a voice saying. " Hello mate, good morning." With a friendly slap on his back. " Want some company?"

Steve looked up and saw Jack and Kristy. " Sure sit right down. Waiter we need two menus and a pot of tea."

" Right away sir."

" You look a whole lot better than you did the other night, when I put you in bed."

" You put me in bed. Wow, I didn't remember that."

The waiter came back with their tea and took their order. When the food came they enjoyed pleasant conversation. Then to Steve's surprise Jack excused himself from the table, saying. " I need to talk to a business associate, I see on the other side of the room."

This was the first time Steve was alone with Kristy. He was very careful what he said for fear she might tell Jack.

" Why are you so quiet?"

" Jack doesn't like when women talk and interrupt men in conversation."

" A little over bearing, don't you think?"

" A lady, should always know her place."

" You do realize your an American?"

" I often have flash backs of a different place and time."

" Maybe because you are from a different time, the future."

" What are you saying. You're confusing me."

Steve decides he may never get another chance to be alone with Kristy, so he tells her the truth.

" Look at me, look in my eyes. Jack took you from the future to be his sex slave."

" That's not true. We sleep in the same bed, but he only holds me. I sleep on my side with my back to him. He puts his arm around me holding my breast. Even when he rubs against me he never gets an erection. He tells me I calm the raging beast inside him. He treats me very well."

" It doesn't change the fact that your from the future. You and I were in love in California 2015. You have to trust me. Jack is coming back, say nothing. Please."

" Did you miss me my dear?" How are you two getting long?"

" Just fine, I was telling Kristy about California where I'm from. Iv'e got enough information to write my story, so I'm going to leave day after tomorrow."

" Well then, we'll have to plan a dinner together tomorrow night. What do you say we meet here at 7:00 pm tomorrow."

" Sounds like a plan, so long as I'm buying dinner."

" Nonsense, your my mate and I've invited you. It's a fair well dinner."

Then Steve turns to Kristy and says. " What do you think is right Kristy?"

Kristy looks at Jack before answering. When he nods his head in approval she says.

" I think Jack is right, he planned the evening so it should be his treat."

" Splendid, well said my dear. Now that, that's all settled we'll see you at 7:00 sharp."

Steve now knows he has to put his plan together on how he is going to get Kristy back on the ship in the proper time zone. Later that night the pub was very crowded. It had been some time since Jack the Ripper had put fear into the hearts of the people of the Whitechapel District of London. Steve thought to himself how quickly a few drinks can make people forget the insane brutal murders that made headlines in the newspapers. Steve got there early and was seated at a table near the end of the bar. Sipping his beer he was surprised to see Jack and Kristy making their way through the crowd.

" Got room for two more at your table?" Asked Jack.

" Always have room for you and your niece. Have a seat, but you better go up to the bar and get your drinks, or you'll never get served."

With that Kristy sat down while Jack went to the bar to get their drinks. Kristy looked to see how far away Jack was so she could talk to Steve in private. Then she said.

" Iv'e been thinking about what you said, that were from the future. I believe you because my memory of you is getting stronger. I can see us together as lovers in my mind. I feel different when I'm near you. What do we do now? How can we get back?"

" I was going to wait until tomorrow at dinner to make a move, and try to get back. Now I'm thinking maybe we should try to go tonight. Here comes Jack, lets talk later."

Jack came back with a tray of boilermakers. Three beers and three shots of whiskey. When he placed the tray on the table Steve said. " The last time I did this you had to carry me up to bed."

" I'll have a beer, but I pass on the whiskey. My stomach is not up to it tonight." Said Kristy. " Okay Steve it's all yours."

" I think I'm going to pass on my whiskey too. Tomorrow is my last day and I need a clear head to put all my notes together for my story."

" I'll drink Kristy's whiskey, but you have to have one shot with me before you go back to America."

" Okay one shot, but Kristy's whiskey is all yours."

" Way to go mate, now your talking. Cheers."

They lift the whiskey and down their shot in one gulp. Then Jack lifts the last whiskey and says." Cheers."

Steve's plan is to get Jack plenty drunk, so they can make their escape. Round after round seems to have no effect on Jack. The pub is now thinning out and they are always in Jack's line of sight. It's almost like he is testing Steve. Daring him to make a wrong move. The cat and mouse game between is getting more intense. It's as if Jack knows Steve has something up his sleeve and he just waiting to strike like the demon he is. When he is far enough away Kristy says.

" I'm getting scared. Iv'e been with him long enough to sense he knows what were about to try."

" If we don't take our chance soon, it may never come."

Jack comes back from the bar and says. " We have to leave. I have important business to take care of."

" Now at this hour of the night." Says Kristy.

" Maybe Steve can walk you back to the flat. I wouldn't want you to walk back by yourself. Never know what's lurking in the night."

" Sure, I don't mind at all."

As Steve and Kristy walk to the front door. Jack stops at the bar to talk to one of the men standing there. When they reach the front door Steve looks back to see if Jack is still standing there. Outside Kristy pulls Steve's hand as to rush away. Steve holds her back not to look conspicuous. Just before they reach the corner, Kristy take one last look back to see if Jack is behind them saying. " He still must be in the pub, I don't see him." Turning the corner Steve stops, pulls Kristy towards him and kisses her in a passionate way. Then he says. " You are my soul mate, I love you with all my heart and soul. Michele we're ready, Michele take us now."

Just as Michele is pulling them back. Jack shows up. A micro second sooner they would have been pulled through. Jack leaps for Steve but fails to hold on to him. In a flash they are both back on the ship, in their suite. Immediately Kristy memory is fully restored. She knows exactly who she is and where she is. Steve hugs her and kisses her. Then he falls to his knees holding on sliding down her body. That's when she sees Jack's knife sticking out of Steve's back. " Oh my God, Steve you've been stabbed."

" Kristy I'll always love you"

" I'll always love you too. Please don't die. Steve hold on I'll call for help."

As his body becomes dead weight, she closes his eyes and gently lays him down. Knowing he gave up his life to save her, she breaks down crying hysterically.

" Why did he have to die God? He was the only man that truly loved me. He had his whole life in front of him, with a promising career."

Then she reached for the phone and dialed the operator. " Send help my boyfriend has been stabbed, suite M 131. Get a doctor he's bleeding bad. Then she pulls the knife out from Steve's back, and rolls him on his back. She begins to caress his face and kisses him as if they were about to make love. " I love you Steve, your my soul mate."

Kristy places the knife under her left breast and throws herself on top of Steve's body. The knife piercing her heart, Killing her instantly.

When security finally arrives they pound on the door yelling out. " Security open the door." (after a few seconds) Security opens the door."

They use the master key to let themselves in. What they find is two dead bodies. They call for the house doctor and the county Coroner. What amazed them was two dead bodies in a suite behind a locked door. Security also informed the police who sent a couple of detectives. They arrived first on the scene and began looking at the evidence at hand. When the coroner came on the scene he examined both bodies saying. " The male was killed by stabbing from behind. The female was killed by stabbing from the front. It looks like the same knife was used on both bodies. The detectives began saying the girl killed the man and then herself. A modern day Romeo and Juliet. The forensic coroner deduced there was a clear thumb print on the handle of the knife that was to large to belong to a women. Security then told the detectives about the fight that occurred the night before, between Steve and an other guest named Eric Von Ellstein. It seemed the fight was over the girl who was Von Ellstein's former girl friend. The detectives immediately asked what room was he in, because they wanted to talk to him. Security took them to Von Ellstein suite. They knocked several times and then told security to open the door. When they went inside the suite was empty, yet all his clothes were still there. Security called the front desk to see if he had checked out. They had no record of him officially leaving the ship. They began a complete search of the ship after sealing closed the exit ramp and elevator. What they did not know was Jack came and got Eric off the ship and back to his time dimension. Eric was now Jack's henchmen to do his bitting. He couldn't replace Kristy, but for now he'd have to do. Security and the detectives could not find Eric any where on the ship. They even searched the lower deck that were off limits to all guest. The detectives now decided that Eric Von Ellstein, was their number one suspect. An all points bulletin was sent out with his description for his capture. They immediately took finger prints in Eric's suite to see if it matched the thumb print on the handle of the knife. The next day the headlines on the local newspaper read.

DOUBLE HOMICIDE ABOARD QUEEN MARY

Rising baseball star Steven Jensen from San Diego found stabbed to death along side female lover Kristy Anderson. Both were found behind lock door of their suite. Does the legend of the Queen Mary live on or is this a modern day.

ROMERO and JULIET!

Eric Von Ellstein named as the number one suspect, cannot be found. A three state manhunt is now taking place. Las Vegas police have been notified to be on high alert.

Soon all the television stations from coast to coast were carrying the story of the haunted ship and the star shine lover killed in a tragic love triangle. When Carol heard the story on television she fell back in her seat and began to cry. She began to think the last time they had talked. Kristy was so happy with her new life. She finally found her soul mate, the only one in Carol's mind had to be Eric Von Ellstein. How could she relate what happen to Kristy when they were on the ship together. She could only hope that they are together in the after life. A week later the forensic autopsy report came back to the detectives. It stated that no drugs or poisons were found in either body. The coroner included his professional opinion that the wound inflected in Steve's body had to be done by a skilled surgeon. Placement of the knife between the ribs to puncture the heart for a fatal stab wound. Kristy's wound was of the ordinary nature. The knife was placed under the breast sliding off the rib cutting several main arteries. The fact her finger prints were on the handle of the knife proved self inflicted. The type of knife used with a serrated edge really aroused his curiosity. He had remembered the story of Jack the Ripper and how he used a serrated knife with surgical sharpness. All of the murdered victims, had the throat cut and their body organs removed like the work of a skilled surgeon. He decided to send the thumb print to Interpol, Police and FBI to see if they had any match on record. One after the other came back negative to any match. It was as if the person never existed. There was no way any records from a hundred and twenty seven years ago would be on file, no matter what agency he went to, they could not help him. There was no way he could put the case to rest no matter how hard he tried. He knew he was on to something strange. When he received a phone call from Carol one day, she began to tell him her side of the story by saying.

" Hello is this Dr. Graham of the Long Beach Police?"

" Yes how can I help you?"

" You are the forensic coroner on the case for Steven Jensen and Kristy Anderson?"

" Yes that's right."

" I'm Carol De Marco from Staten Island, New York. I was very close to Kristy. We were on the Queen Mary together about nine months ago. I was with my husband and she was with Eric Von Ellstein. The man was completely insane, evil to the point he wanted to sacrifice Kristy to evil spirits he believed were on the ship. He claimed there was a vortex on the pool deck that could take you to a different dimension."

" That's quite a story. The trouble is it can't be documented, great story, no proof. A court of law must have hard cold evidence, in black and white. A jury will never believe or convict on a ghost story. Sorry Mrs De Marco, but it's time to close the file on this case and add it to the legend of the Grey Ghost.

EPILOG

J ames questioned Michele what was going to happen now. Michele informed him. "They will have to find their own way. They do not have the ability, to travel between dimensions yet. Their world is now the Queen Mary. Kristy and Steven will feel the same affection we felt for each other. It will take time for them to materialize, in human form."

" How come I could right from the beginning?

" You had the privilege of being with a fifty year spirit. By holding on to me you could do anything I could do. We need to go back in time to the dimension when Queen Mary was the grandest ship on the ocean. When royalty and celebrities walked her decks. We can check in on our friends and see how they are getting along. It is now up to them to protect the Queen Mary, and if they need help to fight the vortex we will always be there. In time we can help them to move between dimension."

In a moments flash they were back in time to 1936, and they were walking the deck with Clark Gable and Carol Lombard, Victor Mature and Bob Hope. This is what Michele had been waiting for all these years. She held James' arm and walked proudly with the man she loved for so many years. As she passed each celebrity they gave their nod of welcome. They had reached the height of success they had hoped for. Hitler had not yet invaded Poland and England's London and France's Paris were still the favorite cities and countries of the rich and famous to visit. Crossing the Atlantic Ocean on Queen Mary was still the way to travel. The Queen still had five years before she would turn into. " THE GREY GHOST"!

THE END!

OTHER BOOKS WRITTEN- by JOSEPH SQUATRITO.

"CODE NAME GINNY" –Biography of the O.S.S. of World War II. The Ginny Mission was the most important mission at that time of the war. What happened to the fifteen American Commandos changed the course of history

" WHERE EVIL LURKS"– Based on a true story of police corruption, murdered and betrayal among best of friends.

" A DESERT OF SIN" – Based on a true story of how the New York Mafia brought sports betting into the casino.